The blanketed old man, Wandering Deer, muttered something in Cherokee, switching to English to add, "Her soul is not at rest."

At Mitch's questioning look, Crying Wolf said, "He does not understand. He was not raised with his father's people."

"He says she is in the ghostland," Rhea translated. "The realm where spirits of murder victims wander until their deaths are avenged."

"She longs to go to the dark land in the west," Crying Wolf explained, "but she cannot go to the Night Land and be at peace until her death is avenged. You must find the evildoer, Mitch Bushyhead. When he is punished the child's soul will be at rest."

"He will be punished," Mitch assured him.

Crying Wolf gazed at his granddaughter, then said to Mitch, "At dawn, I made medicine. The killer is at the tribal school. The smoke has told me this."

———————— ★ ————————

GHOSTLAND

JEAN HAGER

WORLDWIDE.

TORONTO • NEW YORK • LONDON
AMSTERDAM • PARIS • SYDNEY • HAMBURG
STOCKHOLM • ATHENS • TOKYO • MILAN
MADRID • WARSAW • BUDAPEST • AUCKLAND

For Genell Dellin,
a friend for all seasons, with affection and gratitude

GHOSTLAND

A Worldwide Mystery/April 1993

First published by St. Martin's Press, Incorporated.

ISBN 0-373-26117-9

AUTHOR'S NOTE

Since this book was written, the Cherokee Nation of Oklahoma has signed an agreement with state and federal officials to establish cooperative law enforcement among all governments in the Cherokee Nation's fourteen-county service area. The Cooperative Law Enforcement Agreement provides for cross-deputization of federal, state, and tribal law enforcement personnel to enforce common law on Indian and non-Indian land. Had the book been written after the signing of this historic agreement, the question of Police Chief Mitch Bushyhead's lack of jurisdiction on Indian land would not have arisen.

—Jean Hager

ONE

CHARLEY HORN led the gourd dancers into the woods from a corner of the playing field. The path was narrow and meandering, fringed by thickets of native pecan trees and blackjack oaks with stunted sugarberries crowding the bases of the taller trees.

The shady lane was the shortest route to Buckskin High School's football stadium, where junior dancers would kick off the pow-wow. Charley was the head singer for the first round of dances. He was going over the songs in his head, but it was hard to concentrate when he was surrounded by so much racket.

His charges ranged in age from seven to thirteen. Dressed in traditional Cherokee ribbon shirts and fringed moccasins, they chattered excitedly over the noise of eleven rattles. The rattles, used to punctuate the beat of dance songs, were made of hollow, dried gourds perforated at the ends. Dried seeds or stones had been inserted in each gourd before the holes were plugged by a hickory stick long enough to leave a handle extending at one end.

The incessant clamor forced a chuckle from Charley. It reminded him of a colony of chipmunks who'd discovered their burrows were taken over by rattlesnakes.

The boys were students of the tribal boarding school where Charley taught social studies and served as a dorm parent. At forty-two, he'd given up hope of having his own children, and his students were the next best thing. Through the years, a few had come to *feel* like his own, and he tried to keep in touch with them after they left the school.

Seven-year-old Billy Fourkiller, trudging at Charley's heel toward his first Cherokee Heritage Celebration, was one of the special children. Homesick his first year at the school, Billy had quickly cast Charley and his wife in the roles of surrogate parents. When Billy discovered that Charley was leading practice dance sessions for the pow-wow, he'd signed up, eager for Charley's approval and attention.

Pow-wows, though not a part of ancient Cherokee culture, had been appropriated in modern times from other Indians. Nowadays, a pow-wow figured largely in any Cherokee celebration worthy of the name. Like the Cherokee National Holiday each Labor Day weekend in Tahlequah, Buckskin's heritage gala was tribal fair, Thanksgiving, and Homecoming, all rolled into one. It would draw Cherokees from all over the country, including a contingent from the North Carolina reservation, as well as Native Americans from other tribes, and several thousand tourists.

"Billy," Charley called over his shoulder, "where did we get our dances and songs?" Billy, like many of the children whose parents sent them to the boarding school, had come sadly lacking in knowledge of his native heritage and its ancient beauty. Knowing this, Charley rarely lost an opportunity to instruct his students in tribal tradition. The boarding school encompassed only the first eight grades. A few students would go on to the tribal-operated high school in Tahlequah, but most would enter public schools where the old ways were not taught and too often not respected.

Billy responded promptly, "Stone Coat." He gave Charley a gap-toothed grin and shook his gourd rattle fiercely.

"*Na ; yu'nuwi',*" said David Sly, a serious-minded sixth-grader. The Cherokee word translated literally to "stone coat-on."

"He killed the people," said Stanley Dick.

"They couldn't hurt him because he was covered with stone."

"He could make himself invisible."

"He turned himself into an orphan boy to fool the people."

"So he could slaughter the children and eat their livers!"

A chorus of groans and nervous laughter erupted. Charley joined the laughter, satisfied that he'd taught them well. He took up the tale. "After several children were killed, the man who had adopted the orphan boy became suspicious of him. He spoke to the council and they devised a plan to trap Stone Coat."

Upon discovering that blood would weaken and destroy the killer, they had positioned seven menstruating women to lie in wait along Stone Coat's path. Charley decided to skip over that part of the story now.

"Stone Coat grew weak and began to vomit blood. He fell down and was unable to move."

"He was paralyzed," David Sly inserted.

"Yes, and Stone Coat knew he was a goner," Charley continued. "Knowing he was about to die, Stone Coat called the people around him. He told them to build a fire and lay him on it. While he was burning, he sang the songs that we still sing in our dances today, curing songs and songs for hunting and war, all the songs used in our medicine ceremonies. What happened then, Stanley?"

"The people found some stones left in the ashes. They had powerful medicine."

"Right, Stanley. The medicine stones—"

"Mr. Horn," Billy interrupted as he tugged on Charley's sleeve. "I thought I heard someone walking—over there."

AFTER ALL WAS SAID and done, Miss Polly Kirkwood later thought, it was Millicent's fault that she'd stumbled on the grisly scene and fainted dead away from the shock.

Polly was taking her daily constitutional in the narrow strip of woods behind the house she shared with her sister. She walked more rapidly than was her custom, stomping really, with her apple cheeks puffing out with each breath.

It was mid-morning, not the hour she preferred for walking. But she had needed to get beyond earshot of Millicent's litany of complaints about the stomach upset that had kept her awake most of the night. As though she expected sympathy from Polly. Really!

Millicent, Polly had often thought, was her own worst enemy. The silly fool had eaten marinated cucumbers with her supper the previous evening. Millicent *knew* cucumbers gave her gas, a fact that Polly had politely pointed out as

Millicent took an immoderate second helping. Millicent had
paid her no heed, of course. Millicent was obstinate.
"You're not my keeper, Polly," she'd snapped, staring at
Polly's plump hand as it reached for a chicken leg. "But as
long as we're on the subject of diets, isn't that your third
piece of fried chicken?"

Nobody could tell Millicent a thing, least of all Polly, who
at seventy-one was three years younger than Millicent and
had always been considered the flighty sister by their ac-
quaintances. Polly had another name for it. She had con-
cluded long ago that she'd rather be whimsical than mulish.

She stopped and leaned against the tapering trunk of a
cottonwood tree to catch her breath. Honestly, thought
Polly, blotting her damp brow with an embroidered handkerchief, why do I let Millicent's bullheadedness rile me?
How silly to fret because my daily walk has been pushed up
a few hours. Schedules are for retired schoolmarms, not
their fanciful sisters. Since I'm here, I might as well enjoy
the solitude.

She closed her eyes and let the peace of the woods quiet
her spirit. Nearby, a bluejay scolded her for invading his
territory, then flew away, and the woods were still again,
except for the faint sound of insects.

With all the meanness going on in the world, this was one
of the few places where Polly felt safe. When she thought
about it logically, it made little sense. An evildoer could as
easily be in these woods as anywhere else but, as Polly often reminded herself, criminals prefer places where there are
people to mug and houses to rob.

A shaft of sunlight pierced the entwined branches overhead and spilled down her right shoulder and arm. She
looked up at the opening the sun had found and was daz-
zled by the brightness.

Pocketing her handkerchief, she stepped out of the warm
beam and scanned the ground. Occasionally she happened
on some small treasure during her walks—an unusual rock
or a clump of wildflowers that had bravely taken root in a
sunlight-nurtured spot of earth.

Once she had found a cardinal with a broken wing and had carried it home. Over Millicent's objections, she had installed it in the old birdcage she'd hauled down from the attic. She'd fed and watered the bird until its wing healed and then had carried it back to the woods and let it go.

After that, whenever she saw a redbird in the woods, she called to it, imagining it was the one she'd nursed back to health. That had been seven or eight years ago, of course, and she didn't know how long cardinals lived. She had purposely avoided looking it up in the encyclopedia, for if she didn't know she could fancy her redbird flitting through the woods, year after year, endlessly.

Millicent complained about the treasures Polly brought home to add to her collection: wildflowers arranged in fruit jars at first and later included in dried bouquets to decorate her room; rocks of various shapes and hues lined up on narrow plank shelves resting on concrete blocks. Millicent saw no beauty in Polly's "infernal junk," as she called it. To Millicent, the collection was merely something else to clutter up the house and gather dust. For all Millicent's inclination to quote snippets of poetry, Polly was sure her sister's soul was barren of romance.

Polly pursed her lips in pity at the thought. Spying an oddly shaped stone, she gathered the skirt of her faded cotton dress in one hand to keep it off the ground and bent to retrieve her find. Small black insects, their dank world invaded, scuttled in a panicked search for cover. Polly scraped off a crust of dirt with a fingernail.

The stone was mustard-colored, kidney-shaped. Washed and polished, it would be a pretty addition to her collection. She pocketed the stone and walked on, slowly now and quietly, over layers of leaf mold dappled by sunlight. Her scruffy canvas Keds stepped around and between trees, leaving no imprint behind.

The woods' redbud trees had already shed their bright flowers. It was a bit late for wildflowers, too, the last week of May. She had found a few lovely blue blossoms two weeks ago, but none since the days had turned so warm. Spring in Oklahoma was brief at best. Days changed, with hardly a pause, from chilly, punctuated by rain or wind and tornado watches, to swelteringly hot and humid.

Funny, Polly hadn't noticed that particular characteristic of Oklahoma weather as a child. Then, it had seemed to her that summer would never arrive. Unlike Millicent, she hadn't enjoyed her schoolwork. It seemed now that she'd survived school terms only by looking forward to the first day her mother judged warm enough for going barefoot; from then until the start of school in the fall, she had scorned shoes. Except for Sunday morning church services, and that only because her mother had insisted.

She stood still, breathing deeply of the warm, unmoving air. In a few weeks, the dry season would be upon them. The pungent atmosphere of rich growth and the pleasant, moldering scent of past years' vegetation would be quickly leeched from the woods. Leaves would droop in the silent heat and twigs would snap beneath her step.

She felt a sudden urge to share the woods' treasures with someone else before the heat made walking there unpleasant. Millicent, of course, wouldn't be interested. Who might be? Suddenly she had an inspired idea. She would organize a nature walk!

But whom would she invite? She thought of the Indian boarding school, its campus skirting the woods. A year ago, the science teacher had invited Polly to come and show her rock collection to the fourth-grade class. She had enjoyed the hour spent with the children, their dark eyes so bright and interested in her and her rocks.

Today was Thursday, the beginning of Buckskin's annual four-day Cherokee Heritage Celebration. The boarding-school children would be engaged in the festivities. And, though the term for the public schools had ended yesterday, students at the tribal school had another week to go.

Next week would be final exam week, culminating on Friday in Parents' Day and the eight-grade graduation ceremonies. After that, the children would leave to spend the summer with their families. But the Heritage Celebration would end officially on Sunday at noon. The children might have some free time later on Sunday.

Polly clapped her plump hands in delight. Excited, she turned back, taking a shorter route out of the woods than the way she'd come. If she could find the science teacher, Mr. Stand, she'd inquire if any of his students would like to join her Sunday on a nature walk. She would bring her books and show them from the pictures how to identify the various species of flora and insects.

After the walk, she would take the children back to the house and serve refreshments. If Millicent disapproved, she could just sulk in her room until the children were gone and Polly had cleaned up after them. She had learned long ago that ignoring Millicent's sulks was the only way to deal with them.

Chocolate-chip cookies, she thought. She'd omit the pecans—some children didn't like nuts. Chewy butterscotch bars, too, with caramel icing, and vanilla ice cream. Lemonade to drink. She'd noticed party paper plates and napkins at the grocery store. If memory served, there had been a pattern with circus animals in bright primary colors. Perfect.

Lost in plans, she was unaware of the alien object in her path until she'd stumbled over it. She pitched forward, arms outflung, and barely managed to steady herself by grabbing a low-hanging limb.

"Clumsy, feather-brained old woman," she clucked.

Squaring her shoulders, she looked around for the thing she'd tripped over. She thought at first that it must be an exposed root, and she wanted to mark its location so it wouldn't catch her up again, even though this route was not one she ordinarily used. The layer of decayed and decaying leaves and twigs was especially thick and appeared to have been recently disturbed, perhaps by some burrowing animal. Whatever she had stumbled over must be covered by leaves.

She found a piece of fallen limb and poked through the mulch. Her probe struck something solid and she hesitated, feeling an oddly premonitory tingle down her spine. Shaking off the feeling, she used the limb to scrape back the spongy layer until she had uncovered the object.

She went stock-still and gaped, barely keeping back a yelp of amazement. ~~Oddly, the tingle had become a prickling at~~ the base of her skull. Why she had an urge to run, she didn't know. It was merely a deerskin moccasin. A small, gray moccasin with deerhide laces and red and blue beads in a circular design on the instep. It looked hardly worn at all and could not have been there long.

Later, it occurred to her that she should have heeded that premonitory prickling and gone for help. Instead, as she stood there, staring at the moccasin, her mind slowly worked out what had probably happened. One of the students at the boarding school had lost the moccasin while playing in the woods. It and its mate must have been removed so that its wearer could walk barefoot. Thrust into a pocket or dangling from a small hand, perhaps, and this one had dropped to the ground unnoticed as the child reveled in the freedom of going shoeless after the long winter. Polly felt a warm empathy for the anonymous child. She knew exactly how the youngster must have felt.

Faintly, she heard in the distance a sound like that of a chorus of baby rattles. But her mind was intent on the moccasin. She would return it to the school. Bending lower to pick it up, Polly caught a glimpse of red from the corner of her eye.

Straightening, she peered at a piece of red satin ribbon. Her distance vision was not what it once had been and occasionally she saw an optical illusion at the edge of sight. The beginning of a cataract, the doctor said.

She blinked, but the red ribbon was still there. She squinted and moved a step closer. The ribbon was attached to a blue calico sleeve, which stuck out from beneath a pile of leaves and dead branches. Protruding from the sleeve was a small brown hand.

The morning sun, now in its full strength, streamed through a space between branches and flooded the scene like a spotlight, adding to the unreality. Polly's thoughts scattered. A child's arm... a child lying beneath a pile of leaves... buried... This child was surely...

Her thoughts staggered to a halt.

"Oh," she gasped, stumbling back. It was as if she'd been caught and penned by a laser of bright light, and she must free herself. But she couldn't. Everything was pressing in on her, dark squeezing out the light. Through a narrowing tunnel of vision she could still see the sleeve with its red satin ribbon, the small, lifeless hand, even as she sank to the ground.

Darkness swallowed her.

TWO

WHEN BILLY FOURKILLER announced he'd heard someone else walking in the woods, the gourd dancers had paused to listen, their rattles stilled. The abrupt silence seemed eerily threatening.

"I'll bet it was old Stone Coat," said Stanley Dick, a rowdy eighth-grader who liked to hear the younger boys squeal.

After the groans and shrieks had trailed off and another hushed moment passed, Charley said, "You probably heard a squirrel, Billy. Let's go, boys. We're almost out of the woods." They walked on for a while without speaking, the gourd rattles once more keeping time with their steps.

His mind going back to the story Charley had been telling, Billy Fourkiller sighed and said, "I wish the people hadn't lost the medicine stones. They should have been more careful. Why weren't they, Mr. Horn?"

Charley slowed his pace to let Billy catch up with him. He placed a hand on the boy's narrow shoulder. "They were struggling to survive, Billy. The whites crowded into their country back east, stealing it piece by piece. The nation was in turmoil. A few hid in the hills, but most of them were herded into compounds and forced to make the march to this land. I've told you many times about the trail where they cried, what the whites call the Trail of Tears. That must have been when the stones were lost."

Billy looked up at him solemnly and nodded. A few steps behind Billy, David Sly cried out, "Hey, look at that!" In the same instant, Charley saw the old woman lying in the path. Incongruously, a small deerskin moccasin was clutched in her hand. He halted abruptly.

He recognized Miss Polly Kirkwood from the time she had brought her rock collection to school. She'd smiled a lot, as though she were having more fun than the children. The first time he saw her, he'd thought of that plump, motherly Mrs. Butterworth on the TV maple syrup commercial. But now Miss Kirkwood's pink face was the color of ashes.

She's dead, he thought in alarm, she's had a stroke or a heart attack. But even as he hesitated, wondering how to handle this so that the boys in his charge would not be too frightened, he saw the woman's eyelids flutter.

The boys clustered around him, wide-eyed, goggling at the woman in the path. Poor old girl, Charley thought as relief washed through him, she probably got overheated. And how had she come by that moccasin? he asked himself. Aside from the fact that he could not imagine Miss Kirkwood shod in Indian moccasins, it was much too small to belong to her.

"Wait here," he told the boys in the tone he used to quiet a rowdy class, the tone that made the kids doubt he was the pushover he seemed—and too often was. "I think she has only fainted."

Polly Kirkwood groaned and turned her head from side to side. He went forward and knelt beside her. "Miss Kirkwood, it's Charley Horn, from the boarding school. Can you sit up?"

"What happened . . . what . . . oh . . ."

He helped her into a sitting position. Long strands of gray hair had escaped their pins and dangled on either side of her face. She felt warm through the cotton sleeve of her dress, and her plump hand was clammy. Dizzied by low blood pressure, maybe. Or some medication she was taking. She shouldn't be wandering around the woods alone at her age, but he didn't think she'd appreciate being told that.

Her eyes darted all about and widened at the sight of the gourd dancers. Even though no one—not even a disoriented old lady—could take them for a band of no-accounts, he braced himself for her scream. She clearly thought of it but, instead, she grimaced, as though trying to remember where she was and what had happened to her.

She stared at the moccasin still clutched in her hand and, belatedly, she uttered a little yelp, like that of a frightened puppy. One hand flew to her mouth. "Did you see—? *Look!*" The hand holding the moccasin shot out toward the pile of leaves beside the path. Charley hadn't noticed it before.

He noticed it now and sucked in his breath. His first thought was, Get the boys out of here before they see this. He tore his gaze away to say over his shoulder, "The pow-wow will be starting. Stanley, take them to the football field. Tell Abe Byrd that he must be the head singer until I get there."

Stanley seemed frozen in his tracks. "It's a body," he said, deflating Charley's hopes of protecting his charges from grim reality.

Billy Fourkiller pressed against Charley's back, as though the contact made him feel safer. "Who is it?" he asked.

The other boys huddled close around Stanley and stared at the arm jutting out of the pile of leaves.

"I think it's a girl," another of them ventured. "What's wrong with her?"

"Maybe," said young David Sly in a quavery voice, "Stone Coat has been here and taken a liver."

Billy made a barely audible sound of distress.

Charley stood, placing himself between Billy and the pile of leaves. He helped Miss Kirkwood to her feet, then turned back to the boys.

"Stone Coat is dead," he said sternly. "The people destroyed him. Now, listen. This is very important. I will take Miss Kirkwood to her house and we'll call the police. They'll find out what happened here. This is not your business. You must say nothing about what you have seen. Do not let this evil infect you. You must banish negative thoughts so that you will be in the proper frame of mind for the dancing." He looked slowly from one frightened young face to another, gazing into the eyes of each of the boys. Then he looked intently at Stanley Dick, the eldest. "Do you understand?"

With obvious effort, Stanley ripped his gaze from the pile of brush. "Yes, sir."

"Leave this to the police. You dance and think about the words of the songs, what they mean. Do not talk of this. I will surely be with you before the noon break. If I am not, find one of your teachers. They will see that you have something to eat."

"Can we tell about it then?" queried Billy.

"What do you think?" Charley asked gently.

The boy looked down at the ground. "We won't talk about it."

"Good." Charley knew the admonition was probably futile. At least one of the eleven boys, likely Stanley, would be unable to keep such a secret. For that matter, Charley himself would find it difficult since he would think of little else today. Besides, once the police were called, the word would spread through town like a grassfire in a dry Oklahoma summer. He gave Billy a pat on the back. "Stay together. Go now, all of you. Hurry."

As one, they broke into a run, their departure underscored by the clatter of eleven gourd rattles. Charley watched until the last boy passed from sight on the curving path that would take them into the bright sunlight beyond the woods.

Miss Kirkwood looked at him and clucked sorrowfully. Reluctantly, he went to the pile of brush and lifted branches and leaves until he uncovered the child's body. Behind him, Miss Kirkwood uttered a muffled little cry. Charley hoped she wasn't going to faint again. She didn't. He could feel heat from her body as she pressed close and peered around him. Her clothes had a musty violet smell.

The child was Tamarah Birch, a third-grade student at the boarding school. She had come to him only last week, crying because Stanley Dick had taunted her about her Apache blood, told her she came from barbaric stock that even her Cherokee blood probably couldn't overcome. Charley had taken Tamarah to Aggie, his wife, for a cookie and sympathy. Then he'd had a talk with Stanley, who had promised to leave Tamarah alone, a promise the boy had managed to keep less than a week. For there had been that incident in the cafeteria yesterday. . . .

Charley's throat began to ache. Tamarah's head was twisted at an unnatural angle. There were insects in her hair and crawling around her mouth. She was on her back, left arm stretched out, right arm bent, the hand curled on her chest. The hem of her blue calico dress was bunched around her waist, exposing her lower body. The bright sunlight splashing golden on the massed leaves—even the child's dress with its bright ribbon trim—seemed a festive mockery.

He knelt down and placed an ear against her chest. No heartbeat. He pressed his fingers against the artery below her jaw. Her skin felt cold.

For a moment, he crouched over her, unwilling to accept the hard truth. He knew CPR, but it was much too late for life-saving measures. He could do nothing for her now.

A great sorrow filled Charley. Blinking to clear his vision, he reached to pull her dress down and cover her nakedness. Then he hesitated. The police would want him to leave her exactly as he'd found her.

But he could not leave her like that. She seemed too exposed, too vulnerable. He could not think of her as a corpse. To him, she was still the bright-eyed, sensitive child who sat in the first row in his fifth-hour class. He pulled her dress down.

After they called the police, he'd come back to stay with her until they arrived. A small thing, but he felt a need for some final expression of respect and affection for the child.

Even such a trivial decision seemed to push back the whirl of sorrow and confusion in his head. This was so monstrous an evil that he could hardly comprehend it, so there was no point in trying. Some, like Stanley Dick, would say it was the work of Stone Coat or a night stalker—a Cherokee witch—or the *uk'ten'* or another of the monsters of Cherokee tradition.

But anyone with eyes and ears could see and hear enough, even in a backwater like Buckskin, to know that one did not have to resort to the supernatural to explain this. Civilization seemed to degenerate a little more with each passing year. Something was spreading through the world's population, stealing people's consciences and leaving them crueler than before.

Charley didn't know why, but he feared that when more was known about Tamarah's fate, this evil would be revealed to be even worse than what he saw with his eyes. He did not want to know more about it. Fortunately, he could leave to the police the task of discovering what had happened before the broken child was discarded and moldy leaves piled atop her.

The unenviable job of notifying Tamarah's father would probably fall to Porter Qualls, the principal.

THREE

SHORTLY AFTER Charley had returned to the woods, two patrol cars with Buckskin police department insignias on the doors pulled into the driveway of the Kirkwood house, a tall, narrow two-story with long windows and a wide front porch, like many of the first homes built in Buckskin in the early years of the century. An ambulance turned in behind them. Police Chief Mitchell Bushyhead and Officer Harold Duckworth emerged from the cars.

Mitch had taken the call at the station, bracing himself to deal with the usual sort of complaint spawned by the holiday atmosphere of the heritage celebration. An agitated matron demanding protection for her sidewalk craft booth from children running amok or a local barkeep needing help to sort out a drunken argument that had escalated to a fist-flying brawl.

Instead, he'd listened with mounting dismay to a disjointed recital. A dead girl. In the woods. The caller had sounded dazed and had not at once revealed that he knew the child's identity.

Mitch had found himself trying frantically to remember where his own daughter should be at that moment. At the north end of Sequoyah Street, he thought, where Indians, weekend cowboys trying to control their over-stimulated mounts, Shriners, and high school kids were converging on the parade route's starting point. Emily was supposed to march and perform an acrobatic routine with the pom-pom girls.

Mitch had been ashamed of how quickly the grip on his heart had loosened when the caller finally got around to giving the dead girl's name.

As he and Duckworth walked toward the house, they heard the clatter of locks and chains being undone, and then the Kirkwood sisters emerged, squinting, as though the sunlight hurt their eyes. Millicent, tall and gauntly thin, stepped to the edge of the porch. She was in such a state of runaway nerves that she was twitching.

"About time you got here, Chief Bushyhead!" She gripped the porch railing and peered down at him over her rimless spectacles, blinking madly. "This has quite undone poor Polly." Miss Millicent would die before she would admit to being as emotionally wrecked as her sister. "She fainted, you know," she said accusingly, as though Mitch could have prevented it if he'd been on his toes. "It's a good thing she has so much padding, or she'd have broken something."

Polly frowned irritably at the reference to her weight. To Mitch, Polly appeared to have recovered her equilibrium better than Millicent, but then she'd had longer to get used to the idea. She'd found the body, and it was a wonder her old lady's heart hadn't stopped beating from the shock.

"Where is the man who called the station?" Mitch asked.

"He went back to the woods, to where I found the little girl," Miss Polly said.

"Only the worst kind of pervert would harm an innocent child," Miss Millicent shrilled, in case Mitch hadn't grasped the obvious.

"It could have been an accident, Millicent," Polly suggested in a hopeful voice. "She could have fallen out of a tree."

"Pish!" Millicent wheeled on her sister, the nearest available object upon which to vent her distress. "And I suppose she covered herself up with leaves before she died."

"Oh, you're right, Millicent..." Miss Polly fluttered. She waved a plump hand in front of her face, fanning herself. Suddenly her own protected corner of the world had become a dangerous and irrational place. For a long time now, whenever she went out of her house, she would be afraid. "Such a shock. I'll never be able to go into those woods again. There'll be no Sunday afternoon nature walk...no party..."

"What *are* you babbling about, Polly?" Millicent demanded.

Mitch interrupted. "Miss Polly, if you would direct us to the scene."

Miss Polly did, clearly relieved not to be asked to return with them.

"Please excuse us, ladies." Mitch and Duckworth, joined by two ambulance attendants carrying a litter, started around the house.

"I hope you don't waste any time apprehending the fiend responsible for this," Miss Millicent shouted after them. "As for Polly and me, we're taking no chances. I've already phoned the hardware store and ordered new locks for our doors. And I wish to make a formal request for a police patrol of this street on a regular basis." The sisters were obsessed with the notion that Buckskin was rife with burglars and rapists whose chief goal in life was to break into the Kirkwood house.

"'The evil that men do lives after them!' Mister Shakespeare said that!" Miss Millicent's parting shot could probably be heard on Sequoyah Street, over the noise of the high school marching band.

Duckworth sighed. "I knew it was too good to last."

"What?"

"The Kirkwood sisters. We haven't heard from the old gals in two months. Now they'll be driving us crazy again, wanting us to check the house for hard cases panting to jump their bones or steal their Depression glass."

"We'll just make a pass down their street when we're in the neighborhood for a while. Maybe that'll satisfy them."

"Don't count on it."

"Well, that's the trouble with public service," Mitch said. "You have to deal with the public."

"Ain't it the truth," Duckworth grunted. "Here we got some weirdo going around killing kids. And the Kirkwoods are hassling us, on top of a townful of boozed-up good-time Charlies."

"Right now, I'd welcome hauling in a few drunks," Mitch said. He was trying not to think about the child's parents taking the call that every parent dreaded above all others. "Why, in God's name, did this have to happen?"

It was a rhetorical question. Mitch had been in law enforcement for more than fifteen years, long enough to be well acquainted with the seemingly endless variety of cruelty inflicted on men by their fellows. He no longer wasted time on whys. Violence had no reason.

"We could sure use that new officer the city council keeps promising us."

Mitch grasped the change of subject gladly. He would be forced to deal with human depravity soon enough. "I hired one last week. Supposed to report for duty tomorrow for the day shift. Roo's going on the evening shift with Virgil for now."

"What?" Duckworth shot him an amazed look. "What's his name?"

"Who?"

"The new officer!"

"Pitcher. From out of town. Graduated from the Tulsa Police Academy."

"How come I'm just now hearing about it?"

"I thought I'd mentioned it." The fact was, Mitch hadn't told Duckworth because he wasn't sure how Duckworth would take the news that the new officer was female. Correction. He *was* sure, which was why he hadn't mentioned it. Police dispatcher Helen Hendrick's attempts to raise male consciousness around the station had not found very fertile soil in Duckworth's soul.

They entered the woods and found the barely discernible path Miss Polly had described. She'd said the path curved just before they reached the place where she'd found the body. Mitch was in front and as he completed the curve, he saw an Indian man wearing a ribbon shirt and a string tie, secured by a beaded medallion, sitting on the ground. The man rose as Mitch and Duckworth approached.

Mitch's gaze found the child's body lying not far from the path. He had thought himself prepared, but the sight was as horrifying as if he'd come on it unaware.

Charley recognized the tall, slender man in the lead as Buckskin's chief of police. Though Bushyhead moved at a good clip, he didn't seem to hurry. His expression was disturbed, yet watchful at the same time. The kind of man, Charley guessed, who thought more than he said and, therefore, would be easy to underestimate.

The second man, also in uniform, was shorter and heavy set, with crew-cut hair, close-set eyes, and a camera on a strap around his neck. He was breathing with his mouth open and his fleshy face was mottled. Winded, trying to keep up with Bushyhead's long strides, he walked with a lumbering gait that reminded Charley of the bears he'd seen in Yellowstone National Park. If I were a criminal on the run, Charley thought irrelevantly, I'd rather be chased by this one than Bushyhead.

Charley stepped forward. Mitch nodded a greeting. The other officer merely glanced at Charley—his eyes weren't the same color, Charley noticed—before stepping around him to stare at the body. The two young ambulance attendants joined him, squatting beside the corpse.

"Could be a broken neck, Chief," one of the attendants muttered.

Duckworth picked up a stick and lifted the child's dress. "Her panties are gone."

Unsurprised, Mitch nodded, then studied the man who'd waited for them. He looked like a full-blood. He was in his early forties, Mitch judged, starting to thicken around the waist. "You're the one who called?"

"Right. Charley Horn...I'm a teacher at the tribal school."

"Mitch Bushyhead, and this is Officer Duckworth," Mitch said. "You find her like this?" He still hadn't looked at the body again.

"She was under that pile of leaves and branches," Charley said. "Only her arm sticking out. Miss Kirkwood found this on the path." He held up a gray moccasin. "Then she saw the child's arm and fainted. That's when we came along and found her spread-eagled right there, out cold."

"We?"

"Some students from the boarding school were with me. We were going to the football field, for the pow-wow. I sent them on ahead before I uncovered the body—I was praying she would still be alive." He shrugged apologetically. "I recognized her then. She was already dead."

"You said she was a student at the boarding school."

Charley nodded. "Tamarah Birch. Third-grader."

"From around here?"

"No. Colorado. Her mother died last summer. Her father works on construction crews. He's away from home most of the time, so he sent her to us in September." A spasm of regret traveled across his face. The father entrusted his daughter to us, it said, and this is what happened. He looked at the ground. "She seemed to like it here all right, but she was homesick. Her dad was coming for her next week. Only a few more days..." His voice trailed off.

Mitch finished the thought silently: Only a few more days and Tamarah would have been beyond the reach of the one who'd done this. Charley Horn's voice was tightly controlled, but Mitch felt the man's anguish in his own body. "Has she been reported missing from the school?"

"I don't know."

Mitch raised an eyebrow. "You must take regular head counts over there."

Charley Horn seemed to bristle at the statement, as though he heard an implied accusation in it. "There's a room check every night at ten. The students are accounted for again at each meal. Tamarah was in her place at breakfast." Charley had taken the count himself that morning.

"What time was that?"

"Seven." Horn paused reflectively, as though bringing to mind the breakfast scene. "The kids were noisy, excited about two days out of class and the heritage celebration. Most of them are taking part—in the parade or pow-wow or one of the competitions. I think Tamarah was supposed to be in the green corn dance with the younger girls."

"She didn't seem to have anything else on her mind at breakfast?"

"Not that I noticed, but then I wouldn't have."

Mitch nodded, waited.

"I wasn't at her table," Horn explained. "I sat with the junior gourd dancers. I'm in charge of them this weekend. The boys wanted to walk to the football field. They were too restless to wait for their bus, and I thought the walk might work off some of their energy."

Mitch took out a small spiral notebook and ballpoint pen. There was some reassurance in putting events in order, anchoring them to time and place. It gave structure, however illusory, to the deeper chaos of evil. It helped one determine what happened, if not why.

"What time did you leave the school?"

"I saw the buses going out of the bus barn as we crossed the schoolground, so it would have been about nine-thirty."

"Where were you between breakfast and nine-thirty?"

"My apartment in the girls' dorm. My wife and I are dorm parents."

"Go on."

"As I said, I noticed the buses as we left the school grounds. The other children were supposed to board the buses at nine-forty-five in front of the administration building."

Mitch glanced at his watch. It was ten-twenty. "Tamarah should have been missed by now."

"They always call the roll before the buses leave the school. They're probably searching the buildings and grounds for Tamarah right now."

"Officer Duckworth and I will go to the school from here," Mitch said.

"Hey, Chief!" Duckworth held out empty hands. "I've been through these leaves. Her panties aren't here."

Mitch and Duckworth exchanged glances. The missing panties seemed one more confirmation of what Mitch had feared since Horn's call. Disjointedly, he thought of Emily, cavorting down the main street at this very moment, so full of life and hope. And then he flashed to Tamarah's father, who would be going about his business unaware until the phone call came, informing him of this outrage. Mitch's stomach tightened sickeningly.

"Somebody should have noticed this child leaving the school grounds, Mr. Horn." Without his being aware of it, Mitch's tone had taken on an edge. It wasn't directed at Horn in particular, but at the whole damn human race for harboring the animal who had done this.

Horn had no way of knowing it, though. "I had my hands full with the gourd dancers." His dark eyes snapped indignantly.

"You didn't find the panties when you uncovered her?"

"No! Do you think I took them? You can search me if you want to!" Mitch said nothing as Horn paused to collect himself before adding, "I saw she wasn't wearing anything under her dress, but I didn't take the time to look for her underwear. I knew I shouldn't disturb the scene any more than was necessary." Horn was clearly annoyed, as though to find himself explaining, justifying his actions.

"You removed the leaves and limbs that covered the body to see if she was still alive. Then what did you do?"

"Well—I checked for pulse and a heartbeat, but there wasn't any."

"Miss Kirkwood observed all this?"

"She must have. She was standing right there."

He's mighty touchy, Mitch thought, which could mean he had a guilty conscience. Or it could be the indignation of an innocent man. "As soon as you ascertained that she was dead, you went immediately with Miss Kirkwood to her house?"

Horn hesitated. "That's about right."

"About—what does that mean?"

"Tamarah's skirt was up around her waist, for one thing . . . so I pulled it down."

"Oh?"

A muscle in Horn's jaw spasmed. "It seemed indecent to leave her uncovered."

Mitch understood. He turned his eyes and his thoughts temporarily away from the man. He forced himself to stare at the body and imagined little Tamarah Birch, excited about dancing at the pow-wow, running through the woods, eager to get to the football field. Why hadn't she waited for the buses like everyone else? Someone had convinced her to go on foot. Someone had been with her, or met her in the woods. What did he put her through before she died? If Mitch could get his hands on him right now...

"Duck, get the pictures. Then you boys can take her to the hospital. I couldn't get hold of Doc Sullivan before I left the station. I'll catch him later. He'll want to talk to the ME as soon as possible." What a horrible way to begin the Heritage Celebration. On his way to the station that morning, Mitch had felt holiday excitement in the air. Even the weather had cooperated to make the first day of the celebration perfect. Now this.

He rubbed a hand across his chin and returned the notebook and pen to his pocket. He looked at Horn, who had been watching him expectantly, as though he hoped Mitch would pluck the murderer's name out of the air. "Would Tamarah have come into the woods alone?"

Horn hesitated. "Kids are hard to predict, but I doubt it...not this morning, anyway. She'd have been afraid of missing the bus."

Mitch nodded. "I didn't think so. Somebody talked her into coming in here—or forced her."

The attendants began maneuvering the small body into a plastic body bag. Horn averted his eyes. "I should be at the football field. Do you need me any longer?"

"Not right now," Mitch said. "We'll get back to you later." Horn shrugged and looked resigned.

"Leave the moccasin."

Horn glanced down as though he'd forgotten he still held the moccasin. He handed it over. Mitch's fingers crushed the soft leather convulsively as he examined the scene while Duckworth snapped more pictures. He heard Horn leave, followed by the ambulance attendants with the body.

The ground cover had been disturbed, probably by the killer's dragging the body off the path to conceal it. That's when the moccasin must have fallen off. Intent on hiding the body and leaving the scene, the killer hadn't noticed it, or had and kicked leaves over it. Unfortunately, Mitch could detect no footprints.

He would come back for another look when he had more time, but he didn't think the scene would give them anything much. He wanted to get moving, focus his mind on something besides that small, broken body.

"Let's go over to the school." He gestured for Duckworth to follow and led the way. There was only one route into and off the school grounds via automobile—by the main road that was blocked between 11 P.M. and 7 A.M. by tall iron gates. But one could walk in at any number of places where the surrounding wire fence sagged.

"Jeez," Duckworth snarled. "I hate this. If I had the animal who did it in shooting range right now, I swear I'd blow his brains out."

Mitch made no response.

"He took her panties. Like a souvenir." Duckworth muttered an oath. "How does a man get so screwed up?"

"Beats me."

"The hell of it is, these guys walk around, looking like everybody else."

"It sure would help if they wore a sign."

"You know anybody who likes little girls?"

"A pedophile."

"Peda Who?"

"They're called pedophiles."

"I call 'em sickos," Duckworth snorted. "Ever heard of any in Buckskin?"

"Nope. Anyway, we don't know that she was molested. Let's save the speculation till we hear from the ME. Maybe it's something else entirely."

"Yeah." Duckworth plainly didn't believe it any more than Mitch did. "Could be an out-of-towner did this," he added hopefully, "somebody here for the Heritage Celebration."

"If so," Mitch said, his tone fierce, "we'd better get him before Monday. We may not have another chance."

FOUR

PORTER QUALLS, the principal of the tribal boarding school, sat slumped at his desk, his head in his hands. "This is unbelievable," he muttered. "Simply unbelievable."

The desk was the most impressive item of furniture in the room. It was large, crafted of dark, highly polished walnut. Judging from the other furnishings—three uncomfortable-looking straight-backed chairs with seats upholstered in green vinyl, a dark oak library table on which sat a framed color photograph of a middle-aged woman, and well-worn earth-colored carpeting—Mitch assumed the desk was Qualls's personal possession.

This, the administration building, appeared to be one of the older structures on the campus. It had high ceilings, tall, narrow windows, and plastered walls showing tiny hairline cracks like wrinkles in an aging face. The original pine flooring remained uncovered in the hallways.

When Mitch had delivered the bad news, Qualls's face, naturally pale, had turned doughy beneath a receding brown hairline. He was stocky, barrel-chested, and of medium height, with green-flecked brown eyes. Only his high cheekbones and long, hooked nose showed his heritage; otherwise the principal could have passed for Caucasian. Qualls was a quarter-blood, Mitch guessed. He'd even known a few blond quarter-bloods.

Qualls lifted his head. "You say it wasn't an accident. You've no doubt she was murdered?"

"It sure looks that way. The killer hid the body."

"Hid?"

"Piled leaves over it."

"Oh. No wonder she didn't..." Qualls bit his bottom lip. "Forgive me." His voice shook. "Why? Who would want to do such a thing?"

"I thought you might have an idea."

The principal looked horrified, as though Mitch had asked him to confess to the murder himself. He touched nervous fingers to an assortment of ballpoint pens, papers, and books on the desk, finally settling on a glass paperweight. He lifted it in the palm of his hand and shook his head. He stared at the paperweight, where a yellow-winged butterfly was suspended, dead but forever beautiful in its glass prison. Then he set the paperweight down and waited for more information.

When it wasn't forthcoming, he said, "She was missed when the buses were checked. When we didn't find her right away, I sent the students and teachers on to town. Miss Adair and the counselor stayed behind to help Merv Haines, our janitor and groundskeeper, search the campus." He met Mitch's steady gaze for an instant, then glanced at Duckworth who was seated in a chair, taking notes in a spiral pad on his knee. "They're still searching. I should let them know."

"I'd appreciate it if you'd send for them now," Mitch said. "I'll need to question them."

Qualls frowned. "This is Indian land. It's not in the jurisdiction of the Buckskin police department."

Recently, the 10th U.S. Circuit Court had held in an Adair County case that the state did not have authority to make an arrest on Indian land. In fact, in line with the BIA's newly liberalized policies, the Cherokee tribe was in the process of establishing its own courts to handle criminal misdemeanors. It would be the first time federally sanctioned Indian courts had operated in the Cherokee Nation in nearly a hundred years. It was only a matter of time, Mitch was sure, before an agreement was worked out with the tribe, whereby city and county law officers would be deputized to make arrests on Indian land.

"The crime," Mitch said, "wasn't committed on Indian land. When we're ready to make an arrest, we can worry about jurisdiction. Right now, I'm trying to find out what happened. I'm sure, Mr. Qualls, that you want to cooperate in every possible way."

Qualls seemed to be considering the implications of Mitch's words. He didn't want it said that he'd refused to cooperate with the police in investigating the death of a child left in the school's charge, and for whom he was ultimately responsible. He nodded, reached for the phone, and spoke to the young woman in the outer office.

The principal, Mitch observed, had quickly recovered from his shock and spoke authoritatively into the mouthpiece, a man accustomed to being in control. "Darlene, go and find Merv and Mr. Shoemaker and Miss Adair. Tell them to abandon the search. Tamarah has been located." He listened for a moment. "Never mind. Just say what I told you. And tell them to come to my office right away." He paused. "Yes, all three of them."

"What do you know about Tamarah Birch?" Mitch asked when Qualls had replaced the receiver.

The principal's hand closed over the paperweight but he didn't pick it up. The paperweight, Mitch thought, was Qualls's version of worry beads.

"This is her first year with us." Qualls shrugged helplessly. "One of our third-graders. I believe her father is a widower. Beyond that, I know very little, I'm afraid. I don't have a great deal of contact with the students." He removed his hand and stared at the paperweight. "Administrative duties keep me pretty well confined to this building."

"A few minutes ago, you started to say something about Tamarah and stopped yourself."

Qualls looked at Mitch, then dropped his eyes to his desk again.

"You said, 'No wonder she didn't...' What did you mean?"

Qualls expelled a long breath. "Tamarah was supposed to be here, in my office, this morning at eight-thirty, but she never came."

"Why did you want to see her?"

"Yesterday—" Qualls paused, as though trying to get his thoughts in order. "Last evening at dinner, she threw a glass at an eighth-grade boy, Stanley Dick. One of Tamarah's roommates said Stanley had been teasing Tamarah for weeks and...well, I guess she'd had enough. Fortunately the glass missed the boy and shattered on the floor. It could as easily have hit him or another child. Someone could have been seriously injured. I took Tamarah outside the cafeteria to talk to her, and...well, I'm afraid I lost my temper. She started crying, and I realized I was too angry to deal with her then. I instructed her to come to my office this morning and I'd tell her what punishment I'd decided on."

"What about the boy—Stanley?"

"I intended to talk to him later today."

"Did you send for Tamarah when she didn't keep the appointment?"

He shook his head. "I decided I'd deal with her after the weekend. It wasn't as if Tamarah was a chronic trouble-maker. I'm sure she regretted throwing the glass as soon as it happened."

"Were you informed immediately when it was discovered that Tamarah was missing?"

"Oh, yes. Nancy Adair, a first-year teacher here, came to tell me. I went out to where the buses were parked and assessed the situation. As I said, I sent everybody but Miss Adair and Lyman Shoemaker, our counselor, on ahead. I didn't want to make too much of it in front of the children, you understand, until we located Tamarah."

"What do you mean by assessing the situation? What did you think had happened to Tamarah?"

Qualls thrust a finger inside his shirt collar and tugged it away from his Adam's apple. "I assumed—we all did—that she'd simply wandered off and lost track of the time. Occasionally there are students who aren't in their assigned places when we count noses. You expect that when you're dealing with children. We always find them somewhere on campus, engrossed in a game or a book, something like that." He sounded as though he still wanted to believe in such an innocuous outcome, to hold off the truth as long as possible.

"Do you know who saw Tamarah last?"

"Evidently it was Ruthann Blackfox, another third-grader, and one of the three girls who share Tamarah's

room. According to Ruthann, she and Tamarah went back
to the room after breakfast and dressed for the pow-wow.
Then Tamarah asked Ruthann to wait there for her until she
returned. Ruthann knew she was supposed to come here and
assumed that's where she'd gone.''

"What time did Tamarah leave the room?"

Qualls scratched his jaw. "I questioned Ruthann about
that, but she had no idea. You know how children are about
time." He fingered his plaid bow tie, worn with a short-
sleeved white dress shirt. It was a gesture of anxiety, or perhaps irritation at finding himself the object of police interrogation. His suit jacket hung on a hook in a corner of the
room behind the desk. He looked strangely defenseless
without it. "I would imagine it was about eight-fifteen." He
pursed his lips. "An hour and a half at most that she was
unaccounted for. How could—"

Not to be diverted from his line of questioning, Mitch cut
in. "Did you have breakfast in the cafeteria?"

Qualls looked startled by the question. "No. I ate at home
this morning. There's a house provided for the principal on
the grounds."

Mitch nodded, aware that most of the teaching staff were
housed on campus.

"When I eat in the cafeteria, I'm often delayed by having to deal with student misconduct." He grimaced. "Like
yesterday with Tamarah. My wife didn't feel well enough to
prepare a meal, and she wasn't hungry herself. That's the
only reason I was eating in the cafeteria when the incident
occurred."

"You arrived here this morning well before the eight-
thirty meeting with Tamarah?" Mitch asked.

Qualls nodded.

"Did you have breakfast alone?"

Qualls hesitated rather longer than was necessary. "My
wife was there." His gaze had become wary and he fingered
the paperweight again.

"When did you leave your house?"

Qualls's face mottled, but he hesitated not at all this time.
"Eight o'clock," he snapped. "I walked across the campus

to the administration building, reaching my office a few minutes after eight. You might like to check that with my secretary."

In his chair, Duckworth scribbled rapidly, then looked up with pen poised.

Mitch gazed at Qualls a moment. "I'll do that." If the tribal school board was like most such boards, they picked a man to run the school and let him run it, stepping in only when necessary. Qualls was not used to being asked to give such detailed account of himself and he didn't like it. Mitch waited, inviting further comment. Qualls said nothing.

"After you arrived at your office, did you leave it again?"

"I've already told you. I went out to the buses, when Miss Adair came to say they couldn't find Tamarah. That was a little after nine-forty-five."

"Not until then?" Mitch's tone sharpened. He didn't like Qualls's attitude.

"Oh, for heaven's sake," Qualls exploded. "As I recall, I went down the hall to the men's room once."

"I'm sure your secretary can verify that, too," Mitch said.

The look he got in return was hot enough to singe eyebrows. Then, in a flash, Qualls's anger seemed to merge with anxiety. "I am doing my best to cooperate with you," he said, adding, "I can't afford not to. But I don't have to like seeing your people swarm over the campus, questioning everyone and disrupting our schedule."

"Your schedule?" Mitch raised an eyebrow. "A child has been killed and you're worried about your schedule?"

"It's a terrible thing," Qualls said evenly. "You cannot regret it more than I, I assure you. I expect we'll have newspapers calling, reporters showing up unannounced when word of this gets out. I understand that you have a job to do, Chief Bushyhead, but I still have a school to run, parents and a board to answer to..."

Mitch was getting the picture clearly now. Qualls's number one worry was the public relations aspect of this. It explained why he had agreed to cooperate so readily. Paradoxically, by cooperating, he was helping to expedite the wildfire spread of unsavory rumors. The man was be-

tween a rock and a hard place. "Will you get in touch with
Tamarah's father?"

Qualls looked resigned. "Of course. I can imagine how
difficult this will be for him."

Mitch assessed him for a moment. "Do you have children, Mr. Qualls?"

The principal's expression was blank. "No."

"Then you can't begin to imagine what this is going to do
to Tamarah's father." Irritated, Mitch turned and walked to
a row of tall, east-facing windows. From his second-floor
vantage point, he looked down on four people—Qualls's
secretary, a second young woman, a tall man who appeared
to be in his late fifties, and an older man wearing striped
overalls—who were crossing the circular drive where the
students had boarded the buses earlier that morning. They
approached the building and disappeared from his sight.

Duckworth coughed and shuffled his feet, but Mitch
didn't turn around. The three men in the office waited in silence until Darlene tapped at the door. Qualls, seemingly
relieved to have a reason for movement, got up to admit
Miss Adair, Shoemaker, and the janitor.

Qualls made the introductions and Mitch explained what
had happened. All three appeared stunned, especially Nancy
Adair, who gasped and covered her mouth with her hand.
She was slim, an ordinary-looking young woman with
smooth, dusky skin and very white, even teeth. A first-year
teacher, Qualls had said, so she must be twenty-one or -two.
She didn't look a day over eighteen.

Shoemaker was tall and gaunt and the color of tanned
deer hide. He had a smoker's cough. Haines, the janitor,
appeared to be a white man, though appearances could be
deceiving. Haines could easily be on the Cherokee tribal roll,
which required proof of an ancestor listed on the Dawes
Commission Rolls of 1899-1906, a census of the Five Civi-
lized Tribes taken as a prelude to Oklahoma statehood.
Anybody who could provide that information, regardless of
degree of Indian blood, was entitled to all the privileges of
tribal membership, including free use of Indian health care
facilities.

Haines was sixtyish, with a squint that made him look perpetually suspicious. His teeth were as stained as his overalls and a musky body odor wafted from him. He'd taken a toothpick from his pocket and was chewing on it. Haines's body language was defensive, arms crossed over his chest, chin tucked in.

Haines and the other two had remained standing, there not being enough chairs to go around. Qualls had offered Nancy Adair a seat, but she had declined.

Mitch's questions elicited little helpful information from the newcomers. All three had eaten breakfast in the cafeteria that morning. None of them admitted to having seen Tamarah after she left there.

Haines estimated that he'd gone back to his room in the basement of the administration building at seven-forty-five. Shoemaker and Adair had stayed until the last of the children had vacated the cafeteria a few minutes after eight. Then both had returned to their quarters in the row of duplexes lining the west edge of the campus, leaving again in time to meet the buses in front of the administration building at about nine-forty. Since all three lived alone, no one could vouch for their remaining in their quarters in the approximate hour and a half that had passed between breakfast and the discovery that Tamarah was missing.

"Think back," Mitch said. "Can any of you remember something you've seen or heard that might give us a clue to what happened?"

Shoemaker and Haines took little time to shake their heads negatively. Nancy Adair hesitated. "Like what?"

"Did you ever notice a man hanging around Tamarah or any of the other female students?"

She took a moment to absorb the implications of the question. "A stranger, you mean?" she asked.

"Possibly," Mitch said, "or a parent, even a staff member or a teacher whose interest seemed a bit out of line."

Qualls, who had returned to the chair behind his desk and picked up the paperweight, now dropped the glass cube impatiently. "All of our teachers take an interest in the stu-

dents. That's one of the advantages of a small, private
school.''

"I'm referring to interest of another sort." Mitch's tone
was curt. "Behavior that seems exaggerated or skewed."

"I resent these inferences that someone connected with
the school did this," Qualls exploded furiously. "If that's
what you think, you're wrong. We've never had anything
like . . . like what you're insinuating at this school."

"The past is no predictor of the future," Mitch observed
dryly. "Do you check every applicant's background thoroughly before you hire him?"

"Naturally."

"I would like to see your personnel files."

"Oh, now . . . I don't know about that." Qualls tapped a
finger on the paperweight. "There's the matter of privacy
and—no, I can't do that without my board's permission."

"Can you run it by them today?"

He hesitated. "I'm not sure I'll be able to reach them all.
I'll try."

Mitch's gaze returned to Nancy Adair. "You didn't answer my question, Miss Adair."

She frowned and shook her head. "I never noticed anyone taking an inappropriate interest in the girls." She
brushed dark hair off her forehead. "Chief Bushyhead, I
had Tamarah in class. I teach third grade in the mornings—in the afternoon, they go to special classes. I've been
trying to think of something she said or did that might provide a clue to why she went into the woods. Or with
whom . . ." Her voice trailed off.

"And?"

"There simply isn't anything. I'm sorry."

As Mitch turned back to Shoemaker to ask a question,
Nancy Adair pursued her own thoughts. In this, her first
year of teaching, she had prided herself on being able to spot
quickly students who needed extra help. As Porter Qualls
frequently pointed out in faculty meetings, the school's
small classes made it possible for them to provide individual attention, and this was one of the main reasons parents
enrolled their children.

Sadly, some of the faculty members were less conscientious than Nancy. Especially if they had been teaching a number of years. They seemed to get worn down, to give up too easily. They didn't want to be bothered with the students after regular class hours. They said they couldn't be expected to work day and night, not on what they were paid.

Nancy did not consider it a bother, but rather an added opportunity to point students in the direction of productive adult lives. She hoped she never reached the point where she could shrug off students who were doing poorly in class.

Lyman Shoemaker said that after a year or two she would either mellow out or burn out. Lyman had put in enough years teaching to qualify for retirement but planned to work until he could draw Social Security as well as his teacher's pension. Lyman had clearly mellowed out. His relaxed manner seemed to appeal to the students, who found it easy to talk to him. She hoped he was wrong about her concern for the children growing less urgent with the years, although being conscientious had its down side. It made one feel things more deeply. She felt inexplicably indicted by Tamarah Birch's death.

Tamarah had been one of those youngsters who could not seem to grasp the logic of numbers, and Nancy had spent many afterschool hours helping the child with her arithmetic. She had thought she knew Tamarah well, and she would not have believed Tamarah would leave the school grounds without permission. Yet clearly Tamarah had done so, which meant that Nancy hadn't known the child as well as she'd thought. Maybe, as Lyman claimed, her attitude toward the children was not very realistic. Perhaps if she'd been a little more sensitive...

Mitch interrupted her thoughts. "Miss Adair?"

"I'm sorry. I keep trying to think of something to help you, but it's no use."

"Did you see Tamarah at breakfast this morning?"

"I don't recall noticing her. The students are given new table assignments at the beginning of each month. I think she's at Ellis Harlan's table this month."

"He's our coach and PE teacher," Qualls put in.

Mitch nodded. He had the feeling Nancy Adair was holding something back, but she wasn't going to stick her neck out in front of Qualls. Mitch didn't press her. It wouldn't do any good. He'd get back to her later when Qualls wasn't around.

"It might be a good idea," Qualls mused, as though to himself, "to have a security guard on campus round the clock for the next few days, as an added precaution. It would help ease parents' minds."

"Don't you use security personnel on a regular basis?" Mitch asked.

"Only at night. And on days when we're expecting a number of visitors to the campus. We use retired and off-duty sheriff's deputies who want to make a little extra income. It's worked out fine. Our security people are well accepted by staff and students alike."

Mitch knew all the men in the sheriff's department. He'd made it a policy to maintain a good relationship between the city police and the county law enforcement agencies. "What hours do they work?"

"Eleven P.M. to eight A.M."

"Who was on duty last night?"

"Jerry Bookland, I think. He's the only one who works a forty-hour week."

"Yes, it was Jerry," Shoemaker put in. "I spoke to him as I was walking across campus to the cafeteria this morning."

Mitch knew Bookland better than the younger deputies, and liked him. Bookland had retired from the sheriff's department only a few months ago, but Mitch hadn't known he was working at the school. "What was he doing?" he queried.

Shoemaker shrugged. "Making his last round of the campus, I guess. He always does that before going off duty."

Mitch made a mental note to question Bookland, particularly about the male teachers at the school. He also needed to verify Charley Horn's account of his whereabouts that morning with his wife. And talk to Qualls's wife, as well.

Mitch assumed the two women had gone to town with the others, so it would have to wait until the school buses returned students and teachers to the campus.

At this point, he had no reason to suspect Qualls or Horn any more than the other men employed by the school, but he didn't think Tamarah Birch would have gone willingly into the woods with a stranger. She'd have made a fuss. It was difficult to imagine a struggle going on without somebody noticing. No, Mitch told himself, Tamarah knew and trusted her killer. He would proceed on that assumption unless contrary evidence came to light.

There seemed nothing more he could do there now. "When will the students and faculty be back on campus?"

Clearly knowing the reason for Mitch's question, Qualls replied irritably, "Five o'clock. We serve dinner at six."

"I'll be back about seven then," Mitch said. "Right now, I'd like to have a look at Tamarah's room."

Resigned, Qualls said, "Lyman, will you accompany the officers? Get the master key from Darlene."

Mitch gestured for Duckworth, and the three men left the office.

In the reception area, they waited while the gum-chewing Darlene found the master key and handed it to Shoemaker. Duckworth and the counselor headed for the main staircase and started down. Mitch lingered at the secretary's desk. "By the way, Darlene, what time did you get to work this morning?"

She blinked and popped her gum, then pushed blue-framed glasses up her nose. "Eight o'clock. This is about that little girl who's missing, isn't it? What's going on?"

"Tamarah Birch is dead."

Darlene's mouth fell open. She caught her gum in her hand and reinserted it in her mouth. "Good Lord! What happened?"

"I'm trying to find out," Mitch said. "Did you notice what time Mr. Qualls got here this morning?"

"I—I can't say for sure. Five or ten minutes after I did, I guess."

"Did you see Tamarah this morning?"

"No."

"Okay. Your boss got here about ten after eight. When did he next leave his office?"

She frowned. "Uh—well, I guess when Miss Adair came to tell him they couldn't find Tamarah Birch."

"Are you sure he didn't come out of his office before then? To speak to you, maybe, or to go to the men's room?"

"Oh, yes, I remember now. He did come out earlier and went down the hall." She pointed. "You can't see the men's room door from here, but I guess that's where he was going." She took the wad of gum from her mouth and dropped it into a wastebasket beneath the desk. "I can't believe that little girl is dead."

"How long was Mr. Qualls gone, when he went to the men's room?"

"A few minutes."

"One more question, Darlene. I noticed a door behind Mr. Qualls's desk. What's on the other side of it?"

"That's the conference room." She stared at him. "Do you think—"

Mitch cut her off. "Is there a way out of the conference room, other than through Mr. Qualls's office?"

"You can go in from the hall—" She pointed again. "—around that corner."

"So someone could enter or leave the principal's office without your seeing them?"

"Well, sure... Listen, Chief..." She hesitated.

"Yes?"

"Jerry Bookland mentioned something to me the other day." She glanced over her shoulder at the closed office door and lowered her voice. "When my boss is out of the office, I sometimes duck into the guards' office downstairs—for a little chat, you know."

Mitch gazed at her, wishing she'd get to the point.

"It's—well, I wouldn't want to cause trouble for anybody..."

"I'll be discreet."

"Okay." Darlene shrugged. "One day last week, Jerry went with a sheriff's deputy over to Vinita to bring a guy home from Eastern State." Eastern State was a state-funded and -operated psychiatric hospital.

"Few mental patients are violent," Mitch said. "Even fewer are killers."

"The thing is…" Darlene paused to unwrap another stick of gum. "This guy—I can't remember his name—was sent up there for exposing himself to women."

"Dwayne Burns?" Mitch asked.

"Yeah, that's him."

The hospital had agreed to notify Mitch when they released Burns, a mousy-looking man in his fifties. For years, Burns had been self-employed as an appliance repairman. Had a couple of grown daughters living out of state. Lived quietly with his wife in a modest house a few blocks from the tribal school campus. Never gave anybody a bit of trouble until about six months ago, when he had exposed himself to two housewives who'd called him to repair their washing machines.

The first woman, perhaps too shocked or embarrassed, had not reported the incident after ordering him out of her house. She had done so only after the second woman, Bertie Grey, came to the police. Grey, a local florist in her sixties, kept saying, "The whole world's gone crazy, Chief." Mitch had not been inclined to disagree.

Bertie Grey had gone on to say, "I've known Dwayne Burns for years—or thought I knew him until this happened. I turned around, and there he was, showing me his nature. Acted right proud of himself, too. The whole world's gone crazy, I tell you." The other woman had merely nodded vigorous assent to everything Bertie Grey said.

Burns's wife, a soft-spoken Sunday School teacher, had been so mortified she hadn't left her house for weeks. In due time, the judge had put Burns on probation and ordered him to Eastern State to undergo psychiatric evaluation. That had been three months ago.

Mitch thanked Darlene and ambled down the hall far enough to see the door marked CONFERENCE and a second stairway leading to the lower level where there were several exits from the building.

FIVE

"ARE YOU SUGGESTING that Merv Haines had something to do with that child's death?" Qualls's angry bark was directed at Nancy Adair.

After the police officers and Shoemaker had left, followed shortly by the janitor, she had lingered to voice the concern that had instantly come to mind when Chief Bushyhead asked if they had noticed something unusual in anyone's attitude toward the female students.

"I didn't say that. I'm merely pointing out that Merv has a—well, a streak of lasciviousness."

"Upon what," Qualls demanded with a smirk, "do you base such a judgment?"

Nancy Adair blushed but went on staunchly. "He has pornographic magazines in his room. I saw a stack of them a few weeks ago."

Qualls cocked an eyebrow. "You were in Merv's room?"

"I had to go and find him. One of my third-graders threw up all over her desk, and I needed Merv to bring his bucket and disinfectant to clean it up."

Qualls stared at her for an instant. "Pornography. Are you referring to those girlie magazines that can be bought at any newsstand?"

"No, these were—well, cruder. The few pictures I saw were of naked women in lewd poses, or men and women together. I assume they're sold at *adult* bookstores, though if there ever was a misnomer, that's it."

"Why wasn't this reported to me immediately?"

"I didn't want to overreact. I did tell Merv that he'd better get rid of the magazines before one of the students saw them."

"Did he?"

"He said he would."

"I'll check it out." Qualls drummed the desk with his fingers. "I don't see any connection to Tamarah's death here. Even if she was molested, which is only an assumption on your part."

"From the questions Bushyhead was asking, he thinks so. Merv—"

"Merv may have questionable taste in literature," Qualls interrupted, tugging impatiently on his bow tie. "But he's been here for years and he's never paid any particular attention to the female students. In fact, my impression is that he tries to avoid the children, boys *and* girls. I think they get on his nerves, but that doesn't make him a murderer—or a sex maniac, in spite of the magazines you saw in his room."

"At the very least," she persisted, "pornography is an unhealthy preoccupation."

"I said I'd speak to him. Merv has been divorced for twenty years. A man needs an outlet for... for frustration." He cleared his throat as he studied the butterfly imprisoned in the paperweight. "Of course, pornography is a poor choice. But as far as Tamarah's tragedy goes, it's beside the point."

"Beside the point?" She stared. "I must disagree, Mr. Qualls." He looked up at her sharp tone. She went on, "Given the fact that Merv Haines works and lives with children, it would seem to be very much to the point. I think the police would agree with me."

Qualls's gaze narrowed. "Perhaps," he said. "*If* they were to hear about it."

His message was clear. Nancy Adair's shoulders slumped more with sadness than defeat. "No doubt you're right. Merv couldn't have had anything to do with it. For one thing, I can't imagine Tamarah going into the woods with him without a fight. But don't we have a duty to inform the police of the magazines and let them make that determination? It's entirely possible that somebody else has seen Merv's collection and will mention it to the authorities."

"Maybe." Qualls was thoughtful. "But... as far as you and I are concerned, this conversation never took place. Agreed?"

After a moment's hesitation, she nodded.

"If Bushyhead hears of Merv's—er, pastime from another source, I'll handle it." His gaze locked with Nancy Adair's. "You would have to sit in this chair, Nancy, to understand my position."

"I hope," she said bravely, "that I would act on moral principles."

Qualls smiled faintly. "I'm an administrator, not an idealist. There are those who would say the two are mutually exclusive."

She didn't respond, but she clearly didn't agree.

"The school, under my leadership, has a good record. That could be reversed overnight by a few unfounded rumors that would destroy parents' faith in us."

"There are bound to be rumors, anyway, as soon as this gets out."

She would have continued, but he stopped her with a raised hand. "Let me finish. Financially, we walk a precarious line. The money received from the tribal budget is based on the number of students enrolled. Right now we're receiving just enough to maintain our faculty at its current level, which is at the acceptable minimum. We can't afford any significant drop in enrollment. A scandal could ruin us." He gave her a rueful look. "You're too young to have learned the value of prudence, Nancy. One day you'll understand. In the meantime, don't judge me too harshly."

THE GIRLS' and boys' dormitories sat on either side of the cafeteria-auditorium-gymnasium, a barnlike sandstone building. The dorms, rectangular, red brick, two-story structures, had peaked, green, composition-shingle roofs. The cafeteria building faced the only other sandstone structure on campus, the administration building, across a grassy oval studded with pear trees. A paved road circled the oval and stretched north to the school's stone-pillared entrance.

As soon as they left Qualls's office, Shoemaker had tapped a cigarette from the pack in his pocket and lit up, sucking in the smoke like a dehydrated man gulping water.

On the walk from the administration building to the girls'
dorm, he filled Mitch and Duckworth in on a few statistics.

Student enrollment at the school was one hundred and
sixty-seven, a hundred and twenty of whom boarded at the
school. The boarders were about equally divided between
boys and girls. There were twelve full-time faculty members, including the coach, Harlan Ellis, who taught physical education as well as coaching boys' and girls' teams in
basketball and track and the boys' baseball team.

Ten full-time faculty members lived on campus. The art
and music teachers were at the school only a few hours a
week and lived in town. In addition to the principal, the
nonteaching staff included Shoemaker, the counselor;
Haines, the janitor; two cooks; a bookkeeper; and two
clerk-secretaries. Qualls, Shoemaker, and Haines lived on
campus, the others in town.

Two heavily laden lilac bushes flanking the girls' dorm
entrance exuded sweet, heavy perfume. As they climbed the
steps, Mitch trailed a hand along the sloping cement wall
beside the stairs. It was rough and cool.

Tamarah Birch's room had the institutional look of the
dorm facilities Mitch remembered from his college days.
Pale tan walls and a floor of serviceable brown tiles. The
dorm was not air-conditioned, and the room had a stuffy,
closed-up smell but was very clean. Plainly, the girls'
housekeeping was closely monitored. Mitch wished his own
daughter's room was half as neat.

Sturdy oak bunk beds stood against two walls. The bed-
spreads, probably provided by the girls' parents, were of
different colors and styles and there were several stuffed
animals on each bunk. Two oak desks sat, back-to-back,
beneath the single window. Two tall chests of drawers, a
bookcase, and a large bulletin board divided into four sec-
tions occupied the remaining wall space.

Each section of the bulletin board was identified by a
girl's name affixed with a thumbtack. "Jamie"'s space was
wholly taken up with a Michael Jackson poster. On
"Mari"'s section of the board, various mementos were
placed in no particular order: a blue ribbon labeled Okla-

homa City State Fair, First Place, Barrel Riding Competition; a note reminding Mari to "Call Mom Saturday" and
another noting "Theme due May 15"; a snapshot of a
young girl, presumably Mari, astride a bay horse; and other
snapshots of what appeared to be Mari's family—a man
holding the hand of a preschool boy and a woman with a
baby in her arms.

Ruthann's space contained snapshots of several other
girls, including Tamarah Birch; a report card from the previous fall semester, its string of A's marred by a single B in
science; and a certificate, also from the fall semester, stat-
ing that Ruthann had achieved perfect scores on all her
spelling tests.

Tamarah Birch had pinned up a small poster showing the
smiling adolescent faces of the singing group New Kids on
the Block; several photographs of what appeared to be a ski
outing enjoyed by Tamarah and a man, evidently Tamarah's father; a school picture of a girl of Tamarah's age
signed, "I hope we can always be friends, Ruthann"; and a
pencil sketch of a boy's head labeled "Johnny in social
studies class."

Each of the two chests had four drawers, the first and
third drawers being labeled with a girl's name. Tamarah
Birch had shared a chest with Jamie.

Mitch read the names aloud, adding, "Ruthann would be
Ruthann Blackfox, the last person known to have seen Tamarah before she disappeared?"

Shoemaker nodded. "Ruthann and Tamarah were best
friends, always together. Jamie's an eighth-grader and
Mari's in the seventh. We try to put two younger students
with two older ones. The older ones can help the younger
with homework, laundry, things like that. It works out
pretty well."

Duckworth opened the closet door and began rummag-
ing through shoes, books, games, and toys that were piled
on the overhead shelf. "How many adults live in this building?" Mitch asked Shoemaker, who was leaning against the
doorframe, smoking a second cigarette.

"A married couple lives in an apartment in each of the dormitories."

"Aren't Charley Horn and his wife dorm parents?" Mitch asked, vaguely remembering Horn saying something to that effect.

"Yeah. Charley and Aggie have the girls, Stafford and Louise Stand, the boys."

"Are all four on the faculty, as well?"

"Yes. Charley teaches social studies, his wife teaches math in the fourth through eighth grades. Stafford is the science teacher. Louise has the seventh- and eighth-grade girls for living skills mornings and is in charge of the library in the afternoon."

"Living skills?"

"What we used to call homemaking," Shoemaker explained.

Mitch pulled out the two drawers assigned to Tamarah, lifting underwear, socks, folded shirts, and jeans, then putting them all back as he'd found them. Each item of clothing had a tag bearing Tamarah's name sewn inside it. In addition to clothing, the drawers contained several pencil sketches, a box of notepaper and envelopes, three letters to Tamarah from her father, a small bottle of cologne, and a pile of hair ribbons. No notes or diary, nothing done by Tamarah's hand except the drawings. Mitch picked them up and looked through them. There were several attempts at sketching classmates and some of campus buildings.

"Tamarah was always drawing something," Shoemaker offered. "She was pretty good, wasn't she?"

Mitch murmured an agreement. Disappointed, he replaced the sketches in the drawer and turned his attention to the desks. But a careful search turned up nothing helpful there, either. Duckworth came out of the closet, red-faced and sweating.

"Anything?" Mitch asked.

"A stash of gum drops. Somebody doesn't want to share."

Shoemaker chuckled and dropped his cigarette stub on the floor, put it out with his heel, then bent to retrieve it.

Painstakingly, he swept up a few scattered bits of tobacco with his hand and dropped them and the butt in his shirt pocket. When he straightened, he seemed embarrassed to find Mitch watching him. "We're not supposed to smoke anywhere on campus except in our living quarters, the faculty lounge, and rest rooms," he said. "I confess I sneak one now and then when I'm alone in my office."

"That would be on the ground floor of the administration building?"

Shoemaker nodded. "It's across the hall from the guards' office."

"We're about through here," Mitch told him. "I'll make sure the door is locked when we leave."

Shoemaker hesitated, patted the cigarette stub in his shirt pocket, then said, "I'll set up counseling appointments for Tamarah's roommates. They'll need help dealing with what's happened. I can't betray a confidence, of course, but if any of them tells me something pertinent to your investigation, I'll certainly urge her to tell you."

"Thanks. I appreciate it."

"I guess I'll be on my way."

Mitch said, "Wait. I just thought of something I meant to ask you. You must have studied psychosexual disorders."

Shoemaker, who had stepped away from the door, turned back and propped his shoulder against the facing again. "Not in great depth, though the subject was touched on in a couple of my graduate courses." He studied Mitch's face with interest. "Was Tamarah sexually abused?"

"I don't know yet. Certain evidence points in that direction."

"If you're wondering if I've counseled a student with that sort of problem, I haven't. It's not something even a high school counselor is apt to run across."

"I'd like to ask you a theoretical question, anyway."

"Shoot."

"It's my understanding that an exhibitionist and a pedophile are two different breeds of cat. Is that right?"

"More or less. An exhibitionist gets his kicks from exposing himself to unsuspecting people, very often strangers. It's the surprise or shock factor he likes. With a true exhibitionist there's no attempt at further sexual activity, except maybe masturbation. When a pedophile exposes himself, it's a prelude to sexual activity with the child."

"Then there *are* recorded instances of pedophiles who also expose themselves?"

"A few, but it's rare."

Mitch pondered that for a moment. "Could you speak to Tamarah's roommates today and tell them I'd like to talk to them this evening? It might frighten them if they're not expecting me."

"Will do," Shoemaker said. "I'll let the Horns know you're coming, too."

The counselor left then, his leather heels tapping sharply in the silent dormitory.

SIX

MITCH TURNED back to the room as Duckworth emerged from the closet. "What was that about an exhibitionist?" Duckworth asked.

"Dwayne Burns is back in town."

Duckworth's mismatched eyes widened. "No shit."

Mitch looked at him more closely. "What are you eating?"

"Gumdrops."

"You stole a little girl's candy?"

Duckworth shrugged. "One small handful. Big deal." He popped a black gumdrop into his mouth.

Mitch shook his head resignedly. "That's low, Duck."

"The kid's got a quart of 'em hidden in the closet. She'll never miss 'em."

Eyeing Duckworth's stomach, Mitch said, "Looks like you've gained back the weight you lost last winter." Mitch had pressured Duckworth into losing fifteen pounds by instituting weight and fitness requirements for the members of the force. After the January weigh-in, Duckworth had gradually returned to his old eating habits. He knew Mitch might put him on probation following the next weigh-in, but he didn't believe Mitch would ever fire him. Mitch didn't believe it, either, and that took the teeth out of his attempts to impress Duckworth with the importance of weight loss.

Obviously eager to change the subject, Duckworth asked, "What did you find out from the secretary?"

"There's a way out of Qualls's office through the conference room. You can't see the door from where the secretary sits."

Duckworth whistled softly. After a thoughtful moment, he said, "If Qualls left that way, he was taking a big risk.

The secretary could have gone into his office at any time. What if he'd had a phone call?"

"Yeah, it would've been chancy, all right."

Duckworth pondered, then mused, "I like old Dwayne Burns as a suspect." He tapped a finger against his forehead. "The dirty old fart. You think they can cure that kind of thing in three months?"

"I'm not sure they can ever cure it—the urge, I mean," Mitch said. "Maybe they can teach him how to control it." Mitch had serious doubts that Burns had received much help in that direction at Eastern State. The state hospitals were underfunded and understaffed. They'd have socked Burns with tranquilizers and assigned him to a caseworker who might have had time to see him for a few minutes twice a week. If Burns saw a psychiatrist once a month during his hospital stay, Mitch would be surprised.

"I can't really see Burns killing somebody," Mitch said. But he continued to be bothered by what Shoemaker had told him. What if Burns was one of the rare pedophiles who began by exposing himself? What if he'd exposed himself to Tamarah, and she'd panicked and started screaming? He'd have been frantic to shut her up.

"Well, I couldn't believe it when Bertie Grey charged him with exposing himself, either," Duckworth said. "Burns was always such a bookish little wimp. I thought maybe she was exaggerating some innocent incident, like maybe Dwayne forgot to zip up his pants or something. Until the second woman showed up and said Dwayne exposed himself to her, too."

"Yeah." Initially, Mitch had had the same doubts.

"You through here?"

Mitch nodded. They left the room. Mitch closed the door, checking to make sure the lock was engaged.

"What next?" Duckworth asked.

Mitch glanced at his watch. "The parade should be over. You better get to town and help Roo patrol the main drag." It was Charles "Roo" Stephens's last day shift for a while. Starting tomorrow, when Shelly Pitcher came on days, he'd work graveyard with Virgil Rabbit. "Make yourself con-

spicuous. Check with Helen when you get back to the car."
They had left both squad cars parked at the Kirkwood
house. "There must have been an accident or a fight by
now. She's probably been trying to get hold of us."

"What are you going to do?"

"Walk around the campus, see if I can find anybody else
to talk to. Then I'll get my car and stop over at the Burns's
house. I'll drop by the station afterward and check my
messages."

"Mrs. Burns ain't gonna be happy to see you." He ate the
last gumdrop and ran his hand down the front of his shirt
to wipe off the sugar.

"Nope." Mitch hated to bother the prim, retiring woman.
She didn't deserve to have her home and her peace invaded
every time there was a sex-related crime in the county. From
what Mitch had seen of her, she was ill-equipped to deal
with incidents that she couldn't comprehend and that she'd
never expected to touch her life. He sighed as he parted from
Duckworth outside the dormitory, saying, "I'll hook up
with you in town."

As Mitch was crossing the campus, a woman came out on
the porch of a neat brick house to put an out-going letter in
the rack beneath the mailbox. She peered at Mitch curiously. Since it was the only single-family dwelling on the
campus, it had to be the principal's home. Besides, the
woman was the buxom female whose photograph graced the
library table in Qualls's office. Mitch had assumed she'd be
in town with the rest of the school population, but she was
wearing a blue quilted robe and white terrycloth scuffs,
clearly in no hurry to take in the Heritage Celebration.

Mitch walked up to the house. "Mrs. Qualls?"

She clutched the lapels of her robe together with one
hand. Her wispy, graying brown hair was in disarray and the
skin around her eyes was puffy from sleep. "Yes."

"I'm Mitch Bushyhead with the Buckskin police."

"I thought I recognized you. If you're here to see my
husband, you should be able to find him in his office in the
administration building."

"I've already talked to him, ma'am. I gather you haven't heard the news."

She blinked owlishly. "What news?"

Mitch told her. She gaped at him, as though she was waiting for the punch line. Finally, she murmured, "Somebody killed one of the students?" From the way she said it, Mitch guessed she couldn't place Tamarah Birch. "But why on earth would—?"

"We're trying to find out why, Mrs. Qualls. I wonder if I might ask you a question or two."

"Me? I can't help you. I haven't even been out of the house today."

"What time did you and your husband have breakfast this morning?"

She hesitated, looking puzzled, then said, "Porter was up early, before seven, and made toast and coffee. He woke me when he got up, but I dropped off again."

"So you didn't get up until later."

She clutched her robe more tightly and shook her head. "I can't see what this has to do with the little girl's death."

"Nothing, I'm sure, but I like to nail down times and places so I know where everyone was when a crime occurred. Somebody may have seen or heard something pertinent without knowing it. If I know who had the opportunity, I might be able to jog some memories."

"Oh," she said doubtfully. "Well—I suffer from migraine headaches, and yesterday afternoon about six I felt one coming on." She touched the back of her head gingerly. "It starts with a dull ache right at the base of my skull. When I get that feeling, I have to take one of my pills and go to bed in a perfectly dark room. If I'm lucky, I can sleep it off. I wake up feeling sluggish because of the pill, but the pain is usually gone."

"Were you lucky this time?"

"Pardon?"

"Were you able to sleep it off?"

"Yes, I finally fell asleep about eight."

"When did you wake up?"

She bit her lip. "After nine. The pills often put me to sleep for twelve hours or more."

"So you didn't see your husband at all this morning?"

"No, not after he left the bedroom." She frowned, then added an afterthought. "I found the remains of his toast and his coffee cup on the kitchen table, though. The paper was there, too. Porter always reads the *Tulsa World* with his breakfast."

"I see. Thank you, Mrs. Qualls. You've been very helpful."

"I have?"

"Yes, ma'am. You'll let me know if you think of anything else?"

"I won't—think of anything else, I mean. I don't interfere with the running of the school or in the affairs of the students."

A telephone rang inside the house. "That's probably Porter," she said, turning to go back inside, "calling to tell me about the student's death."

And too late to brief her on what she should say to the police. Mitch thanked her again and continued toward his patrol car. It was clear now why Qualls had hesitated when Mitch had asked if he'd been alone that morning before going to his office. He hadn't been in the house alone, but he might as well have been. Qualls's whereabouts could not be precisely accounted for from before seven A.M. to nine-forty-five, roughly three hours.

UNLIKE MRS. QUALLS, Mrs. Burns looked as though she had slept very little the previous night. Her eyes were bloodshot, and there were dark half-moons like bruises beneath the bottom lids. Her cotton dress hung on her body, which appeared to have about as much shape as a clothes hanger. She had lost at least twenty pounds since Mitch had last seen her three months ago.

She had cracked her front door a few inches, taking a stiffly inhospitable stance when she saw Mitch. "Don't tell me he's done something else," she said, lifting a hand as though to ward off evil. "I can't take any more."

"I don't know that Dwayne's done anything, Mrs. Burns.
I merely want to talk to him."

She eyed him with deep suspicion. "Don't try to pull the
wool over my eyes, Mitch Bushyhead. You didn't come here
to pass the time of day with Dwayne."

"I merely thought I'd check in with him. The hospital was
supposed to notify me when they released him. There was a
note in his file. They overlooked it, I guess. I learned only
this morning that he's home."

She made a sound of disgust. "That doesn't surprise me.
The people in the hospital business office can't keep up with
the work load. They need more help, but there's no money
for it." She sighed. "I've never seen such a terrible place in
my life. Dwayne's doctor up there was a Cuban. He could
barely speak English. The few times Dwayne saw him, he
didn't understand a word the man said. Will you tell me
what earthly good somebody like that is to mental patients?"

"I don't know, ma'am."

She answered her own question. "None whatsoever. All
they care about is herding people in and out of there like
cattle. They turn them loose on the street and most of them
have nowhere to go."

"Yes, ma'am. Could—"

"They gave him some pills and told him to get into a
counseling program. Of course, they didn't tell him how to
pay for it. I've lived on our savings while Dwayne was in the
hospital. Now that he's out, he can get unemployment
compensation for a few months. After that, I don't know
what we'll do. It's a sure bet nobody's going to call Dwayne
to fix their appliances." Mitch had never heard the quiet
Mrs. Burns say so many words at the same time before. Six
months' worth of bottled up resentment had wrought a
transformation.

"Social Security—"

"Dwayne won't be eligible for Social Security for three
years. What are we supposed to do in the meantime?"

Good question, Mitch thought. "I don't know, ma'am. Dwayne could check with the county mental health office in Tahlequah, see if they have any ideas."

Her anger wavered. "How could they help?"

"They provide counseling on an ability-to-pay basis, for one thing. Once they've evaluated a patient, they're sometimes able to place him in a job," Mitch said. "They vouch for him and cooperate with the employer in monitoring his progress. It's part of the rehabilitation process."

She eyed him warily. "I don't know if I can get Dwayne to talk to them. I can't say boo without him losing his temper."

"Perhaps if I suggest it to him."

She glanced behind her into the living room. "He isn't here right now. He should be back any time, though."

Mitch considered for a moment. "May I come in and wait for him, Mrs. Burns?"

She seemed to wilt. "I don't care," she said with a heavy sigh and stepped back far enough for Mitch to enter. She shut the door and leaned wearily against it. "I don't really know when he'll be back." She gazed at Mitch with undisguised despair now. "He was so mad when he left, he might not come back at all."

Mitch wished he knew words to reassure her. "There are bound to be adjustments the two of you have to make, after what's happened."

She shook her head. "How do you adjust to something like that? I thought I knew Dwayne, but—" She gestured helplessly. "I can't trust him now. Every minute he's out of my sight, I wonder what he's doing. When he leaves the house, I ask where he's going and when he'll be back. I can't help it. This morning, he blew up at me. Said I was going to drive him crazy, if he wasn't already. I thought he was going to hit me, but he slammed out of the house instead. He was on foot, so I don't suppose he's gone far."

"What time did he leave?"

"About seven-thirty. He didn't even finish his breakfast." She paused, watching Mitch. Her gaze sharpened as a thought occurred to her. "Why? Has something happened to Dwayne?"

Mitch shook his head. "Honestly, I haven't seen him."

"But something *has* happened, hasn't it?" She moved listlessly to a chair and lowered herself into it, her eyes never leaving Mitch's face. "Has he—done that to another woman?"

"Not that I'm aware of."

"Then what?"

"There's a problem," Mitch said carefully, "at the tribal boarding school involving an eight-year-old girl."

She stared at him. "What has that to do with Dwayne?"

"Probably nothing, but since I wanted to see Dwayne anyway—"

"You think Dwayne exposed himself to one of those little girls." She began to cry silently.

"No, ma'am, I don't." Mitch shifted uncomfortably. The denial sounded hollow. Tears continued to stream down her cheeks unchecked. "I'll be questioning a number of people who live near the campus."

She wiped her eyes with the back of her hand and looked up at him, angry again. "We're a half-mile from the school. Have you talked to any of our neighbors?"

"Well, no, not yet, but—"

"No, of course you haven't. They haven't been in a mental hospital."

There was something hopeless about her anger now. She's not sure herself that Dwayne wouldn't molest a child, Mitch thought. When she found out the child had been murdered, would she still be unsure? Conceivably. Dwayne had become a stranger to her. She must feel like a prisoner in this house, in this town, Mitch thought. She must lie awake half the night, trying to think of a way out, and wake up in the morning, hoping it's all been a nightmare. But it's real, and she can't be sure of anything any more.

If Burns had left in a temper, there was no telling when he might show up. Or what he might have done in the meantime. "I don't think I'll wait for Dwayne, after all, Mrs. Burns."

Silence.

"Please tell him I'd like to talk to him. Merely as a matter of routine."

She gave him a disgusted look but said nothing.

"Sorry to bother you, Mrs. Burns." Mitch let himself out of the house.

SEVEN

MITCH PAUSED on the porch to look up and down the street. A gray tomcat ambled down the sidewalk, stopped and stared at Mitch with yellow eyes. A blue jay squawked into startled flight from the mimosa tree in the Burns's front yard. The cat's eyes followed the jay's flight and he trotted off in that direction, disappearing behind the house next door.

Mitch went down the steps and hesitated before walking around the house. Neither the cat nor the blue jay was in sight.

The Burns's property backed up to the narrow stretch of woods that, six blocks to the north, skirted the tribal school campus. A redwood picnic table and two webbed chaise longues on a brick-paved patio spoke of more companionable days in the Burns's marriage.

A detached one-car garage sat at the back of the lot. Mitch wondered if Dwayne had been sulking in the garage since storming out of the house that morning. The padlock, which was hooked through the slotted end of the hasp, hung open. He pushed back the hinged, double doors and saw the Burns's '79 Chevy, and tools hanging on hooks along two walls. The car was empty, and there was nowhere else to hide.

After shutting the garage doors, Mitch walked around to the alley separating the Burns's property from the woods. The trash barrels behind the garage were empty. The refuse truck must have picked up the trash that morning. As Mitch was replacing the lids, he noticed something sticking out from beneath one of the barrels. Bending he pulled out a small pair of white cotton panties. They were stained with soot from the barrel. Sewn inside the waist band was a tag with TAMARAH BIRCH printed on it in permanent black ink.

Had the trashmen dropped this when they emptied the barrel?

As Mitch started back to the house, Dwayne Burns walked out of the woods. He halted when he saw Mitch. How long had he been in there? Mitch wondered. He could have thrown the panties into the trash can earlier, and gone back into the woods to think about what to do next.

The man who had always held himself very erect, to appear taller, was stoop-shouldered now. During Burns's three-month stay at the state hospital, his hair, which had been peppered with gray before, had gone completely white, and he had the pasty pallor of an invalid.

Burns stiffened, then blanched with outrage. "What do you think you're doing, nosing around my property?" he demanded.

Mitch said, "I've been waiting for you, Dwayne. Where have you been?"

"Walking, not that it's any of your business. I've been released."

Mitch opened his hand and held up the panties. "Look what I found under your trash barrel. Any idea how they got there?"

Burns stared at the panties and went even paler than before. *"Oh, my God,"* he choked out before he wheeled and ran back into the woods.

Mitch gave chase, catching up with Burns about a hundred yards into the woods. It wasn't difficult since Burns was in poor physical condition. Mitch grabbed him from behind, holding him against his chest. "Come on now, Dwayne. You don't want to run."

Burns was panting heavily. Mitch's arm was wrapped around the man's chest, and he could feel Burns's heart pounding frantically. "I had nothing to do with that child. I never even laid eyes on her."

"Then you don't have anything to be afraid of. Now, let's go on down to the station and have a talk." Mitch loosened his grip. Burns didn't move. Mitch took his arm and led him, unresisting, across the yard and to the patrol car parked at the curb. There was no sign from the house that Mrs. Burns noticed them.

"WHY DID YOU RUN?" Mitch asked. He and Dwayne Burns were alone in Mitch's office at the police station. Mitch had instructed Helen to hold his calls. Burns sat slumped in a chair, his hands clasped loosely between his knees, his eyes downcast.

Burns had not spoken since Mitch had put him in the police car and now seemed to be considering maintaining his silence indefinitely. His eyes darted to Mitch and then away. He bit a thumbnail, his face sullen.

"This could take all day," Mitch said, "if you won't cooperate. Shall I call your wife and let her know where you are?"

Burns jerked forward in the chair. "No! I don't want her to know."

"Well, then . . ." Mitch half-sat on the side of his desk, folded his arms, and waited for Burns to go on.

Burns sighed and slumped back in his chair. "As soon as I saw those panties, I knew what you were there for."

"You already knew about the girl's death?"

He nodded glumly.

"How?"

"I heard it in town. I was standing on the sidewalk in front of the jewelry store, after the parade. Two men walked by and I heard them talking about it."

"Did you recognize the men?"

"One of them works at the Indian school. I think his name is Horn. I didn't know the other one. Horn acted pretty shook up. They were intent on their conversation, and I don't think they noticed me."

"What did they say?"

Burns pinched the bridge of his nose before continuing. "Horn said he had found the girl, Tamarah something, in the woods under a pile of leaves and called the police. He said he thought her neck was broken and he thought she'd been molested because her underwear was gone." Burns didn't look at Mitch.

"I can check with Horn, you know, and find out if he had such a conversation."

"Go ahead and check," Burns muttered, picking at his thumbnail.

"You know what I've been thinking, Dwayne? You could have seen Tamarah Birch in the woods and decided to expose yourself."

"No—"

"Maybe she started screaming and you had to silence her."

"No!"

"What else did you overhear Horn say?"

"Nothing else."

"Why did you immediately assume the panties belonged to the dead child when I showed them to you? I had my thumb over the name tag."

Burns looked up, then dropped his head again, went back to picking at his nail. "I'd been thinking about Horn's conversation. About the little girl being molested and all. When I saw you behind my house with those panties—well, somehow I just knew they belonged to that poor child and that you were going to try to pin this on me." He looked up at Mitch again. "I've learned to expect the worst and lately I've not often been disappointed. I'm never going to live down what happened, am I?"

"I'll ask you one last time. Did you take that little girl to the woods, Dwayne?"

He flinched as though recoiling from a blow before he said gravely, "I swear I never touched her. Yes, I had some trouble before. I don't know what got into me, but I never tried to touch those women. I didn't even want to. And I wouldn't harm a child. Not for any reason."

Mitch reached for a memo pad and pen. "When did you leave your house this morning?"

"It was after seven. I didn't notice the exact time but I'd been up about an hour. That would make it seven-twenty or seven-thirty."

That jibed with Mrs. Burns's account. Mitch made a note and said, "Tell me where you were, to the best of your recollection, from then until you returned to your house."

"I walked to town."

"By way of the woods?"

"No. I went down Third to Sequoyah, then down Sequoyah to the coffee shop. I sat in there, drinking coffee a long time, an hour maybe."

That would be easy to check with the owner of the coffee shop. "You left the coffee shop about eight-thirty?"

Burns hesitated, then nodded.

"What did you do then?"

"Walked."

"Where?"

Burns closed his eyes and scooted farther down in his chair, as though trying to disappear. After a moment, he seemed to realize that wasn't going to work and opened his eyes. "Back down Sequoyah to the highway. I walked west beyond the trailer court, almost to the industrial park. When I got back to town, people were gathering for the parade. I'd forgotten about the Heritage Celebration." He shot Mitch a grim look. "I wasn't exactly in a holiday mood."

Mitch nodded. "Go on."

"Once, out by the industrial park, I thought about walking on, hitching a ride somewhere else. I don't have any work and my wife watches me like a hawk. She can't sleep at night for fear I'll slip out and do something to humiliate her again." He made an ironic sound. "Daisy seems to think I did what I did simply to embarrass her in front of her friends. I can't talk to her. I think she'd be relieved if I left."

"Why didn't you?"

He shrugged. "No money. No place to go. My brother lives in Stillwater, but he doesn't want to see me."

"All right." Mitch looked down at his pad again. "People were gathering on the street when you got back to town. Did you see anyone you know?"

"Sure. They acted like they didn't know me, though."

"I need names, Dwayne."

He thought, then said, "Jim Hampton."

"The mechanic at the Ford garage?"

Burns nodded. "Sandra and Frank Murdock, too. Up-right Christian folks," he observed sarcastically. "Used to go to church with Daisy and me—when we were still going. Lots of school kids. I could probably give you some more names after I think about it."

"That will do for now," Mitch said.

"I hung around in front of the jewelry store for about half an hour and watched the parade. After that, I stopped at one of the booths for a cold drink. Then I went back home, the long way this time, through the woods. You know the rest."

"Except how those panties came to be in your back yard."

Burns's fingers curled over his knees, clenching and un-clenching. "I have no idea. I swear it. Obviously somebody left them there, but it wasn't me. Should I call my lawyer now?"

Mitch reached behind him for the phone on his desk and handed it to Burns. "Call him, get him over here. I won't detain you now if he will guarantee that I can find you again when I need you."

The fact was, even though the panties were strong cir-cumstantial evidence, they weren't enough to warrant an arrest. Mitch was going to have to trace Burns's movements that morning very carefully.

From Burns's end of the conversation, it seemed clear that the lawyer was not pleased to hear that Burns had been questioned by the police. He apparently said he'd have to speak to Mrs. Burns before he decided what to do. Burns tried to talk him out of it, but got nowhere, and slammed down the receiver.

While they waited for the lawyer to call back, Mitch went through the mail on his desk. It consisted mostly of flyers from other police and sheriff departments. The authorities in Fort Smith were looking for an albino firebug who had torched several business buildings. If the guy had any sense,

Mitch thought, he'd be long gone. It wouldn't be too hard
to spot a pale, pink-eyed guy smelling of smoke.

The sheriff over in Creek County sought a runaway four-
teen-year-old, daughter of an Okmulgee couple. There were
several descriptions and requests for information on robbery suspects. Robberies across the state had been up
sharply that spring. The epidemic hadn't touched Buckskin, but it had come close. Within the past two months a
bank in Grove, a bank and savings and loan in Tahlequah,
and a Muskogee bank had been robbed by a man wearing a
ski mask. During the last robbery, a security guard had un-
wisely tried to stop the robber and been shot for his pains.
The guard had died later in a hospital.

Burns's lawyer called back with the information that he
would be by to pick up Dwayne Burns and drive him home.
He and Mrs. Burns would take joint responsibility for him.
Burns went out to the common room to sit on a bench and
wait with his head in his hands.

Helen Hendricks, the dispatcher, watched him uncertainly for a moment. "Would you like a cup of coffee, Mr.
Burns?"

"No," Burns muttered.

Mitch felt sorry for him. "Why don't you go over to
Tahlequah and talk to the people in the mental health office," he suggested. "They might be able to help you find a
job."

"Sure. Like cleaning out stalls at the stockyards?"

"You won't know until you try, Dwayne."

Burns mumbled something unintelligible without looking up. Helen caught Mitch's eye and shook her head sadly.

EIGHT

LISA MCDOWELL was curled in the corner of a booth at the Three Squares Cafe, reading a book, when Mitch arrived for their tentative lunch date. Tentative because he hadn't been sure he could find time for lunch. He was fifteen minutes late and should not have left his duties on that particular day to come there at all. But he had needed to see her.

She was leaving tomorrow to attend a six-week seminar at Boston College, having been one of thirty teachers chosen from among hundreds of applicants. The credit hours she would earn there would complete the requirements for her master's degree. Mitch had tried to appear happy for her, but he didn't think he'd fooled her.

The news that she would be away for half the summer had been bad enough, but not as unsettling as what she'd told him last week. Contingent on completing her master's requirements, she had been offered a position on the faculty of a junior college in a small northern California town within commuting distance of Berkeley. If she took the job, she had pointed out, she could apply for admission to a doctoral program in educational administration at UC.

He had not known she was looking for another job. He wasn't sure which distressed him more, the fact that she hadn't told him or the possibility of her moving to California.

The café's tables and booths were occupied and about a dozen people were waiting to be seated. Even though he was late, Mitch hesitated in the doorway to study the woman he had been seeing for more than eight months. She was his daughter's English teacher and, in his eyes, beautiful. Lisa was ten years younger than he. Having turned forty two months previously, he was more conscious of the age gap than ever before. Sometimes when he passed a mirror, he was caught up short by the thought: You're forty. It didn't seem possible.

Lisa sat with head bowed, absorbed in what she was reading, her shining hair falling across her cheek to half-obscure her face.

Behind the thin curtain over the window above the booth, the midday sunlight shed a muted glow over Lisa. It settled on the slender hands holding the book, giving her skin the sheen of ivory, and transformed her blond hair into curling strands of spun gold.

When Emily had discovered that her father was seeing her English teacher, she had reacted with furious outrage. Fortunately, Emily had already come to like Lisa before a classmate had told her about the relationship. That liking had finally won her over. In time, Emily had come around, and lately she had begun to drop Lisa's name into conversations casually, almost as if Lisa were a member of the family.

In fact, two weeks ago, Emily had insisted that Mitch invite Lisa to dinner and had spent all day Saturday preparing the meal. The evening had been an unqualified success. Except that Mitch hadn't known Lisa wanted to leave Buckskin. Ever since he'd discovered it, he had been wondering how many other things he didn't know about her.

He had been dreading the six weeks that she would be away but, until a week ago, he had been able to look beyond that and see a promising future. The past few days, when he looked to the end of summer, he saw a void filled with questions that he had closed his mind to. Even as he watched her, his body yearning for her, he felt the separation that was already beginning.

As if sensing his eyes upon her, Lisa stirred and lifted her head. A smile lit her face when she saw him, and she closed the book. He made his way to the booth. Her hand rested on his arm as he bent to kiss her cheek. Her skin was warmed by sunlight.

"I thought you'd stood me up," she said as he slid into the booth across from her.

"No way."

"Herschel has been putting a guilt trip on me for holding a booth with so many waiting. He keeps giving me the evil eye from the kitchen." Herschel Lee owned the Three Squares and did most of the cooking.

"We'd better order then." Mitch waved at the nearest waitress, who happened to be Duckworth's wife, Geraldine. She already had her eye on the booth and came right over. Mitch braced himself for a spate of questions about Tamarah Birch's death. If Buckskin had a gossip columnist, it would be Geraldine Duckworth or one of the other waitresses at the Three Squares Cafe.

To his relief, Geraldine didn't mention the child, which could only mean the news hadn't spread from the main street to the Three Squares yet. They chose from among the café's plate lunches, the fastest food on the menu.

As soon as Geraldine left, Lisa reached across the table to lace her fingers through his. "Busy day?"

He brushed his lips across her knuckles. "Hectic."

"Was that rider badly hurt?" He looked puzzled. "A man was thrown from his horse and taken to the hospital," she explained. "Didn't you see the parade?"

"No." He wasn't surprised to hear that someone had been thrown from a horse. Round-up club cowboys hauled their horses in cramped trailers from country pastures to a crowded parade route and spurred them in among equally nervous, strange horses with kids dashing across the street in front of them or yelling from the sidelines. It was a wonder more people didn't get hurt.

"Duck and I were called to the tribal school."

"What happened?"

Lowering his voice, he outlined the bare bones of his morning's activities.

"Good God," she murmured, and her eyes filled with dismay.

"I'm surprised you haven't already heard about it."

"I haven't talked to anyone but Janet. We watched the parade together." Janet Harden was the art teacher at the high school.

Lisa shook her head as though to deny what he'd told her. "It's incomprehensible to me how anyone could hurt an innocent child—even though I read about it in the newspaper all the time. It makes me want to *do* something. When there are so many people who would give anything to have a child to love and care for—" She faltered and looked down at their linked hands.

Mitch had not thought how the news of Tamarah Birch's death might stir Lisa's private regret. Her marriage had ended because of her inability to have a child—Lisa believed that was the reason, anyway. Mitch thought any man who would divorce his wife on those grounds was looking for an excuse and would have found another if that one hadn't been handy. Early in their relationship, Lisa had revealed to Mitch the pain she carried with her because of what she saw as a lack in herself. She had never spoken of it again.

"I know," he said gently.

She collected herself and said, "Catch him quickly, Mitch. Do you have a suspect?"

"Several." They fell silent and Mitch released Lisa's hand as Geraldine approached the booth with their food. She set their plates down and hurried to another booth to take more orders.

Mitch said, "I have to go back out to the school this evening." Don't go to Boston, he wanted to say. Instead, he said, "It may be late before I can get by your place."

"It doesn't matter." She picked up her fork. "I'll be up half the night packing. Too excited to sleep, anyway." He wondered if the reminder that she was so eager to go was deliberate. But when he saw her ingenuous expression, he realized that she was simply caught up in the adventure. "Six weeks to explore the Boston area. All that history. Lexington, Plymouth, Concord...oh, and Cambridge, Mitch," she said, her blue-gray eyes sparkling. "Think of it."

He nodded, wanting to be glad for her. To him, Boston was just another big city where he wouldn't want to live,

Cambridge another college town, and Harvard, for all its grand Ivy-League tradition, another university.

"If only you were going with me," she said.

"I'd be like a fish out of water."

She smiled indulgently. "Emily's going to cheerleading camp soon, isn't she?"

"Next week."

"Do you think, if you've tied up this investigation by then, that you might come up for a few days?"

She had suggested once before that he visit her in Boston. He didn't understand his reluctance to do so. Too many unanswered questions between them, he guessed. The day after she had told him about the job offer in California, she had asked idly how he would feel about leaving Buckskin. Not any time soon, she had hastened to clarify, but some day.

He had avoided a direct answer by saying he'd never given it much consideration. Since then, he had thought about it quite a bit. Except for the first few weeks after his wife's death, the idea of leaving Buckskin had never held any appeal for him.

He couldn't take Emily away from the only home she could remember, from her friends. After the death of her mother a little more than a year ago, Emily needed stability and roots more than ever. To be honest, he doubted that he'd give serious thought to leaving even when Emily went away to college. Maybe he needed stability as much as she did.

There was a part of him that took comfort from the Victorian house on Pawnee Street where he and Ellen had been happy for so many years. At first, the house had been a painful reminder of her and he hadn't been able to sleep in their bedroom, but that had passed as the grief had faded. Now it was just home again.

"I can't promise I'll come to Boston," he told Lisa. "This case could drag on. Any number of other things could make it impossible." He saw the disappointment on her face. "But I'll try. I really will."

She studied his face for a moment. "You won't come," she said simply. "I know you won't."

"You don't know that. You can't."

Briefly a smile drove the resignation from her eyes. "Ever since you learned about this Boston thing, I've felt you withdrawing from me." She didn't mention the California job offer, though it was in both their minds. "I can't abandon my career aspirations, even for you."

He realized suddenly that neither of them had eaten much of their food, and he wasn't hungry any longer. He reached for her hand and enclosed it in both of his. "I wouldn't want you to. I know how important your work is to you."

"I don't know what's going to happen to us, Mitch, and it frightens me."

"That's nonsense, Lisa. There aren't enough miles to separate us if we don't let them. No matter where you go, there are airplanes and telephones and weekends and vacations. We'll work it out."

But he was frightened, too.

NINE

AFTER NOON, a northwest wind swept down Going Snake Mountain and swirled into town, stirring up dust and discarded food wrappers and shaking the craft booths that had been quickly knocked together for the Heritage Celebration. Sequoyah Street swarmed with people strolling from one sidewalk booth to the next and children darting in and out among them. Boothkeepers anchored their wares with whatever was handy. Teenaged girls tried to hold their hair in place with their hands.

Mitch parked beside a NO PARKING sign and got out, ignoring glances from passersby, some merely curious, others resentful because they had had to leave their cars blocks away and walk.

The wind wasn't strong enough to prevent the food and craft booths doing a booming business. People waited all year for this. Only handcrafted Indian items were given booth space during the Heritage Celebration. Every year, people came from miles around to buy.

Mitch saw his daughter and her best friend, Temple Roberts, standing in front of a booth halfway down the block. The two girls, in their crimson and gold pom-pom uniforms, were hard to miss.

An eddy swooped by, stirring their short skirts, revealing red tights. Mitch made his way to the booth, returning greetings from several townspeople. His cousin Callie Roach was tending the booth, which was sponsored by the local Cherokee Historical Society and offered for sale traditional Indian food and Indian cookbooks compiled by the society.

Coming up between the girls from behind, Mitch draped his arms over their shoulders. "Now, here's a couple of good-looking dames."

Emily was leaning on her elbows over a styrofoam cup
with a plastic spoon half way to her mouth, her other hand
holding her long brown hair out of the way. "Watch it,
Daddy. This is my lunch and I don't want to spill a drop of
it." She slid a sideways glance at him. "Dames, Daddy?
Really."

"Chicks, then, or whatever the current vernacular is."
Emily uttered a despairing sigh. Mitch peered into her cup.
"Connuche, huh?" Callie was known for the soup made
from ground hickory nuts and hominy. With rice substi-
tuted for the hominy and sugar added, it made a tasty pud-
ding, also. "Is that recipe in the cookbook, Callie?"

Callie was staring hard at him. She's heard, Mitch
thought. Apparently she hadn't told Emily and Temple,
though, or the girls would be bombarding him with questions.

"It's in there," Callie said, allowing her thoughts to be
diverted for the sake of a sale. She lifted a jar of jelly that
anchored a stack of spiral-bound cookbooks, picked up one,
and held it out to him. Decorating the book's cover was the
official seal of the Cherokee Nation, a seven-pointed star—
one point for each of the seven ancient clans—surrounded
by a wreath of oak leaves reminiscent of the days before the
removal when wood from the live oak tree kept the sacred
fire burning in the Nation's centrally located "town house."

"You need one of these, Mitch," Callie said, "Trust me."

Temple nodded, her red curls bouncing like springs.
"Auumunnch duh." She held half of a flat, plate-sized circle of fry bread in her hand and appeared to have the other
half in her mouth.

"She says to buy the book," Callie interpreted.

Temple swallowed and licked her lips. "My mother
bought one." She rolled her blue eyes. "This is scrump-
tious. I'm going to try the bean bread next. That recipe's in
there, too."

"I want to learn how to make connuche," Emily said, and
lifted the cup to swallow the last of the soup.

"It's for a good cause," Callie put in.

Mitch gave in without protest, knowing the odds against him were too great. He took out his wallet. "How much?"

"Ten dollars." He handed Callie a bill. She tucked it into a metal cash box beneath the counter. Straightening, she said, "Mitch, Aggie Horn told me—"

"Who made that possum grape jelly?" Mitch interrupted.

Callie gazed at him for an instant before she replied. "Patsy Glass."

Mitch lifted a jar and looked at it critically. "Will you vouch for it?"

"Sure will," Callie said. "Not everybody can make good possum grape jelly, you know. If you don't pick the grapes when they're just right, you get a weedy taste. Patsy's jelly is always perfect."

Mitch took out another bill. "Give me two jars." When Callie handed him a sack containing the cookbook and jelly, he passed it to Emily. "Take care of this, honey. I'm working."

Emily accepted the package.

"Listen, I don't want you girls wandering off alone, hear?" Mitch said. Callie gave him a knowing look and nodded her head approvingly. "And stay together."

Emily glanced at Temple and grinned. "He still thinks I'm six years old."

He tugged on a strand of her brown hair. "No, I don't. I guess you haven't heard about the dead girl found this morning."

Callie leaned across the booth eagerly to join the conversation. "Aggie Horn told me just a few minutes ago. A student at the boarding school, wasn't it? Somebody dragged her into the woods and mutilated her."

Emily and Temple stared at Mitch with horrified expressions. "She wasn't mutilated, Callie," Mitch said. "Nor do we know that she was dragged anywhere. She was dead, though."

"Aggie said it was murder," Callie said.

"That's for the medical examiner to determine." Mitch didn't want to add any more fuel to the rumors. "But I want you girls to be careful. Is Kevin driving you home?"

Emily shook her head. "Now that school's out, he has to work for his dad every day but Sunday. He says he can't get off for anything."

From her aggrieved tone, Mitch suspected that Emily and her boyfriend had had words over it. Maybe they'd break up, he told himself. Actually, Mitch would be relieved if they'd cool it for a while. He thought they saw far too much of each other, but then he was Emily's father.

"If you decide to go home and need a ride, find me and I'll drive you."

"Mrs. Roberts will take us." Emily's brown eyes were troubled. "How old was the dead girl, Daddy?"

"Eight."

"Oh, how gruesome!" Temple breathed.

"Really," Emily agreed.

"Stay together," Mitch reiterated.

"We don't plan to go home for hours yet," Emily said. "Not till suppertime. We're supposed to meet Mrs. Roberts in front of the coffee shop at two o'clock and go with her to the blow-gun competition. She'll drop me at the house about five."

"Good," Mitch said. "I'll try to get there before six." He kissed the top of his daughter's head. "See you then, honey."

He left the booth and headed for the coffee shop where he would begin tracing Dwayne Burns's movements that morning.

The wind rose and moaned down the tunnel created by buildings on either side of Sequoyah Street, then fell. A small black dog dashed across the sidewalk in front of Mitch, chasing a Hershey bar wrapper.

TEN

BURNS'S STORY CHECKED OUT. The owner of the coffee shop confirmed that Dwayne had been in the shop early that morning for a long time. "As long as an hour?" Mitch had asked.

"Could have been," the man said. "I thought he'd never leave, to tell you the truth, and I had customers waiting. I didn't want to hassle him, you know, with him just out of the hospital and all. So I let him be. Dwayne don't look too all together to me, Chief."

At the jewelry store, a clerk said that Burns had been in front of the store during the parade. In fact, she'd seen him "loitering" there some time before the parade started. Mitch suspected the woman had watched Burns like a hawk, once she'd spotted him. In case he did something outrageous, she didn't want to miss it.

The parade had started at ten. If Burns had been in front of the jewelry store a half hour before, that left the hour from eight-thirty to nine-thirty unaccounted for, the time period when Burns claimed to have walked out to the industrial park and back. Unfortunately, it was the crucial hour during which Tamarah Birch had probably been killed.

Burns would have had to hurry to walk to the tribal school, lure Tamarah into the woods, murder her, cover the body with leaves, and get back to town by nine-thirty. But the scenario wasn't inconceivable. In fact, if Burns had killed the child, he'd have hastened back to town as quickly as possible in order to establish an alibi. With his recent history, he could count on being noticed on the street by several Buckskin residents.

At mid-afternoon, Mitch managed to get a breather from breaking up schoolboy fights, investigating fender benders, and collaring a few drunks in order to turn them over to family members with instructions to take them home. He returned to the station and checked in with Dr. Sullivan.

The medical examiner, Ken Pohl, had been in town for the Heritage Celebration. Sullivan had looked him up and Pohl had already done a preliminary examination of the body at the local hospital and sent it to the county morgue for more extensive forensic tests. Tamarah's clothing had been sent to the forensic laboratory in Tulsa for examination. Mitch had already packaged the panties he'd found in the Burns' yard and forwarded them to Tulsa, as well.

According to the medical examiner, Sullivan told Mitch, death by strangulation would be the probable finding. During his examination of the corpse at the hospital he had found pinpoint hemorrhages in the whites of the eyes.

"That's usually an indication of strangulation," Sullivan said. "The hemorrhages come from capillaries bursting when blood pressure rises. The blood enters the head from the artery in back of the neck and can't get out."

The image created by Sullivan's words gave Mitch a sick feeling in the pit of his stomach. "What else did Pohl say?"

"She wasn't raped, Mitch. There was no penetration. No blood or bruising in the genital area. The only bruises he found were the fresh ones on the neck and older ones on the upper arms."

"How old?"

"At least eighteen hours. Could be older. The bruises appear to be left by human fingers, as though somebody had grabbed her arms and squeezed hard. Adult fingers, by the way. They were too big to have been left by a child."

"Did Pohl say when he could do the autopsy?"

"Today. He's going to postpone another autopsy in order to do it. Seeing that little girl shook us both up."

Mitch thanked Sullivan and hung up. He took off his shirt and mounted the stationary bike he kept in his office. He began pedaling furiously. He was still pedaling and sweating twenty minutes later when Officer Roo Stephens poked his head in.

"I got a guy back there in a cell sleeping off a drunk, Chief. He's from Stilwell. I called his brother and he said he'd come after him when he gets off work, but he wasn't going to be in any hurry. I think he was glad to hear we had him in jail. Guess he's had to clean up after him before." The gangly, young officer came farther into the office. "Anything new on that little girl?"

Mitch climbed off the bike and flopped in his chair. "According to the ME," he panted, "there was no vaginal penetration."

"Where does that leave us?"

"Maybe in limbo." Mitch ran his hands over his face, wiping away perspiration. His eyes felt gritty. "Dwayne Burns's story checks out, as far as I can tell, Roo." He had run into Duck and Roo earlier in town and had brought them up to date on the investigation to that point. "There's an hour unaccounted for when he *could* have been in the woods murdering Tamarah, but it's tight time-wise. Especially since he was on foot. And Tamarah didn't know Burns. It would have taken some time to gain her trust and coax her into the woods with him. Otherwise, she'd have raised a ruckus that would have brought teachers and students running."

Roo lowered himself into a chair, rested his elbows on the arms and made a tent of his long fingers. "He had her panties, though."

"Not in his possession. And if he tossed them in with his own trash with the name tag still attached, he's dumber than I thought."

"Why take them at all if he was going to turn right around and throw them away?" Roo asked.

"That's what I keep asking myself. He could have taken them on impulse and later decided it was too risky to keep them, but why didn't he burn them or bury them? Why toss them out practically in plain sight? I went right to them. It all feels too damned convenient to me."

Roo nodded. "Dwayne may have lost a few shingles in the last storm, but he's not stupid. Sure coincidental, though. Burns gets released from the hospital and a few days later, a little girl is killed."

"Well, I can't arrest him solely on the strength of Tamarah's panties being found beneath his trash barrel. Anybody could have planted them there."

"You got any other ideas?"

"No clear ones. I need the results of the forensic tests and I'm going back out to the school later to interview teachers and Tamarah's roommates. Virgil will be too busy in town to do it after he comes to work. He's sure happy to be getting your help on the second shift starting tomorrow." He watched Roo run a finger down his long, freckled nose. "What does Laura think about you working evenings?" Laura Tucker, a local librarian, and Roo had been dating steadily for more than a year.

"Aw, she was kind of ticked off at first. But when I told her the pay was better, she calmed down. We're saving up to get married."

"Really?" Mitch studied Roo's glum expression. In his early twenties, he still looked like a kid fresh off the farm.

Roo shifted uncomfortably in his chair. "Don't tell Duck, okay? I get enough razzing from him as it is."

"Okay, but I didn't know you and Laura had gotten that serious, Roo."

He shrugged. "Laura wants to get married, and she's not gonna wait around forever."

"She tell you that?"

He ducked his head. "Sort of. In a roundabout way."

"Don't let yourself get railroaded into something, Roo."

He looked up quickly. "Oh, I'm crazy about her. It's just that she wants a big church wedding with a white gown and tuxedos and all that stuff. I'd rather save the money. Go to the preacher's house and get it over with."

Mitch smiled. "Sounds like you're talking about taking a dose of medicine." He reached for his discarded shirt.

"I guess I'm getting scared. Marriage is a big responsibility."

"Don't do it till you're good and ready. If she loves you, she'll wait."

"I don't know," Roo said doubtfully. "You wouldn't think it, Laura's so quiet and all, but she's kind of like a bulldog when she gets her head set." He chewed the inside of his jaw and raked a lock of red hair off his forehead. "I never had much experience with women before Laura, Chief, but I don't think I'll ever fully understand 'em."

Mitch nodded sympathetically. "They're a whole different species. Speaking of women, Roo, I need to tell you something about the new police officer."

"Pitcher?"

"Shelly Pitcher."

"Shelly?" Roo's eyes widened. "Pitcher is a woman?"

"Right. I haven't told anybody else except Virgil."

He grinned. "She's gonna be Duck's partner?"

"Yeah. Kind of boggles the mind, doesn't it?"

A bark of laughter erupted from Roo. "Lordy, I love it, Chief!"

"I'd just as soon Duck didn't find out until he meets her tomorrow. You have to promise not to tell him."

Shaking with laughter, Roo pulled a handkerchief from his pocket and wiped his eyes. "Shoot, Chief, I don't think I can keep it in."

Mitch struggled to keep a straight face. "Yes, you can. Now, swear to me you won't say a word to anybody about it."

Roo blew his nose and laughed some more. Finally, he nodded and stuffed his handkerchief back in his pocket. "Okay, I swear. But I'm gonna be biting my tongue for the rest of the day."

Mitch chuckled. "What do you think I've been doing for the past two weeks? But I didn't see any sense in letting myself in for Duck's whining a minute before I had to."

"I see your point."

Briefly, the two men sat in companionable silence, contemplating Duckworth's reaction to his new partner. Then Roo said, "I better get back to town and give Duck a hand. Wouldn't want him to work so hard he can't make it to work tomorrow."

"Sure wouldn't want that," Mitch agreed.

"Last time I saw him, he was taking a statement from a clerk at the drugstore. Some kids ripped off a bunch of rap tapes."

"Figures," Mitch muttered. Shoplifting was always a problem during the Heritage Celebration.

"Don't know what they see in that rap stuff. It drives me crazy."

"That's what adults said about rock and roll when I was a teenager," Mitch said. "Come to think of it, that's probably one of the main reasons kids like their music so much."

"There was a stack of Willie Nelson tapes right next to the rap. They didn't even touch 'em."

"Incredible."

Roo left and Mitch began writing a report for the Tamarah Birch case file. He'd been at it about fifteen minutes when a man knocked on the open office door and strolled in. "The eternal paperwork, eh?"

Mitch half-rose from his chair and grabbed the big man's hand. "Hey, Claude. What's happening?" Claude Dunn was an officer in the Muskogee police department.

"I'm looking for a place to rest my aching feet for a few minutes."

"You found it. Grab a seat."

Dunn settled his meaty buttocks into a chair. He looked to Mitch to weigh fifteen pounds more than the last time he'd seen him. The man must tip the scales at close to two-fifty. No wonder his feet hurt.

"The wife dragged me over here, kicking and screaming."

"Ah, the Heritage Celebration."

Dunn nodded. He took out a handkerchief and swiped his damp, flushed face. "I left her to do her shopping. She's got her heart set on a genuine handmade Indian basket. Have you checked those prices?"

"No, but handmade doesn't come cheap."

"Nothing does these days."

Mitch leaned back in his swivel chair. "Not enough crime to keep you busy over in Muskogee, eh?"

"Actually, things have been pretty quiet lately. Except for a robbery at the First National Bank."

"I read your flyer this morning," Mitch said. "Sounds like your man had a similar MO to recent robberies in Grove and Tahlequah."

"Except he didn't kill anybody till he got to us."

"A bank guard tried to be a hero?"

"Yeah, stupid old cuss. The man was sixty-two years old and stove up with arthritis. Don't know what he was thinking of, making a move on a guy with a gun in his hand. Witnesses said the guy was acting real nervous, too. That guard didn't use good judgment." He sighed heavily. "He paid for it, too."

"Are you making any progress in the investigation?"

"Not much. You know how accurate eyewitness accounts can be. According to them, the guy's between five feet eight and six feet two, bulky build to on the skinny side. He wore a ski mask and gloves. No bare skin showing that anybody noticed. So he could be black, white, or Indian. The ski mask had red stripes around the eyes and mouth, according to the witnesses of the first three robberies. Nobody at the Muskogee bank could recall any red stripes, which doesn't mean they weren't there. In other words, we've got very little to go on."

"He'll probably do it again."

"That's our best guess. These guys never learn. He's already taken more than half a million. Got three hundred thou of it in Muskogee. That ought to be enough for anybody, right? But then it's not just the money. It's the risk, thumbing their noses at the honest folks and the law, and getting away with it."

"If criminals were smart, the prisons wouldn't be overcrowded."

"True. What about you, Mitch? From what I hear, you people over here must be busy as birddogs."

Mitch snorted. "Running in circles with our tails in the air, you mean?"

Dunn grinned and stuffed his handkerchief in his shirt pocket. "What's the scoop in your investigation of the little girl's murder?"

"You already heard about it, over in Muskogee? It happened less than seven hours ago."

"Somebody from here called my sister. As soon as she hung up, Sis called me. Bad news has wings, Mitch."

"Yeah. As a lady told me this morning, the evil that men do lives after them. I think she lifted that from Shakespeare."

"Well, he got it right. Any good suspects?"

"We've talked to a lot of people, but the pieces aren't fitting together yet."

Dunn nodded glumly and asked about Emily. Mitch reciprocated by inquiring about Dunn's two children. Finally, Dunn said, "Don't guess you have time for me to buy you a piece of pie and coffee somewhere."

Mitch shook his head. "Wish I did, Claude."

Dunn pushed himself out of the chair with a grunt. "Well, the soles of my feet have stopped burning, so I better amble on out of here and find my wife before she charges our Visa card to the limit."

"Next time you're in town, try me again. Any other day, I could probably take off for half an hour."

"I know how it is. See you later, and good luck on your investigation, Mitch."

He would need good luck, Mitch thought. He stared at the unfinished report he'd been writing before Dunn arrived, and shoved it in a folder. He wanted to check in with Duck and Roo before their shift ended, then fill in Virgil on the day's business, and still get home by five. He could just about make it if he left for town now. He would finish the report later.

ELEVEN

THE WIND DIED during the afternoon as if lured away by a wind-chasing *i:gawe':sdi*. Now that no breeze brushed Charley Horn's skin, he could feel the sun's heat on his bare arms. He could smell a faint grassy scent and the enticing aroma of popping corn from the booth behind the bleachers where he sat.

The last dance of the pow-wow's afternoon session was in progress. It was the warrior dance in which the participants carried ceremonial war clubs colored red, for blood, and black, for anger. A singer with a drum sat at the edge of the dance ring. The dancers stood abreast in a line facing east with clubs in their right hands. Leaning forward, they moved with slow steps forward and backward. This first movement ended with a prolonged war cry.

"Ye! Ye! Yeeee!"

Then the drumbeat changed to faster time and the dancers went through the motions of striking enemies with their clubs. This was followed by a dance in quickstep and four war whoops.

"Ye! Ye! Ye! Ye!"

While following the movements of the dance, Horn was keeping half an eye on the boys in his charge, who were seated around him on the bleachers. Fortunately, at four o'clock, they had little energy left for rowdiness and horseplay. This allowed him to transfer most of his attention to the words of the song, which he was trying to commit to memory. The warrior dance was one he hadn't taught the junior dancers, and he wanted to add it to the lessons next year.

With the scant remainder of his attention, for the last quarter hour, he had been scanning the audience in search of the medicine man, Crying Wolf.

He dipped a hand into his shirt pocket and touched the small wool mitten to assure himself it was still there. At noon, he had told his wife to keep an eye on his students and had slipped away from the celebration and hurried back to the school. The eerie silence of the girls' dorm had made him hurry even faster, down the hall to the room where Tamarah Birch had lived. He had let himself in, slipped the mitten from the drawer marked "Tamarah" and returned to town at a run. Apparently nobody but Aggie even knew he was gone.

As the warrior dance was ending, he caught sight of Crying Wolf crossing the field behind the opposite bleachers with a young woman. He recognized the woman as the medicine man's granddaughter, Rhea Vann, who, after going east for her medical education, had returned to take charge of the tribal clinic. A write-up accompanied by her photograph had appeared in the *Cherokee Advocate*, the official tribal newspaper published in Tahlequah. She must have come to the pow-wow to take her grandfather home in her car.

Charley twisted around to speak to Stanley Dick and David Sly, who were seated behind him. "I have to leave for a few minutes. I'm putting you two in charge. Keep the boys here until I get back."

He clambered down the bleachers and circled behind them to intercept Crying Wolf and his granddaughter before they reached the car.

"Grandfather!" he called. The two stopped and turned to wait for him.

"It is Charley Horn," said Crying Wolf to his granddaughter, adding gravely as Charley reached them, "he found the dead child in the woods."

Rhea nodded. "I heard. I'm Rhea Vann, Mr. Horn."

They shook hands. "I recognized you," Charley said. "I saw your picture in the newspaper."

"She makes medicine. Like me." A grin briefly rearranged the leathery wrinkles in the old man's face. "Her medicine has much power. She learned the secrets of the white man's medicine in Baltimore, Maryland."

Smiling, she took her grandfather's arm, adding for Charley's benefit, "I did my medical residency at Johns Hopkins."

"She has come home," Crying Wolf said, "and now I must go everywhere in her car with cold air blowing in my face. I tell her to stay in her clinic and make people well. I have no need of cars. My feet have carried me everywhere I want to go for seventy-five years. But she doesn't listen to an old man. They must have taught her that in Baltimore, Maryland, too."

Charley couldn't tell if he was insulted by her insistence upon chauffeuring him or merely poking fun. Rhea Vann, however, appeared undisturbed by his words. "I listen to old men when they make sense," she responded lightly.

"So now I am loco," Crying Wolf said.

"No, only stubborn." She glanced at Charley. "Did you wish to speak to my grandfather alone?"

"If it's not too much trouble," Charley told her.

"No trouble at all. I'll wait for you in the car, Grandfather."

Crying Wolf waved her away, but his eyes remained fixed on Charley's face. "You wish to speak of the dead child?"

"Yes."

"Do you know who did this evil thing?"

"No, sir. I have no idea, and I don't think the police do, either."

"The unseen world cannot be at peace until payment is made for the child's life. Ahhh...," Crying Wolf sighed, "in the old days the child's clansmen would have quickly hunted down her murderer and taken blood revenge to free her ghost. Blood for blood. It was the law of the people." He shook his head regretfully. "Now we must wait for the working of the white man's justice. It is very slow. Sometimes it does not work at all."

"I understand that, sir. But I've been thinking, maybe we could help the white man's justice work a little faster."

Crying Wolf studied Charley with his intense, black eyes and waited for him to explain himself.

"I know a little about Cherokee medicine," Charley said.
"As a child, I witnessed a few medicine ceremonies. But I've
been told that you know more about the old ways than anyone in Cherokee County."

"You want me to make medicine."

Charley nodded. "If you think it would help, and it sure
couldn't hurt. Could it?"

The old man was silent for a long moment, thinking. Finally, he muttered, "No, but I will have to study on it. Tell
me where you found the body."

Charley had hoped for more enthusiasm from the medicine man, but he gave him careful directions. Then he pulled
the mitten from his pocket and offered it to Crying Wolf.
"This was Tamarah's. I took it from her room."

Crying Wolf accepted the mitten without comment and
stuffed it in his jeans pocket. Charley watched him walk
away, his head bent. Well, he'd done all he could, and it was
time to collect his students for the bus trip back to school.

TWELVE

AFTER A HASTY SUPPER with his daughter, Mitch called Mrs. Morgan, the widow who lived next door and who cleaned for them. She agreed to stay with Emily while he went out again. Ordinarily, he would have gotten heated opposition to the plan from Emily. It wasn't that she didn't like their neighbor, but, as she'd told Mitch several times, she'd die if her friends suspected she had a baby sitter. Mrs. Morgan doesn't baby-sit, Mitch had said, she's just here to keep you company. Emily had not been mollified and, in fact, Mitch had left Emily alone at night a few times when Mrs. Morgan was away. But he didn't like it. He still had trouble thinking of her as old enough to date and almost old enough to drive.

To his surprise, Emily didn't even offer a token argument. What had happened to Tamarah Birch had frightened her.

It was night by the time Mitch arrived at the tribal school. The campus was quiet. In the dim silence, as Mitch crossed the oval to the girls' dorm, he could smell the sweet perfume of the lilacs flanking the entrance.

Most of the windows in the dormitory stood out as muted yellow rectangles. Mitch rang the bell at the main entrance and waited for several moments before a woman's voice from the other side of the door asked him to state his name and business. After he did so, she said, "I need to see some identification."

Mitch was pleased with her caution. He pulled out his wallet and waited. The wood panel covering the small square of glass in the door at eye-level moved to one side.

"Place your ID against the glass, please."

He flipped open his wallet, took out a card, and held it up to the window. She took several moments to study it before

she was satisfied. The panel slid back into place and the
door was opened.

"Come in, Chief Bushyhead. I'm Aggie Horn. I was told
to expect you."

She was a short woman with a trim, compact build suited
to the tailored slacks and blouse she wore. "Tamarah's
roommates are waiting for you in their room. I'll show
you." She led the way briskly, evidently unaware that he'd
been there earlier that day and could find his own way.

"After I talk to the girls, I'd like to ask you a few questions, also," Mitch said. "Where will I find you?"

She had started up the stairs ahead of him and didn't look
back. "I'll stay with you. The girls will feel more comfortable if I'm there."

"I'd prefer to talk to them alone."

She hesitated briefly, one foot poised on the next step,
then went ahead. "I don't know how they'll react to a
stranger questioning them, especially Ruthann. She was
distraught when she learned about Tamarah. And all the
girls are frightened now, of course."

"I'll give it a try, anyway."

They reached the second floor. She paused outside the
room that Mitch and Duckworth had searched that morning. She looked up at him worriedly. "I'll be in the apartment. It's on the ground floor to the right of the lobby as
you enter. Knock on the door when you're finished here."

Mitch nodded and she tapped lightly and said, "It's Mrs.
Horn, girls. I have Chief Bushyhead with me. Let us in,
please."

The tall, athletic-looking girl who opened the door was
one of Tamarah's older roommates—Mari Ketcher, sev-
enth-grader, Mitch learned when he was introduced to all
three of the room's occupants. Though Jamie Walkingstick was a year older, Mari was taller and clearly the leader.
Mari's black hair was cropped short, pixie-style, and she
stood, her fingers pushed into the hip pockets of her jeans.
Her dark eyes fixed on Mitch's face as Aggie Horn told the
girls that she would be in her apartment if they needed her,
then left the room.

Jamie, a silky-haired, round-cheeked girl, perched on the edge of a lower bunk close beside Ruthann Blackfox, as though to protect the younger girl. They also wore jeans. Mari—the horsewoman, Mitch recalled, from the snapshots on the bulletin board—wore hand-tooled western boots, the other two, white Nikes.

Ruthann's wary eyes followed Mitch as he crossed the room and pulled a chair from the kneehole of one of the desks. He straddled the chair and rested his arms on its back, hoping the relaxed pose would put them more at ease.

"As Mrs. Horn will have told you, I'm investigating Tamarah's death," Mitch said, his fingers curled loosely around two rungs of the chair back. "I know this is upsetting for you, but I have to ask you a few questions. Okay?"

The two older girls looked at Ruthann, then all three nodded.

"Good. Were all three of you here when Tamarah left the room this morning?"

The girls exchanged another look and Mari moved to the bed to sit beside Ruthann. Three little Indians all in a row, Mitch thought.

"After breakfast, Jamie and I stopped downstairs to talk to some other girls and hadn't come back to the room yet," Mari said. "When we did, Ruthann was the only one here."

"What time was that?"

"Before eight-thirty, but not much. Isn't that right, Jamie?" Jamie nodded.

"Did you see Tamarah leaving the dorm?"

"No," Mari said. "We were in our friends' room with the door shut."

"What about when you were coming from the cafeteria? Did you see Tamarah on the grounds? Jamie?"

Jamie touched a shirt button, as though to assure herself it was fastened, and shook her head. "No, sir," she said softly.

"Ruthann, how long had Tamarah been gone when Jamie and Mari got here?"

Ruthann's bottom lip trembled a little. "I—I don't know." She dropped her head and bit her lip.

"Was it a long time or a short time?"

She took a deep breath. "Short, but I don't know how many minutes. She made me promise to wait here for her . . . she was supposed to come right back after she talked to Mr. Qualls, but she didn't. I should have gone with her. I could have waited for her outside the principal's office."

Mari put a comforting arm around Ruthann's shoulders. "It's okay, Ruthann."

"You know, don't you, that she never reached the principal's office?" Mitch asked.

Ruthann nodded grimly.

"Have you any idea where she might have gone instead?"

"Huh-uh. But she was scared. Mr. Qualls has a really bad temper."

"Oh?"

"His face gets red when he's mad," Mari said. "Nobody wants to be called to his office, that's for sure."

"Maybe Tamarah meant to stop somewhere else before seeing the principal."

"She would have told me," Ruthann said.

"She might have had her reasons not to," Mitch said.

"Nobody has any secrets around here," Mari put in. "There's no privacy. You can't make a phone call without the whole dorm knowing about it. If you want to keep something for yourself, you have to hide it." Mitch noticed the faint flare of her nostrils and thought of the gumdrops hidden in the closet.

"Tamarah was my best friend," Ruthann said earnestly. "Best friends don't keep secrets from each other."

"Did Tamarah tell you a secret recently?"

Ruthann chewed absentmindedly on a thumbnail. Either she was searching her mind in order to be absolutely accurate or something had occurred to her which she was reluctant to reveal. Finally, she said, "No."

Mitch turned his attention to Jamie Walkingstick. "What about you, Jamie? What did you think when Tamarah didn't come back?"

Jamie looked at him blankly. "I didn't think anything about it. I had to get ready to go to town."

"And when it was time to get on the bus, what did you think then?"

"I guess I was worried. Kind of," Jamie said. "Tamarah and Ruthann were always going off together and whispering. It was weird that Tamarah went off alone, but I knew she had to go to Mr. Qualls's office. I thought it had turned into a long meeting—and then we went to our bus and she wasn't there."

"What did you think, Mari?"

Mari shrugged. "When Tamarah missed the bus, I knew something must have happened. She'd been going on for weeks about dancing at the pow-wow. I couldn't see her missing the bus on purpose."

"Did you mention that to any of the teachers?"

Mari rolled her eyes at this. "They'd have thought I was just being dramatic. They never take us seriously."

"Mrs. Horn does, usually," Jamie said.

"She's better than the others," Mari conceded, "but she's our dorm mother. She's supposed to keep tabs on us."

"But none of you has any idea who might have killed Tamarah?"

The girls shook their heads in unison. Their bewilderment looked genuine. Mitch glanced at his wristwatch and asked them a final question.

"Can you think of anybody who makes you feel uncomfortable when you're around him? Somebody who works at the school, or maybe somebody you've seen in town? Even a stranger that you saw only once or twice?" They were all watching him intently. "Any of you?"

Nobody spoke for a moment. Then Ruthann said in a small voice, "Mr. Haines."

Mari and Jamie turned their heads to look in surprise at the small girl between them.

"I don't like to be around him because he smells bad," Ruthann explained.

Jamie and Mari tittered. "Behind his back, we call him Slop Bucket," Mari said.

"I can see where getting too close to Mr. Haines could make you uncomfortable," Mitch told them. "Can you think of anybody else? Maybe he makes you uneasy by the way he touches you, or even just the way he looks at you."

"Stanley Dick," Ruthann said.

"He's an eighth-grader," Jamie interjected.

"He's always picking on somebody," Ruthann went on. "At supper yesterday he pulled Tamarah's hair hard, and she threw a glass at him. That's why she had to go the principal's office."

"Okay. Anybody else?"

No, they all agreed with a shake of their heads.

Mitch was disappointed, but he didn't think anything would be gained by persisting. He rose and pushed the chair up to the desk. "I appreciate your answering my questions, girls. Later, if you think of something you want to tell me, call me at the police station."

Mitch had reached the door when Mari said, "I do have one question."

He turned back quickly. "Yes?"

She stood to face Mitch. "It's not about anything as important as Tamarah, but—well, how do you go about getting a crime investigated?"

"What crime?"

"Stealing. I guess you'd call it theft."

Jamie hid a smile behind her hand.

"Has something been stolen?" Mitch asked.

"She thinks somebody took some of her old gumdrops," Jamie told him.

"I know somebody did." Mari's expression was quite fierce.

Jamie didn't hide her grin this time. "She counts them. Can you believe it?"

"I didn't touch your candy," Ruthann said.

Mari glanced at her. "No, I don't think you'd have the nerve. And I know it wasn't Jamie because only the licorice ones are gone and she hates licorice."

Mitch was having trouble hiding his own grin now. "Where was the candy, Mari?"

She jerked her head toward the closet. "In there."

"It's out of my jurisdiction then. If I were you, I'd report it to Mrs. Horn." He had the door open by the time he finished speaking. He stepped into the hall and let the door swing shut on Mari's disgusted response.

"Big hairy lot of good that'll do."

Chuckling, Mitch made a hasty retreat.

Downstairs, Aggie Horn searched his face anxiously as she admitted him to her apartment. "How did it go?"

"All right, but they couldn't help me much."

"I didn't think they could. I called all the girls together as soon as we got back to the dorm to talk about Tamarah. None of them saw her leave the campus. They were all in their rooms, getting ready to go to town."

"Has anybody asked the boys?"

She nodded. "The Stands, the boys' dorm parents. With the same result as I got. Fifteen or twenty minutes earlier or later, and somebody would have seen Tamarah. She just happened to pick the few minutes when everybody was inside, getting ready to board the buses." She led him into a small sitting room furnished with worn but comfortable-looking chairs and loveseat. "Would you like to sit down?"

Mitch took a well-padded recliner with the permanent impression of a head and back in the cushions. Aggie Horn perched on the edge of the loveseat.

"I'm trying to track everyone's movements this morning," Mitch said. "I need a run-down on you and your husband, from the time you left your apartment to go to breakfast until you learned Tamarah was missing."

"You'll want Charley, too, then. He's over at the library, working on semester tests."

Mitch took out his pad and pen. "If you'll give me your account, I can probably fill in the holes from what your husband has already told me."

According to Aggie Horn, she and Charley were together until nine-fifteen, when he left the apartment to meet the junior gourd dancers in front of the administration building. By that time, several students were outside on the grounds, running around, engaging in horseplay, or simply talking and waiting for the buses.

"In your position as dorm mother, you must have known Tamarah pretty well."

"Yes. She was terribly homesick the first weeks of the school term, and I brought her here several times to give her a snack and a hug and just let her talk. Her mother's dead, you know. That's why her father sent her to us, in the first place." Mitch nodded, and she stared at her hand, which rested on the arm of the loveseat. "Mr. Qualls hasn't been able to reach Mr. Birch yet. He's out in a jungle somewhere, overseeing the building of a bridge. That poor man." She looked at Mitch bleakly. "Tamarah was an only child. He has no one now."

"He's going to blame himself for sending her here," Mitch observed, knowing that's how he would react in Birch's place.

"It could have happened anywhere," she said in a weak protest, rubbing her index finger across a dim stain on the loveseat's arm.

"He'll come around to that in time."

She nodded and looked toward the framed Jerome Tiger print above a small bookcase. It was *Hardship Journey,* a horse pulling a travois uphill through snow with an Indian brave astride him, head and shoulders bent low against the wind. When her eyes returned to Mitch, they shone with unshed tears. "I keep thinking I should have noticed when she left the dorm. I should have—"

"Even if you had, Mrs. Horn, you wouldn't have suspected anything amiss, would you?"

She blinked rapidly and shook her head. "No...I knew she was due in Mr. Qualls's office." Her voice sounded thick.

Mitch closed his pad and gave her another minute to compose herself before he asked, "Where will I find the other faculty members?"

She cleared her throat. "Some of them will be at the library with Charley, doing last-minute work—making out tests or averaging grades. That's in the stone building between the two dorms. Otherwise, you'll probably find them at home. Do you know where the duplexes are?''

"Yes, but not who lives where. Could I trouble you to make a list?"

"Of course." He tore a sheet from his tablet, and she wrote down names with the appropriate duplex number beside each one. "I wish I could be of more help to you," she said as she handed him the list. She followed him to the door. "Chief Bushyhead...it can't be anyone at the school."

"You're sure about that?"

She stared at him for a moment. "Yes. I know these people. This school is a separate little world. We work together and eat together and see each other socially. I can't believe anybody here could have done such a thing."

"Yes, ma'am." Mitch shrugged. "We can never think that of the people close to us."

THIRTEEN

FIVE PEOPLE were seated around a long table when Mitch entered the library. The relative darkness or lightness of their skin indicated varying degrees of Cherokee blood. The single woman was engaged in paperwork. The men had papers and books in front of them but they seemed to be merely talking and drinking coffee. Everybody looked up alertly as Mitch opened the door. Evidently, they'd been expecting him.

Lyman Shoemaker touched his fingers to his forehead in a little salute. "The long arm of the law has arrived."

Charley Horn rose and introduced Mitch to the others. Stafford Stand, the science teacher, about thirty-five and muscled from lifting weights, regarded Mitch, his hands clasped behind his head. Ellis Harlan, coach and physical education instructor, in his forties, a slim, physically fit man, took in Mitch with hooded eyes that were shrewd and intelligent. They met Mitch's briefly as they were introduced, then slid away. He had a Cherokee face, long and rather bony.

The woman was Katherine Hildebrand, English and speech, who must be past sixty. She acknowledged Mitch in a quiet but firm voice and looked him straight in the eye, clearly a woman who knew how to keep order in a classroom.

Mitch pulled out a chair at the end of the table. "Mr. Harlan, I understand Tamarah Birch was seated at your table this morning at breakfast."

After a small hesitation, the coach nodded.

"How did Tamarah seem to you?"

Harlan's eyes remained guarded. "She didn't seem any different from the others. She was present at breakfast. Beyond that—" He shrugged.

Mitch felt the man was being deliberately obtuse. "You didn't notice that she was a little excited? Nervous? Unhappy? Talkative? Silent?"

"There were a dozen children at my table," Harlan countered. "This morning they were on a tear, even noisier than usual."

"Because they were going to the Heritage Celebration?" Harlan gave a curt nod.

"And Tamarah was rowdy, like the rest?"

"I'm afraid I don't recall." Harlan rubbed a hand against the back of his neck. "She must have been. I'm sure I would have noticed if she'd behaved differently from the others." Mitch found this hard to believe. Tamarah would have been thinking about the dread visit to the principal's office. She must have been anxious. "Frankly," Harlan was saying, "I wasn't feeling very well this morning. I have allergies and the pollen count was off the charts. I had a sore throat and stuffed-up sinuses, and the noise gave me a pounding headache."

"Did you take one of the buses to town later?"

"Yes."

"Where were you from about eight A.M. until you boarded your bus?"

Harlan's nostrils flared. "Am I a suspect?"

"At this point, everyone's a suspect. Where were you during the time in question?"

"I went home after breakfast."

"Was anyone with you as you crossed the campus?"

"There were people about, but I wasn't with anyone. As I said, I felt ill. I wanted to get home and take an antihistamine tablet."

"What time was it when you left your house to go to your bus?"

"I don't know. I didn't notice."

Mitch didn't believe him. "It seems reasonable that you would have been watching the time, knowing you had to get to your bus by nine-forty-five."

Harlan made an impatient movement with his shoulders. "It may seem that way to you but, as rotten as I felt, I wouldn't have cared if I'd missed the bus. Anyway, I knew they weren't going to leave without me. We were all needed today to corral the students."

"Was Tamarah Birch in one of your PE classes?"

"Yes. All students are required to take phys. ed. if they don't go out for a team sport."

"Did you have any contact with Tamarah outside of class, other than at meals?"

Harlan rubbed his palm across the back of his neck again. He looked chary for an instant, then blurted, "Are these poorly veiled questions your normal interrogation procedure, Chief? Why don't you just come right out and ask me if I killed Tamarah?"

Shoemaker touched the coach's arm. "Take it easy, Ellis."

Mitch smiled. "I'm merely trying to find out who among the faculty knew Tamarah best."

"Well, I'm not the person you're looking for. I had her in PE for fifty minutes, five times a week, that's all. I don't know what she did or with whom at other times. My wife and I don't make a habit of socializing with students. Faculty, either, for that matter. We prefer staying at home with our children."

"That must be difficult, seeing as how you live in such close proximity to other faculty families on campus."

Harlan's temper frayed. "It isn't difficult at all," he snapped. "It seems to me your time would be better spent trying to jog Nancy Adair's memory. She's the third-grade teacher. She spent more time with Tamarah than any other faculty member. Are you finished with me?"

"For now."

Harlan grabbed a gradebook and got to his feet. "Then you must excuse me. I have work to do." He stalked across the room and sat at another table, his back to the others.

The four remaining teachers watched Harlan's retreat with expressions ranging from surprise to resignation. "Is he always this testy?" Mitch asked.

"The Harlans are very private people," Katherine Hildebrand told him. "As Ellis said, they don't mix with the rest of us much. They're very protective of their privacy."

"The faculty and staff have monthly potluck dinners," Shoemaker put in. "I don't think the Harlans have been there more than twice all year. They didn't even come to the retirement party we gave for Katherine the other day. This is her last year to teach, lucky woman."

Katherine Hildebrand smiled a bit wistfully, as though she would miss teaching, after all.

"The Harlans may have skipped the party because of their daughter," Stafford Stand said. "They probably didn't want to bring her—she'd have sat around and scowled. And they don't like to leave her alone. Kendall's going through a rebellious stage."

"We may be giving Chief Bushyhead the wrong idea here," interjected Charley Horn uncomfortably. "Sure, Kendall's been a bit of a problem this year, but it's nothing more serious than a lot of parents go through with teenagers. I think the Harlans simply don't enjoy being with people. My impression has been that Ellis and Serina find whatever they need in each other. In a couple who've been married for twenty years, that's kind of admirable."

"Or unhealthy dependence," Shoemaker mused, "but I don't know the Ellises personally well enough to judge which it is."

"Nor do I," said Katherine Hildebrand, "even though I share a duplex with them."

"Did you go back home after breakfast, Ms. Hildebrand?" Mitch asked.

She nodded. "I think it was close to eight-thirty before I got there. I stopped to talk to Jerry Bookland as he was leaving campus."

"What did you talk about?"

"Nothing important. The Heritage Celebration. The weather."

"Did you see Harlan as he was going home?"

She made a helpless gesture with her hands. "I'm afraid not. He must have passed as I was talking to Jerry."

"How long has Harlan been employed at the school?"

"This is his second year."

Mitch realized the teachers were getting nervous, wondering why he was concentrating on Harlan and if what they said might be construed as evidence against the coach. He got out his tablet and made a few notes. "Let's see if we can pin down times and places for the rest of you this morning."

That took several minutes, at the end of which the sound of Ellis Harlan's chair being pushed back jarred in the quiet room. Clutching his gradebook and a sheaf of papers, the coach left the library.

After the door swung shut behind the coach, Mitch asked, "What kind of administrator is Porter Qualls?"

No one said anything for an instant. Finally, Stafford Stand ventured, "He's rather old-fashioned in some ways."

"He means he's a strict disciplinarian," Katherine Hildebrand explained. "It's only the younger teachers who view that as old-fashioned. Personally, I believe children need discipline. If you love children, you must set limits, for their own good."

Shoemaker chuckled. "We all love children, Katherine. We sure don't teach for the money."

"Yeah," agreed Stand. "Most of us have to work at a second job during summer vacation just so we can keep doing what we're doing."

FOURTEEN

"ELLIS, TALK TO ME. Please. Why are you so upset?"

Ellis Harlan didn't look at his wife as he removed a can of root beer from the refrigerator and popped the tab.

"Earlier you said the police would be on campus this evening. Have you talked to them?"

He sat down at the kitchen table and took a long swallow of his drink. He tried to ignore the gentle but insistent pressure of her hand on his shoulder. It was a plea for reassurance. For absolution. But he was fresh out of indulgences.

Upon entering the house, he had walked straight through the living room, past his family, with a nod and a grunt. They had been watching a television movie.

Before the murder of Tamarah Birch, he'd been happier than he'd been in months because his son was home. Three days ago, nineteen-year-old Cody had returned for the summer from his first year at Northeastern State University in Tahlequah. A star athlete at Buckskin High School last year, Cody had distinguished himself on the junior varsity football team at NSU. His performance had virtually assured him of a starting position with the varsity in the fall. A natural athlete, handsome and outgoing, an A student, Cody was the son parents dreamed of having. The way Cody had turned out was a perfect irony that Harlan still marveled over.

No matter how dark things looked, and Harlan's marriage had been characterized by many black periods, Cody had always been the candle that kept the darkness from enveloping him totally.

Kendall, his seventeen-year-old daughter, was another story. If not for Cody, he'd consider himself a dismal failure as a father. The last time he'd really looked at Kendall—and he tried not to look at her more often than was necessary—she had a wide streak of dyed purple hair down the middle of her head. As if that weren't bizarre enough to stop him in his tracks, she had been wearing safety pins as earrings, ragged jeans with one leg ripped off just below the knee, and tennis shoes with holes exposing both big toes. The toenails had been painted black. He doubted that there had been a noticeable improvement in her appearance since Kendall seemed never to change clothes. He wasn't even sure she undressed to go to bed.

The happy glow that had been with him since Cody's return had evaporated. He didn't want to deal with his daughter's incomprehensible penchant for making herself as unattractive as possible or with his wife's everlasting anxiety. At the moment, he merely wanted to be left the hell alone, but clearly it was not going to happen. Serina had followed him to the kitchen and she was hovering over him. Were it anyone else, he might have said what he was thinking: *For God's sake, get out of my face!*

"I can't bear it when you won't talk to me, Ellis."

Harlan realized he could not avoid this conversation. The first few months after they had come to the tribal school, she had seemed more relaxed, almost happy. It was the ideal environment for Serina, he'd thought. Out of the way, a close society.

Then, a few months ago, the problems with Kendall had started and naturally Serina had seen them as retribution for their sins. Now one of his female students had been murdered, and Serina would manage to see something ominously personal in that, too.

To add to his problems, he had bungled the meeting with Bushyhead. He'd come across as defensive and angry, a man with something to hide. After he'd moved to another library table, he'd considered going back and apologizing to the police chief for his behavior. In the end, he had decided that whatever he said would call even more attention to himself. Instead, he'd left the library without a word to anybody. He had only hoped to have time to marshal his thoughts so that he could put the best face on it for Serina.

Twenty years ago, he hadn't realized that guilt was not something you could confront and defeat, once and for all. It had eaten relentlessly at his marriage almost from the first day. It had turned his wife into a fearful, chronically depressed woman who, every year or so, went off the deep end into religious fanaticism and spent hours each day on her knees. Sometimes he felt as though the main function of his entire life had been bucking her up.

He had to remind himself that this was the woman he loved. Twenty years ago, he had believed he couldn't live without her. He would have done almost anything to make her his wife. Now, even though he still loved her, he wasn't sure he'd fight so hard for her again. Be careful of what you wish for, his mother used to say. You might get it.

"We can't talk here, with the kids in the next room," he told her.

"Then let's go to our bedroom."

Her natural beauty was masked by worry lines in her brow and around her mouth that were becoming permanent. Her skin was unhealthily pale and her eyes were bloodshot. Even her blond hair, though always squeaky clean—Serina was obsessed with cleanliness—was lank and lifeless.

A twinge of compassion pierced his despair. He got to his feet, leaving the root beer on the table, and followed her to the bedroom.

He braced himself. She would pronounce doom on them again. She always did at times such as this. Harlan couldn't stifle the sarcastic voice in his head that said: Too bad hair shirts are no longer an acceptable method of mortifying the flesh. Serina would live in one.

She closed the door. "It's happening all over again, Ellis," she said despairingly. "It's never going to end. I don't know what to do. I just don't know."

Her head was bowed, her eyes on the dark green carpet. Looking at her fine, pale hair, Ellis was reminded of how it felt, slipping through his fingers like strands of pure silk. He had always been fascinated by her hair.

He touched it now. "Don't, Serina." He lifted her chin gently until her moist eyes met his. "There is nothing to do. You know that."

"I thought love would be enough," she said, her voice catching. After twenty years she could still say that with a sense of incredulity.

"So did I. I do love you, Serina."

"I know, and I love you. That has always been the problem, hasn't it?" She brushed hair off his forehead. Then, overwhelmed by hopelessness, she dropped her hand. "Did you talk to the police?"

He nodded. "Chief Bushyhead came to the library. Five of us were there, and he questioned us about where we were this morning when Tamarah was killed."

"All of you together?"

He nodded. There was no need to tell her how he'd reacted. It would only be something else for her to worry about.

She clutched his hand and held it against her breast. "Then he didn't single you out." There was a pathetically hopeful note in the words. "Do you think he'll let it go at that?"

He looked down at her hand, so fragile and white against his tan skin. "There's no reason why he shouldn't." She wanted to be reassured, and he could see that his words accomplished this. Soothing words were easy, rote after so many years. How many times had similar scenes been played out during their life together? Too many to count.

He pushed down the resentment he felt at having *always* to be the strong one, the one who supported and comforted and calmed her. He had accepted that role willingly when they married. It was illogical to chafe under the burden of her dependence when he was its chief cause.

He put his arms around her and she rested her head on his shoulder. "I don't think I can cope with having to move again," she murmured.

He wished she wouldn't say things like that. Implied in the words, whether consciously or unconsciously, was a reminder that she was always on the verge of breaking apart and he alone was responsible for holding the pieces together.

There were times when he felt close to implosion himself, times when he'd give much for just a little encouragement. He was tempted to tell her so, but she'd only cry and talk about people having to atone for their sins.

As Mitch was leaving the library, he ran into Nancy Adair in the hall. She clutched a stack of folders to her chest. "Good evening, Miss Adair."

She halted. "Oh, hello. Are you looking for someone?"

"I've been talking to a few of the teachers in the library. Actually, I'm glad to have the chance to speak to you again, too."

"Oh?"

"When we met in Mr. Qualls's office, I sensed you might have something you'd like to tell me."

Her arms tightened around the folders. "I can't imagine what gave you that idea."

"It was a feeling."

"I—it was just the shock of learning about Tamarah. She was a sweet child. To think of that happening to her—well . . ."

"Miss Adair," Mitch said, "It doesn't matter how trivial it may seem, anything you know or suspect might prove useful in the investigation."

She ducked her head for a moment, as though arguing something in her mind. When she met his gaze again, she said, "If Mr. Qualls finds out I told you, I could lose my job."

"He won't learn it from me."

She studied him intently for a moment. "It's probably not pertinent, but Merv Haines—the janitor—keeps pornographic magazines in his room. I know that doesn't make him a pervert, certainly not a child killer, but that's what popped into my mind when you asked if we'd noticed anything suspicious."

"Kiddie porn?"

She shook her head. "Just your regular garden-variety trash, from what I saw."

"Well, it's probably not relevant to my investigation, but thanks for telling me."

As he left her, he realized he was disappointed. He wasn't even surprised to learn that Haines was into pornography. If he tried to pin a crime on every man in town who occasionally looked at girlie magazines, he'd have a suspect list as long as a football field.

As he crossed the campus, he heard the faint bass rhythm of a rock tune. It seemed to come from the boys' dorm. The only other sound was the high-pitched drone of a cicada.

The night was cool enough that Mitch was glad for the long sleeves of his uniform. Noticing the lights on in the south side of Duplex #2, Mitch altered his course to make one last call.

FIFTEEN

ELLIS HARLAN had finally succeeded in calming his wife, when there was a tap at the bedroom door. "Dad, Mom," Cody said, "there's a policeman here to see you."

Returning to the living room, Cody said to Mitch, "They'll be right out." He glanced at his sister, who was sprawled in a chair in front of the television set, one leg thrown over the arm as though to display her filthy bare foot. "Kendall, shut that thing off, will ya?"

"Shit," the girl mumbled and stretched out a foot to stab the off button with her toe. She unwound her leg from the chair arm and got to her feet. She looked like one of those punk rockers Mitch had seen on TV. Wild, brown hair with a wide purple swath down the middle. Safety pins dangling from her earlobes; it looked as though it ought to hurt and made Mitch wince. Clothes that a street bum would reject. She started to leave the room, having yet to acknowledge Mitch's presence.

"Kendall, I'd appreciate it if you would stay," Mitch said. "I'd like to talk to all of you."

She rolled her eyes in a world-weary expression. "Shit," she mumbled again and collapsed on the nearest piece of furniture, which happened to be the couch.

Cody looked at Mitch and shrugged, eschewing any responsibility for his sister's rudeness. He was a good-looking kid. Clean-cut, lean and muscular, his dark hair short and neat. His jeans and red knit shirt, in contrast to his sister's clothing, were clean and unfaded. He was a teenager any adult could approve of.

Mitch looked around the living room. Harlan's attitude earlier had made him curious about his home and family. A large painting of Christ, purple-robed and haloed, was prominently displayed over the couch. The room itself was spotless and smelled of lemony furniture polish. Kendall was the only unkempt thing in sight.

Ellis Harlan came into the living room, scowling. He was followed by a pale, blond woman wearing a blue satin, quilted robe. Not exactly the welcoming committee.

"I thought you'd finished with me," Harlan said.

"I need to ask your family a couple of questions," Mitch told him.

"There's no reason to involve them in this."

"It's all right, Ellis," Mrs. Harlan said nervously, her eyes fixed on Mitch like a fawn poised to dart away at the first hint of danger.

"Mitch Bushyhead, ma'am." Mitch extended his hand. Hers was cold, and she dropped her gaze.

"Won't you sit down? Can I get you something—coffee, maybe?"

"No, thank you."

Serina Harlan wrapped her bathrobe around her self-consciously and lowered herself to sit beside her daughter, who threw her a contemptuous glare and scooted farther into the corner of the couch. Cody settled on the arm of the couch, the other side of his mother, as though to protect her. Mitch took the chair nearest the door.

Ellis Harlan remained standing, not about to do anything that might appear hospitable. "You should have called first," he said.

"I was crossing the campus on the way to my car and I saw your lights," Mitch told him. "I want to talk to as many of the people on campus as possible tonight, to save time."

With a loud sigh, Kendall propped a bare foot on her knee and began picking at a black toenail. The sole of the foot was almost as black as the nail. Her father threw her a furious look, which she made a great show of ignoring.

Mitch removed his notebook from his shirt pocket and thumbed through the pages. "I'll try not to take up too much of your time." He poised his pen above the notebook. "Mrs. Harlan, where were you this morning between eight and ten?" He caught Serina Harlan's gaze and was shocked to see naked fear leap into her eyes.

She plucked agitatedly at the tie belt of her robe and a muscle beside her left eye twitched involuntarily. "Here, I haven't been out all day, in fact." She studiously avoided looking at him again.

"Is there anyone who can verify that?"

Harlan drew himself up. "Just what is it you're trying to imply here?" he demanded. "I was given to understand you're looking for a man."

Mitch rested the notebook on his knee. "I'm not implying anything. And, at this point, we're not sure what we're looking for." He studied Harlan's rigid face. "You don't seem very cooperative, Mr. Harlan."

Icy silence.

"This will go faster if you'll let me ask my questions."

"You've no right to come into my home and harass my family. If it continues, I'll speak to a lawyer."

Serina Harlan looked at her hands. Kendall sniffed loudly and continued picking at her toenail. "Listen to Mister Upright Citizen," she mumbled. Cody shot his father a worried sidelong glance, but Harlan pretended he hadn't heard his daughter's sneering remark.

"Why are you so defensive, Harlan?" Mitch asked.

"This is an outrage!" Harlan's hands balled into fists at his sides and he glared at Mitch. "I demand that you leave my house at once!" He took a menacing step toward Mitch.

Mitch remained seated. He raised his hand. "Hey, let's don't either of us do something we'll regret. Nobody's making any accusations here. It's my job to find out where everyone on this campus was when Tamarah Birch was killed. Until I know that, I can't proceed with the investigation."

Harlan relaxed slowly but he remained standing. "Then do it quickly and leave us alone."

"Now, Mrs. Harlan," Mitch said, "I gather you didn't eat breakfast in the cafeteria with your husband."

"No. I hardly ever have a meal there. Kendall doesn't like the cafeteria food, so I cook for the two of us here." She gave her daughter a curiously pleading glance. Kendall ignored her. "When Cody's home, he often eats here with us, too."

"Did you eat at home this morning, Cody?"

"Yes, sir. I got up about eight and Mom cooked a waffle for me."

"What did you do after breakfast?"

"I went to town to look for a summer job. I might as well have stayed in bed, though. Nobody had time to talk to me, with the Heritage Celebration going on."

"Did you drive?"

"Yes, sir. I have my own car. An eighty-four Ford."

"Specifically where did you go?"

"All the grocery stores, hardware store, filling stations. Like I said, nobody had time to talk. A couple of people told me to come back next week."

"Before you left the house, did you see your father?"

"What the—" Harlan sputtered.

Mitch raised his hand. "Let the boy answer, please."

Cody shot his father a questioning look. "Yes, sir. He came back from the cafeteria while I was eating break-fast."

"Did you talk to him?"

"Not really. He had a sore throat, so he took something for his allergies and said he was going to lie down."

"You didn't see him again before you went to town?"

Cody hesitated, looking to his father for direction. Har-lan nodded curtly. "No, sir," Cody said. "He was still in the bedroom when I left."

"What time was that?"

"About nine, I guess," Cody said uncertainly.

"Kendall, do you know when your father left the house the second time this morning?"

"Nope."

"Did you happen to notice what time your brother left?"

Kendall crossed her arms and scooted down in the couch. "Nope."

"You didn't have breakfast with Cody?"

"Nope."

"Did you have breakfast elsewhere?" Mitch asked, his patience straining.

"Nope. Don't eat breakfast."

"Let me put it this way. Where were you this morning between eight and ten?"

"In my bedroom."

"Asleep?"

"You got it." She stared at him stonily.

"You seem awfully angry about something, Kendall, if you don't mind my saying so."

She heaved a sigh, rose and headed down the hall. "Say whatever the hell you feel like saying. I'm going to my room till this joker leaves."

Serina Harlan's hand fluttered to her breast, as though she'd suffered a sudden pain there. Her expression was fearful.

"Dad," Cody said, "can't you make her at least put on some decent clothes?"

"She's trying to get a rise out of somebody, son. Ignore her." Harlan's tone was placating. It was the first softening Mitch had seen in him all evening.

"I'm sorry, Chief Bushyhead," Serina Harlan said weakly. "Kendall is going through a very difficult period. She's mad at the world."

"I'd say it's you and her father she's mad at."

Harlan bristled. "She's failed three of her classes this spring. She's going to have to repeat her senior year. She has managed to rationalize that until it's our fault."

Serina swallowed convulsively. "She wants us to speak to her teachers. She seems to think we could talk them into giving her D-minuses so that she could graduate."

"We couldn't and we've told her that," Harlan put in. "Even if we could get the grades changed, we wouldn't. We feel that Kendall must experience the results of her own misguided choices. Some people—" regret flickered in his eyes as he glanced at his wife "—have to learn their lessons the hard way."

Serina stood, clutching her robe around her. "I'd better go and talk to her." She practically ran from the room.

Harlan watched his wife leave, then turned to follow her. "Excuse me. Serina can't handle the girl by herself."

Mitch was left alone with Cody.

"Dad would have beat the tar out of me if I'd treated Mother half as bad as Kendall does," Cody observed sourly. "I can't believe what they let her get away with. She needs her butt kicked around the block a few times."

Mitch couldn't have agreed with him more. He closed his notebook and tucked it back into his shirt pocket. "Did you know Tamarah Birch?"

Cody hesitated, searching Mitch's face as though for a clue to the proper response. Here's a boy, Mitch thought suddenly, who seeks approval from people around him. "Not really. I knew who she was."

"You never had any reason to talk to her?"

The boy frowned. "Sure, I talked to her once or twice. Well, not really talked. I spoke to her. I filled in for Dad in his phys. ed classes a few times this year when I was home from college. So he could spend extra time working with the basketball teams. That's really where his heart is. He played college basketball, you know."

Mitch eyed him thoughtfully. "I may want to get back to you if I think of more questions."

Cody nodded. "Any time. Only, could you lay off Mom? She's under a lot of pressure with Kendall and all."

Which, from Mitch's point of view, meant she was a weak link, the likeliest to crumble under questioning. Which wouldn't help him unless she knew something.

It didn't take Sherlock Holmes to deduce that Serina Harlan was stressed to the breaking point, Mitch thought as he left. The tension in that family was thick enough to choke on.

Something was going on in the Harlan house besides a teenager's rebellion. Mitch could smell it.

ELLIS HARLAN stood in the darkened hallway for a few minutes to collect himself and get his temper under control. Then he stepped into his daughter's bedroom and closed the door. His wife was sitting on the side of the bed, looking lost and helpless. Kendall lay on her stomach, her face turned to the wall.

Serina glanced at him and seemed to draw strength from his presence. "Kendall—talk to us. You need to get rid of this anger."

"Forget it."

"If you can't talk to us, maybe we could find somebody—a professional."

"Serina!" Harlan's voice rose. "That's not a good idea."

"We have to think of what's best for Kendall now," Serina said pleadingly.

"Don't worry, Daddy dear," Kendall snarled. "I have no intention of talking to a shrink."

Serina touched the girl's shoulder. "Sweetheart, don't be like this."

Kendall jerked away from her mother's touch. "Get away from me. You make me sick."

Harlan's temper snapped. He strode to the bed. "You are not to talk to your mother like that, young lady," he hissed furiously.

Kendall rolled over on her back and glared up at him. "Back off, you—you degenerate." The words trembled.

Rage exploded in his head. He grabbed her by the shoulders and jerked her to a sitting position. "If you don't shut your mouth, I'll do it for you!" In his anger, he shook the girl until her head bobbled and she yelped in pain.

Serina pulled at him frantically. "Stop it, Ellis...*stop!*"

With an oath, he released Kendall and she fell back on the bed like a limp rag. Her eyes filled, but behind the tears the irises burned with hatred. "Don't you ever touch me again," she said brokenly. "Don't you *ever.*"

They stared at each other for a long moment, both understanding the threat that remained unspoken. He ached to strike her across the face, to feel the brutal sting of his palm smacking against her cheeks again and again. Until he broke her spirit and she pleaded with him to stop. But he didn't dare.

Instead, he uttered a string of low curses, every vile one he could think of. It didn't help.

"YOU'RE AWFUL QUIET, Mitch." Lisa slid from the bed and reached for her robe. "Get dressed and I'll make some herbal tea."

Mitch lay in the darkness of her bedroom for a few minutes after she had gone, fighting a feeling of panic. He had arrived at her apartment a half hour earlier and they had grabbed each other like a couple of teenagers. After a few hot, feverish kisses, they'd made it to the bedroom, tearing at each other's clothes.

But their lovemaking had not been as free and releasing as it usually was. Not for him, anyway. He'd sensed she was holding back, too. As though her mind were already in Boston, waiting for her body to catch up. Was she bored with him? You're forty, that damned voice in his head reminded him.

But he knew his age wasn't really the problem. He and Lisa had never talked about commitment, about a future together, although he supposed he'd been taking it for granted. Evidently that had been a mistake, but this wasn't the time to bring it up with Lisa.

Not tonight of all nights when he probably wouldn't see her again for six weeks. His sense of being unable to say what was on his mind seemed ominous. A wave of sadness engulfed him. He knew it was an extreme reaction, out of proportion to the situation. Yet he felt as though he'd lost Lisa. What we have here, he told himself, is male ego running amok. He climbed out of bed and began searching for his clothes.

He came out of the bedroom buttoning his shirt. She went to him and wrapped her arms around his waist. Tilting her head back, she asked, "You okay?"

He cleared his throat. "Yeah. Sure."

"How come I don't believe you?"

"I'm sorry, I guess I'm preoccupied."

"You don't need to apologize, Mitch." She framed his face with her hands. "I'm going to miss you."

"Lisa." His hands went to her hair. He pressed her head against his shoulder. His throat felt thick. "I miss you already."

"I'll be back before you know it," she murmured. No mention of his coming to see her in Boston. The omission seemed depressingly significant.

"For how long?"

She went very still. "I don't know. Let's not talk about that now." She took a deep breath and stepped out of his arms. "The water's hot. I'll fix our tea."

"No, thanks."

Having moved to the stove, she turned her head to look at him over her shoulder. "I have to go home," he explained. "A neighbor woman is at the house with Emily. I didn't want to leave her alone tonight."

She turned off the flame beneath the tea kettle. Her back still to him, she said, "I'll call you as soon as I get settled in Boston."

He brushed her hair aside and kissed the back of her neck. "Okay." Not trusting himself to say anything more, he walked out.

When he arrived home, Emily was in bed and Mrs. Morgan was nodding in her chair. She jerked awake when he spoke to her. "Mercy," she gasped. "You gave me a start." She gathered up her needlework. Mitch stood on the front porch until the neighbor crossed their yards and unlocked her door. She waved to him before disappearing inside.

Then he walked through the silent house, out the back door, and cracked his shin on the frame of a canvas deck chaise beside the steps. He cursed softly and dropped into it, rubbing his shin with the heel of his hand until the pain eased. Heaving a sigh, he stretched out with his hands behind his head.

The moonlight danced on the links of the chain fence and the honeysuckle vine on the trellis beside the kitchen window poured out its fragrance. He thought of the many nights he'd sat in the back yard like this with Ellen, talking. They used to talk for hours. Now he wondered what they had talked about.

She used to say that she didn't want him to die before her, that she wanted them to live to be a hundred and then drop dead of simultaneous heart attacks. He had always said that the life expectancy statistics were against that. "You'll be a sexy widow with all the available men in town to choose from." But the statistics hadn't applied to them, and he was the one left behind.

He thought of his mother, who'd died five years ago. After losing his father, when Mitch was eight years old, she had never remarried. Mitch couldn't even remember her spending time with another man. If she had, she'd done it when Mitch was occupied elsewhere. And there couldn't have been many such occasions or he would have suspected. Twenty-seven years she had been alone. There must have been times when she felt incredibly lonely and abandoned.

Funny, Mitch hadn't given it much thought before. To his child's eyes, she had seemed a little quieter and more serious after his father died, but not obviously unhappy. Only since losing Ellen had he been capable of understanding how his mother must have suffered. But she had coped, working hard in a department store, raising her son, and then been truly alone after Mitch left home. He wished she were here so he could ask her how she did it. She had been a practical woman; maybe she would say that, when you strip life down to its core, all of us are alone.

It seemed a long time that he sat there, taking slow, deep gulps of air to dislodge the weight of depression that sat on his chest. He looked at the stars, thinking about the vastness of the universe and the insignificance of human loneliness by comparison.

Long after midnight, he re-entered the house and locked the back door. He found his bed and undressed in the dark. Though he hadn't expected to, he fell asleep quickly.

SIXTEEN

WHILE IT WAS STILL DARK, Crying Wolf rose from his bed to dress and gather the supplies needed for the medicine ceremony. Then he left his cabin in the woods near Going Snake Mountain. It was about a mile and a half from his cabin to the place where the child's body had been found.

Using a flashlight to show the way, he walked slowly. From long practice, he knew exactly how to pace himself so as to arrive at his destination with breath left in his lungs. It was, he thought unhappily, the pace of an old woman. Even though his mind was as young and clear as ever, his body had failed slowly with the years.

He would never admit it to Rhea, but he was grateful she had been around the past few months to take him where he wanted to go in her car. Of course, he had not told her of his present mission. She would have tried to talk him out of it. "Let a younger man do it," she would have said. But he did not want to shift the danger surrounding the morning's work to somebody else. If Rhea had realized that, she would have insisted upon getting out of bed at four A.M. and driving him.

Knowing that the spirits could be capricious, he feared the noise made by her automobile might disturb them. And they might withdraw, refusing to communicate with him. This was something he had to do alone.

Rhea was his youngest grandchild and the dearest to him, though he would never have admitted that aloud, either. She had grown up in Cherokee County, had scarcely traveled a hundred miles from home until she went away to the state university. Crying Wolf's daughter, Rhea's mother, and his son-in-law had died in a car crash the week of her graduation from the university. After the funeral, she had gone to Indiana for more schooling, and then to Maryland. He

loved her as much as ever, even though he suspected she had
lived in the white world for so long that she now thought
more like a white woman than a Cherokee.

He pushed aside these troublesome thoughts and con-
centrated on the ceremony he was about to perform. Yesterday, after Rhea had left him at his cabin to return to the
clinic, he had taken out the manuscripts that he kept in a
box beneath his bed. The roll of papers written in his own
hand in the Sequoyah syllabary included health remedies,
stories told to him through the years by the old people of the
tribe, and magic formulae.

His manuscripts did not include a specific ceremony for
identifying a murderer, but there were several for suppress-
ing evil and for turning evil back upon the evildoer. And
there were divining ceremonies. After long consideration, he
had decided on a ceremony to return the evil by fire. Instead of remaking tobacco to infuse it with magic power, he
would burn the lightning-struck wood that he carried in a
cloth sack slung over his shoulder. He was convinced that
only by such an extreme measure could the present evil be
dealt with.

He had not reached this decision lightly. Returning the
evil by fire was a terrible weapon. But he had had no other
choice. He had already performed a ritual to protect himself and, during this morning's ceremony, he would make
certain the smoke did not touch him.

At the edge of Buckskin, he turned toward the woods that
separated several blocks of houses from the tribal school
campus. The trees enclosed him in early morning stillness,
as though to protect him from unseen forces.

He had no trouble finding the place, which had been described to him by Charley Horn. There was the curve in the
path and there, alongside, the scattered pile of leaves and
brush. He set his sack on the ground and scanned the gray
patches of sky showing between leafy branches. Dawn, he
judged, was still a half hour away.

First, he cleared leaves and twigs from the spot where the
child's body had lain. Next, he gathered stones from the

surrounding woods and arranged them in a circle on the cleared ground. Finally, he laid the lightning-struck wood he had brought in the center of the circle and pushed handfuls of dried leaves beneath the pile for kindling.

His preparations completed, he closed his eyes and let the scents and the silence of the woods seep into him. Slowly, the syllables of the *i:gawe':sdi* emerged from the darkness of his memory and became black marks against the whiteness of his mind.

He opened his eyes and announced in Cherokee to the woods and its creatures, "I have come to restore peace."

Reverently, he took the child's mitten from his pocket and placed it on the small pile of wood in the circle. He struck a match on the heel of his boot and touched it to the dead leaves beneath the wood.

He stepped back as the leaves caught and flames leaped up and curled around the wood. The dry wood crackled and burned quickly. As the flames devoured the mitten, he chanted in Cherokee:

Listen! You Thinker of Evil, you will take it back!
Listen! Destruction will return to the One who
    brings it!
My name is Crying Wolf. I am of the wolf clan.
Listen, you Seven! Peace I have restored.

He repeated the incantation four times, his eyes fixed on the slowly dying flames and the smoke they left behind.

The smoke hovered over the glowing embers. It did not move for so long that he began to fear the spirits would not answer him. In his mind, he reviewed each step of the ceremony, each word of the incantation. Finally, he felt sure that he had made no mistake, and so he waited.

And then the smoke began to move. It drifted slowly southeast in the direction of the tribal school, staying low to the ground. Crying Wolf watched until the smoke was dispersed, but it never altered its course. He could not see the school buildings from where he was, but he trembled as he piled stones over the ashes of the fire, making sure no embers were left burning. The evil was at the school. The murderer was harbored there.

SEVENTEEN

SHELLY PITCHER stood in the doorway of Mitch's office and waited for him to look up from the report he was writing and acknowledge her.

Sensing her presence, Mitch glanced toward the door. "Hi, Shelly." He rose and came around the desk. "Come on in. Sit down." He glanced at his watch and saw that nearly an hour remained before the time he'd told her to report. Even Helen Hendricks, the dispatcher hadn't come in yet. "You're early."

"Yes, sir..." She took a chair and smoothed her new khaki trousers over her knees. With the trousers, she wore a tailored, khaki shirt and brown oxfords. She was twenty-nine and single, according to her employment application. She had worked for a suburban Tulsa police force for a couple of years after graduating from the police academy. At five feet nine inches, she was boyishly thin. Short sandy hair framed her angular face. She wasn't pretty, but the combination of cleanly drawn features and brilliant green eyes made her face arresting. She would probably photograph well, and Mitch wondered idly if she'd ever considered modeling as a career. Why police work?

She said, "I ordered a couple of uniforms from the place you told me. UPS delivered them last night. I haven't had time to sew on the patches you gave me. I'll do it tonight."

"Good." Mitch took a shiny badge from a drawer and slid it across the desk. He leaned back in his creaky swivel chair as she pinned the badge to her shirt pocket. "Did you find a place to live?"

"Finally. It's a four-room house on Osage Street. I moved in Tuesday."

"You getting settled in okay?"

"Yes. I like the house fine. Seems like a lot of room after living in a two-room apartment."

"In Broken Arrow?"

She nodded.

"Where are you from originally?"

"Born and raised right there in Broken Arrow."

"Is your family still there?"

She hesitated briefly. "My stepfather is. I haven't seen much of him since my mother died."

"When was that?"

"Almost a year ago. There was nothing to keep me in Broken Arrow any longer, and some painful memories to make me want to leave. That's one of the reasons I took this job."

Mitch wondered about the painful memories. "Well, I'm glad you're here."

She gave him a grateful smile. "I came in early, hoping you'd be here, so you could brief me on the routine, before anybody else gets in."

"For the next few days, anything resembling a routine will be purely accidental. We're in the middle of the annual Cherokee Heritage Celebration plus a murder investigation. Things could get pretty crazy."

"I heard about the child's murder."

"Sorry you won't have time to get your feet wet gradually—on the one hand. On the other, we've needed another officer for a while and never more than now." He picked up the report he'd been writing. About the murder investigation. "As you probably know, the victim was an eight-year-old girl . . ." He went on to give her the pertinent details.

When he finished, her face looked pinched and her expression was grim. "The fact that the panties were removed points to a child molester," she said, "even if he didn't actually get that far."

"I haven't kicked out the possibility."

"Child molesters are the worst kind of criminal. They're why I'm in favor of the death penalty."

"They almost never get death. They're nuts."

"Yeah, I know all about our enlightened court system," she said bitterly. "Even if you concede that all child molesters are crazy—and I don't—that doesn't make them any less dangerous. There are people who are just plain evil. Or so screwed up they can't be fixed. I attended an FBI seminar on sex crimes and perpetrators. The record of our attempts to rehabilitate pedophiles is dismal."

"So we should snuff them?"

"You bet," she said vehemently, "if we're not willing to lock them up and throw away the key. In today's climate, that's not going to happen. It's a case of choosing between the best interests of perverts and children. I'll come down on the side of the kids every time."

Mitch wondered if her vehemence had anything to do with her stepfather. Maybe when he got to know her better, he'd ask. "I can't argue with what you say. I'm just not sure it's that simple."

She started to disagree, then changed tracks. "So, who do you like as a suspect?"

He gave her a rundown on the people he'd interrogated so far. "For a little while, after I found the panties in Burns's yard, I thought I had our man. But I've checked out his alibi. I can't see how he'd have had time to kill that child. And he never exposed himself to children that we know of, just women."

"That FBI seminar included a session on exhibitionists. They're not the same as pedophiles. Of course, you know that..."

"Yeah, but I'm told it's not unheard of to find both disorders in the same individual."

"Yet you're confident Burns isn't your man?"

"Almost. I sure scared the crap out of him, anyway," Mitch said with a wry smile.

"Maybe it'll make him think twice about exposing himself again any time soon. That could wear off, though, if he's under stress."

"Dwayne's sure stressed," Mitch said. "So's his wife. I don't think she can hang in there with him if it happens again."

"Won't matter if the impulse becomes strong enough."

"I suggested to both of them that he should get some counseling at the county mental health clinic. I'll follow up on it again when I can find the time. At the moment, my top priority is to talk to the men who work as security guards at the tribal school. Starting with Jerry Bookland."

"You said he was on duty the night before Tamarah was killed?"

Mitch nodded. "As best we can pin it down, Bookland was leaving the campus about the time Tamarah went into the woods."

She sat forward in her chair eagerly. "Can I go with you if I keep my mouth shut?"

Mitch eyed her with doubt. "Sorry. I need you in town."

She wasn't very successful at hiding her disappointment. "Whatever you say."

"I'll include you in the investigation when I can."

She nodded. "Could you tell me something about the other members of the department?"

"Two officers, Virgil Rabbit and Charles Stephens, who goes by Roo, work the four-to-midnight shift. I'm shifting Roo off days and you'll be taking his place. We rotate being on call from midnight to eight A.M. Calls to the station are automatically transferred to the officer on duty."

"And the fourth officer?"

"That's Duck—Harold Duckworth. He'll be your partner to start with. Should be here any minute."

"Great. I'm looking forward to meeting him."

EIGHTEEN

"DUCK, meet your new partner, Shelly Pitcher."

"Get out of town, Chief." Duckworth glanced at the police badge pinned to Shelly's shirt. He did a double take and his grin faded. "You're kidding, right?"

Mitch shook his head.

"You're *serious*?"

"As a heart attack."

Watching Duckworth's face grow pale, Shelly hesitated, then stuck out her hand, her expression resolute. Duckworth's face quickly turned from pale to purple. Shelly wondered if he had a blood-pressure problem. "Pleased to meet you, partner," she said.

Helen Hendricks, at the dispatcher's desk, having met Shelly before Duckworth arrived, examined the fingernails of her left hand and turned her head to hide a grin.

Duckworth stood there dead still for a minute. Then he shot a look at Mitch. "Okay, what's the joke?"

"No joke," Mitch said. "Don't look so surprised, Duck. You *know* there are women police officers, don't you?"

Shelly glanced at her still extended but unshaken hand and let it fall. Her face had gone absolutely unreadable.

"Where'd she come from?"

"*She* came from Broken Arrow," Shelly said. Duck's head swung back around. "Yeah," Shelly added, "she walks, she talks, she's almost human."

Mitch had never seen Duck knocked so totally for a loop before. He almost felt sorry for the guy. Maybe he should have warned Duck.

"In Broken Arrow, I worked in burglary, after I graduated from the Tulsa Police Academy," Shelly said.

"Shelly won a couple of commendations for bravery," Mitch added.

"Uh—" Duck said.

"I worked with two partners while I was in BA," Shelly elaborated. "Both male. After they got used to the idea, they kind of liked me."

"That's uh—interesting, but what's it got to do with me?"

"Duck, you won't mind showing Shelly the ropes, will you? The two of you can work out who'll have possession of the squad car when you're off duty. Now you better hit the main drag."

"Yes, sir," Shelly said. Duckworth's mouth opened and closed, opened and closed. Like an oversized guppy, Shelly thought. He seemed to have lost the power of speech. She watched him for a moment, then threw her shoulders back and headed for the door.

"I'll wait outside, Duckworth." She opened the door with such force that it swung back and clanged against the wall. Duck stood there, gawking like a just hatched gosling waking up in a new world.

Finally, he said, "We gotta talk, Chief."

"Can't do it now," Mitch said briskly.

"Hold on. I want to put in a request for the evening shift."

"Later," Mitch said and retreated to his office.

Helen had taken out an emery board and was filing her nails. "I like her," she remarked, studying a thumbnail critically before starting on an index finger.

"Who asked you?"

"I'm merely making an observation. Just off the top of my head, I'd say your new partner is a tad ticked. Way to go, Prince Charming."

"Stuff it up your nose," Duck snarled.

"Tsk, tsk," Helen murmured to his back as he slouched out of the station.

SPOTTING ONE OF THE county patrol cars parked at the Three Squares Cafe, Mitch went in and found Jerry Bookland seated at a booth with a young deputy, Mike Farnwell. Mike was in uniform.

"How's it going, men?" Mitch slid in beside Bookland.

"Can't complain, Mitch," Bookland said. In his late fifties, Bookland had gone through a rocky period a couple years previously when his wife left him and, a few months later, his mother died. He'd apparently come out of it all right and, at the moment, was the picture of a contented man. He wiped a piece of biscuit through sausage gravy and popped it into his mouth. From the evidence remaining on their plates, Mitch deduced that both men had ordered the Grand Slam breakfast: fried eggs, gravy, sausage patties, buttermilk biscuits, and hash brown potatoes.

"Can't complain? Har-har," Mike Farnwell said. Farnwell was married with two young sons. He had a way of looking at you that reminded Mitch of the pictures he'd seen of James Dean, the late teen movie idol. "Ever since we sat down, Jerry's been griping about the price of everything from gasoline to cherry chocolates." Farnwell reached for his coffee cup. "Oh, and I mustn't forget the Middle East terrorists and the Central American drug lords. Jerry thinks we ought to haul the whole bunch of 'em to a deserted island, dump 'em out, and let 'em kill each other. How's that for a foreign policy?"

"It works for me," Mitch said.

Dicey, one of the two waitresses on duty, appeared at Mitch's side. "You having the Grand Slam, Chief?"

Mitch held up both hands and ducked behind them. "Get thee behind me, Satan. I can feel my arteries clogging up, just looking at their plates. Bring me coffee and a Danish."

"Empty calories, Mitch," Bookland said as the waitress left the table. He sat back and patted his stomach. "I decided I'd rather enjoy life now and give up a few years at the end when I won't be doing anything, anyway, but starving on my paltry pension."

"We don't die of heart trouble in my family," Farnwell put in. "We're accident-prone. My old man was killed by a bucking horse, trying to be a rodeo star. My grandpa fell off a roof and landed on his head. Splattered like a ripe melon, my dad always said. Never knew what hit him."

Bookland made a face. "You have to talk about it at the table, Mike?"

Farnwell grinned. "Never knew you were so delicate, Jerry."

"I'm sure glad I've finished eating." Bookland pushed his plate back.

Dicey brought Mitch's order. He waited for her to leave before he said, "Jerry, I understand you were the security guard on duty at the tribal school night before last."

"Figured that's what you had on your mind, Mitch." Bookland sipped his coffee and set his cup down. "Yeah, I worked that night. Went off duty a little after eight yesterday morning. I left the campus and went straight home to bed. Never saw Tamarah at all before I left. Wish I had. I'd have stopped her from going into those woods. She wasn't supposed to leave the school grounds without a chaperone."

"Had she ever done that before?"

"Not that I know of, but I wouldn't necessarily have heard about it."

Mitch looked across the table at the young deputy. "Do you pick up extra money working security at the school?"

"Sure," Farnwell replied. "I usually do four or five shifts a month. More if I can get it. The extra money comes in handy with two kids."

"Let me put a question to both of you," Mitch said. "Did your mind make any kind of connection when you heard about Tamarah? An incident? A name?"

They were silent for an instant. Then Farnwell said, "Nothing. I don't have a clue who might have done it. I almost feel guilty having to admit that. If somebody at the school did it, I mean."

Bookland nodded in glum agreement. "Somebody like that," he added, "seems like we should have noticed something different about him."

Nobody spoke for a moment. Bookland and Farnwell exchanged a look and Bookland said hesitantly, "I guess you know, Mitch, that Dwayne Burns is back home."

"I talked to Dwayne," Mitch said. "It doesn't look as though he's involved. I understand you had to go over to Eastern State and pick him up."

"Mike here asked me to go with him. Burns's wife called the sheriff and requested the department provide transportation. Said her car needed new spark plugs or something."

"To tell you the truth," Farnwell put in, "I think she just didn't want to go after him."

"She's having trouble coping," Mitch said.

"Heck of a thing," Bookland observed. "Don't know what makes a man all of a sudden start hauling out his dong in public. What's he thinking of? You've seen one, you've seen 'em all. Am I right?"

"Maybe something like a short circuit happens in his brain," Farnwell suggested.

"To understand it, I guess you'd have to be a psychiatrist," Bookland said, "or as screwy as Dwayne Burns. You sure Dwayne didn't do it, Chief?"

"I haven't eliminated him completely, but he's way down the list. What do you guys think about the coach at the tribal school—Ellis Harlan?"

Farnwell frowned. "As a suspect?"

"In general."

"Well, he's not a friendly sort," Bookland offered.

"And the rest of the Harlan family?"

There was a moment of silence before Bookland said, "The boy, Cody, is the only one of the whole bunch who will give you the time of day."

"I worked out there a couple of months before I ever saw the coach's wife," Farnwell added. "Before we go off duty in the morning, we usually see the faculty members and their families going to the cafeteria for breakfast. But not Mrs. Harlan. I wonder if she's got that disease that makes you afraid to go outside. Acra something."

"Agoraphobia?" Bookland said. "No. I'm there more than you are, and I see her out every once in a while. She'll say hello if she comes face to face with you, but she's not one for idle chatter, that's for sure." He scratched his jaw contemplatively. "I can't put my finger on it, but there's something about the woman makes me think she's afraid."

Mitch found Bookland's observation interesting, since he'd had the same impression. "I was at the Harlan house last night. I think the daughter's antics are making the coach and his wife crazy. The kid's got safety pins stuck in her ears. Not to mention purple hair and dirty feet."

"Some adopted kids go nuts when they find out," Farnwell mused.

Mitch darted a startled look at the young officer. "The Harlan children are adopted?"

"The daughter is," Bookland said. "Cody's the Harlans' biological child. It's common knowledge."

Now that Mitch thought about it, Kendall didn't appear to have Indian ancestry. But Cody's Cherokee blood, about one-quarter, Mitch guessed, was detectable in the boy's facial features and his dark hair and eyes. "It's odd," Mitch reflected, "the Harlans didn't mention that when I was out there. They explained Kendall's belligerence by saying she was upset over having to repeat her senior year in high school. I wonder when she found out she was adopted."

"I assumed she'd always known," Bookland said. "She doesn't look like either of her parents, for one thing. And everybody at the school knows, so the Harlans must have mentioned it when they came there."

Still, Mitch thought it was strange that the Harlans hadn't mentioned it to him. Even if Kendall *had* grown up knowing she was adopted. She might have handled it all right until she hit adolescence and started having problems in school. At which point she could have started to feel that she didn't belong—at school or in her family. Under those circumstances, some kids withdraw, others strike back at the most convenient target. Kendall wasn't the passive kind.

"What's your opinion of Porter Qualls?" Mitch asked.

There was no hesitation this time. "He'll never win any popularity contests," Farnwell said.

"From what I hear," Bookland added, "he's got his bluff in on the teachers. He says jump, they ask how high."

Farnwell said, "I heard one of the young female teachers tell another that Qualls sits up there in his office like a king in his tower."

"In other words," Mitch summed up, "he holds himself aloof from the teachers and staff. More of a dictator than a team player." The two men nodded. "How is he with the students?"

"Same way," Bookland said. "Those kids would rather walk across hot coals than be called into Qualls's office."

"Scare tactics," Farnwell observed. "It seems to work because they don't have many discipline problems."

So, Mitch pondered as he finished eating his Danish, if Tamarah was frightened enough of facing Qualls, she might have easily been diverted to the woods by someone she knew. Anything to put off facing the principal. Which reminded him. He had a few more questions to put to Qualls some time today.

"I'd better check on Duck," Mitch said, "see how he and the new officer are getting along. This is her first day on the job."

"Her?" Farnwell asked.

"Yep. We're an equal opportunity employer."

Bookland threw a dollar bill on the table. "There was a woman who applied the last time the sheriff hired a deputy. She didn't get the job, but she was in the running. Tough as nails. If you don't get to work, Mike, the sheriff might decide to hire her to replace you. Mitch, if I can be of any help to you in the investigation, give me a holler. I want to see that little girl's killer behind bars."

Farnwell voiced similar sentiments. The two men said good-bye to Mitch at the cash register counter, after paying their checks. Mitch paid and exited the restaurant as they were driving away.

The weather was as pleasant as yesterday, without the wind. Mitch drove toward the main street. Before he reached Sequoyah, Helen's voice crackled on the radio. "BPD One, this is base. Are you there?"

Mitch reached for his speaker. "BPD One here. What's up?"

"The medical examiner called. He'll be in his office for the next hour."

"I'm on my way back to the station. This is BPD One signing off."

NINETEEN

SHELLY PITCHER handed Duckworth coffee in a plastic cup through the open window of the squad car. He accepted it with a grunt. She opened the passenger door, got in, and rolled down her window to admit any idle breeze that happened by.

Parked at the corner of First Street and Sequoyah, they could see about half the booths that lined the sidewalk. At ten A.M., pedestrian traffic was already brisk. They'd written a couple speeding tickets. Otherwise Friday's crowd to this point seemed to be law-abiding.

Duckworth drank his coffee while drumming the fingers of his left hand on the steering wheel. His conversation since leaving the station had consisted largely of grunts and monosyllables. Shelly hated to see a grown man pout. So far she had managed to hold her tongue, but it didn't appear things were going to improve until they cleared the air.

She threw him a sideways glance. "Why don't you just spill it and get it over with?"

His eyes flickered, but he remained impassive. "What're you talking about?"

"All the bad stuff you've been thinking about me for the past two hours. Go ahead and say it before it eats an ulcer in your stomach."

"What gave you the idea I'm thinking about you?" he grunted.

"Hey, call me psychic."

"You women are all alike."

"Golly. In what way, other than the obvious, Officer?"

"You don't want to know."

Shelly expelled a long, low huff of air. "When you're finished jacking me around, would you mind getting real?"

"Whadda you mean?"

"Come on, Duck, cut the crap. Obviously, you didn't know your new partner was a woman until the chief introduced us. I'm sorry about that, but it wasn't my doing. I can see where it might come as a shock if you've never worked with a female officer before. But if you think this silent treatment will send me slinking back where I came from with my tail between my legs, think again."

Duckworth leaned back, took a swallow of coffee, and surveyed the view through the windshield. "You sure you can take it?"

Shelly allowed herself a slight smile. "Lay it on me."

"Okay, but, remember, you asked for it. If I get in a situation that calls for physical force I now gotta worry about my partner getting hurt in addition to subduing the perpetrator. Plus I gotta deal with female stuff I don't want to deal with, like PMS. Furthermore, I got people laughing at me behind my back due to this predicament I'm in. I could go on, but that's the gist of what I been thinking. Am I being real enough for you?"

"It's a start," Shelly said. "At least we have the beginning of a conversation here. First, I've got quick reflexes and I have physically subdued men twice my size. Second, I don't suffer from PMS. Just lucky, I guess. As for people laughing at you, I can't help you there, pal. That's your problem. And as long as we're sharing our innermost thoughts, let me just say I'm not thrilled about my new partner, either."

"What the hell do you mean by that?"

"You're overweight and out of shape," Shelly said bluntly.

"Now, looky here, my weight ain't none of your damn business."

"It slows reaction time. What if we have to pursue a criminal on foot? You can't keep up and I'll be left with my butt hanging out."

Duckworth's face turned red, but the squawk of the radio prevented his answering.

"Calling BPD Three. Come in, BPD Three."

Duckworth snatched the speaker off its hook. "BPD Three here."

"BPD Three to the old Stoney Point school. Fight in progress. At least one unidentified male reported to have a knife in his possession . . ."

"Hang on." Duckworth shoved the car into reverse and squealed from the curb. They zig-zagged down Sequoyah Street, skirting cars, siren blaring, hit the highway, and sped east.

"How far's the school?" Shelly asked.

"Three miles out. It's used as a community center now. Hasn't been a school for years. They've got some competitions scheduled out there this weekend."

Shelly reached for her holstered gun from the back seat and strapped it on. By the time they arrived at their destination, a small crowd had gathered to the south of the old stone building. Their attention was on something at the back of the building, but whatever was happening there could not be seen from the road. As the two officers got out of the car, a young Indian man ran up to them.

"Guy pulled a knife. He's using a woman as a shield."

"What's he riled up about?" Shelly asked.

"He was competing in the cornstalk shoot with an Indian bow. The competition's wide open, always has been. You can use any kind of bow you want. All of a sudden, this guy started yelling that he was getting cheated because two contestants were using expensive factory-made bows. We tried talking to him first, but he just got more worked up. So we asked him to leave and that's when he pulled the knife."

"What's his name?" Duckworth asked.

"Don't know. He's a Sioux from Lawton."

"First, we have to get those people away from there," Duckworth said and started across the grassy field toward the old stone one-room schoolhouse. Shelly headed in the other direction, running around the front of the building to the opposite side.

"Police!" Duckworth shouted as he approached the crowd. "You people get back away from there."

As Shelly crept along the side of the building, she could hear Duckworth trying to negotiate with the knife-wielding Sioux. Edging up to the back corner of the school house, she saw the man. With his left arm, he clutched a young woman back against his chest, and with his right he held an open switchblade poised close to her face. Shelly could hear the woman sobbing.

She didn't have time to think it through. She saw her chance and took it. Drawing her gun, she ran quickly up behind the man. She jammed the barrel against the back of his head. "It's all over, Sitting Bull. Let the woman go." The man froze. He reeked of whiskey. When he made no move to obey instructions, she shoved the gun barrel hard against his skull. He yelped and dropped his knife.

She had him cuffed by the time Duckworth reached them. Furious, Duckworth shoved the prisoner from behind. "Move it," he snarled and the man stumbled forward, all defiance gone.

Shelly followed a few steps behind. She had stolen Duckworth's thunder and he was boiling. Congratulations, Shelly, she told herself. First day on the job, and you're right out there winning friends and influencing people. She should have given Duckworth a chance to handle it his way, but she hadn't thought. In her admittedly limited experience, such standoffs were best solved as quickly as possible. The longer it lasted, the more likely it was somebody would get hurt. Okay, so she'd been a little too eager to prove her mettle to her partner. In the process, she'd humiliated him in front of the crowd.

By the time she climbed into the car, Duckworth had secured the prisoner in the back seat and was gunning the engine. The prisoner spat something in a language Shelly didn't understand. Evidently Sioux.

"Shut up, puke face," Duckworth said. He stuck his head out the window. "Jeez, you smell like a brewery."

Nothing else was said during the drive to town. Duckworth put the prisoner in a cell and returned to the common room to book him for drunk and disorderly and assault with a deadly weapon. "I jumped the gun, partner," Shelly said. "I'm sorry."

"There was no need to draw. I could have talked him into cuffs. You're lucky he didn't panic and hurt the woman."

"I said I was sorry," Shelly said meekly.

"One thing I don't need," Duckworth mumbled, "is a hotdogging cowgirl for a partner."

Shelly swallowed hard. It wasn't easy to keep admitting she was in the wrong, especially to this redneck lard bucket. "You're right. It won't happen again."

"It better not. I knew you were gonna be trouble the minute I laid eyes on you."

"You've made it pretty clear that you don't like me."

"Don't like you," Duckworth snorted. "That don't hardly cover it."

"So what are you trying to tell me? We can't go steady, or what?"

"You're a laugh a minute."

Mitch's office door opened. "I thought I heard voices."

Duckworth whirled around. "We brought in a drunk Indian. He pulled a knife and threatened to cut a woman."

"Anybody hurt?"

"No."

"I heard from the medical examiner on the Birch case," Mitch informed them. "Come into the office and I'll tell you what he said."

Shelly and Duckworth took the two chairs facing the desk and Mitch went behind it to consult his notes. "Cause of death was strangulation evidenced by a fractured windpipe and hemorrhages in the neck caused by pressure on the Adam's apple."

"At least it was quick," Duckworth muttered.

"We already knew she wasn't raped," Mitch said. "But Pohl confirmed it. No traces of blood, semen or saliva any where on the body. Or on Tamarah's clothing—Pohl checked with the forensic lab before he called me. The only bruises on the body were on the neck and arms."

"Wait a minute," Duckworth said. "Why'd he take her panties off then?"

"Several possibilities," Mitch said. "He was scared off before he could do what he'd lured her into the woods to do. He heard somebody coming—or thought he did—and had to kill her fast and get out of there."

"Didn't you say the body was covered with leaves?" Shelly asked.

Mitch nodded. "Yeah, and that doesn't seem to jibe with the quick kill and getaway theory."

"Maybe he was only trying to shut her up, not kill her," Duckworth suggested.

"Possibly. Say that's what happened. He's not into necrophilia, so when he realized he'd killed her, he hid the body and left."

"Maybe he's impotent," Shelly said.

For an instant, Mitch imagined a scene where the killer's impotence so infuriated him that he killed the child in a rage. "That's the third possibility. He's drawn to little girls as sexual objects, but he can't do anything about it."

"Except destroy an innocent child," Shelly said through clenched teeth.

TWENTY

THE SUN WAS HIGH by the time Mitch could leave the station for the tribal school. His sense of urgency had increased during the morning. Too soon, Friday would be gone. Visitors in town for the Heritage Celebration would begin leaving in less than forty-eight hours, and most of them would be on the road before sundown Sunday. Would the killer be among them?

He tried to shake off his sense of time rushing past, getting away from him. He would still give odds on the murderer being connected to the tribal school. Even so, a week from today virtually all the professional staff and faculty would desert the campus for the summer. Most of them, needing to supplement their school salaries, took summer jobs elsewhere. If he didn't nail the killer within the week...

But he would, he told himself as he parked in front of the administration building and shifted his mind from worst-case scenarios to the interview ahead of him.

He didn't much care for Porter Qualls, but somehow he had to put his instinctive dislike aside and concentrate on the vital question: Had Qualls, directly or indirectly, contributed to Tamarah's death?

Qualls wore a dark scowl as Darlene ushered Mitch into his office. Rankled at seeing Mitch again, he made no effort to hide it. Qualls was accustomed to calling the shots, beckoning and dismissing at his pleasure, and he clearly felt threatened when he sensed his control slipping. Mitch found himself wanting to rattle the man a little more each time he saw him.

"I'm very busy this morning, Bushyhead."

"I'm busy, too," Mitch said.

"What do you want? I can spare you only a few minutes."

"A few minutes should do it." Not waiting for an invitation, Mitch turned one of the straight-backed chairs to face Qualls's desk and sat down. "Have you reached Tamarah's father yet?"

Qualls pursed his lips and his left eyelid twitched. "Unfortunately, no. He's to hell and gone, out in some South American jungle. I had to reveal to a woman in the company's office what's happened to impress on her how important it is to get word to Birch quickly. She said they'd send a messenger out to him as soon as they could. Radio contact has been poor to nonexistent and transportation not much better. Apparently it's the rainy season there and off-road travel is chancy." He placed his palms flat on the desk, fingers spread, as though to prove he had no cards up his sleeves. "There's nothing more I can do to reach Birch."

Birch would hear a bare-bones report of his daughter's death third-hand. What a way to learn your only child has been murdered, Mitch thought. Once word reached Birch, how long would it take to get out of that jungle and on a plane for the States? Perhaps he should alert the funeral home that they might have Tamarah with them for a while.

Qualls shuffled some papers. "If that's all..."

"It isn't." Mitch waited until Qualls looked up. "I'd like to go over that incident at dinner the evening before Tamarah was killed."

Qualls leaned back in his chair and crossed his arms. "I've said all there is to say about that." He spoke testily.

"Sometimes people remember a detail they forgot the first time around. So if you don't mind, run through it again for me."

Qualls frowned, shifted in his chair and finally heaved a long-suffering sigh. "Tamarah threw a glass at Stanley Dick." His words were clipped short with impatience. "It missed, hit the floor, and shattered. That's it."

"I understand the Dick boy had been tormenting Tamarah for some time, and just before she threw the glass he pulled her hair."

"I've dealt with Stanley."

"Oh?"

"He'll be helping the janitor clean the bathrooms in the boys' dormitory next week. He'll think twice before he torments another child. But Stanley's behavior is no excuse for what Tamarah did. That glass could have struck a child in the face—the eye, even. We could have had an extremely serious injury."

"Where were you when the glass was thrown?"

"Seated at a table across the room, but I had a clear view of what happened."

"So you took Tamarah out of the cafeteria immediately."

"Yes."

"Did you go to her table or call to her, or what?"

"Oh, for heaven's sake!" Qualls exploded. "What difference does it make?"

"I want to be able to picture it in my mind," Mitch said. "Humor me."

The principal rubbed the space between his eyebrows with his thumb, as though he felt the beginning of a headache there. "Very well. I left my dinner to get cold. This, by the way, is a good example of why I prefer eating at home. I'm invariably interrupted mid-meal. Anyway, I immediately went to Tamarah's table and told her to come outside with me."

"Did she try to argue or justify herself?"

Qualls raised an eyebrow as though the suggestion was ridiculous. "She didn't say a word. She simply did as she was told."

I'll bet she did, Mitch thought, remembering his conversation with Jerry Bookland and Mike Farnwell. The students were terrified of Qualls. Tamarah wouldn't have dared talk back to him, particularly when he was angry.

"Did you touch her?"

He bristled. "What?"

"When you told her to come outside with you, did you touch her?"

"What are you implying?"

"I'm not implying anything. I'm trying to visualize the scene. It seems reasonable that you might have taken her arm to help her out of her chair."

Qualls's lips twisted into an angry slash. "It wasn't necessary to 'help her,' as you put it. She got up at once and followed me from the cafeteria." He reached for the butterfly paperweight, tapped it restlessly on a stack of papers. "Bushyhead, what has this to do with Tamarah's death?"

"I don't know, Qualls. Perhaps nothing. That's what I'm attempting to settle in my own mind. You said Tamarah followed you from the cafeteria. What happened then?"

"I reprimanded her." Qualls sounded resigned now. "And I told her to come to my office the next morning."

Reprimanded, of course. But had the reprimand been merely verbal? "This was in the hall outside the cafeteria?"

"Isn't that what I just said? As you know, she didn't keep the appointment."

"No. She was busy getting killed about that time," Mitch said dryly.

Shrugging off whatever resignation he'd been feeling, Qualls stared at Mitch, annoyed.

"Yesterday you said you put off talking to Tamarah because you were too angry to handle it at that moment."

"That's true." He lifted the paperweight in his palm, as though testing its weight. Mitch wondered if he was considering throwing it. Qualls set the paperweight down and his eyes moved back to Mitch. "It's always best to think through whatever punishment is to be meted out to a student. It must fit the crime, you see."

"Like cleaning bathrooms for tormenting little girls?"

Qualls nodded curtly.

"I'm curious, Mr. Qualls. What punishment did you decide on in Tamarah's case?"

"She would have been confined to her dormitory room next week, except for classes and meals." He met Mitch's gaze aggressively. "Obviously, you think I'm too harsh with the students."

"I'm not here to form an opinion about that."

Unmollified, Qualls snapped, "I can assure you, if you sat in this chair for a few days, you would change your mind."

No you don't, Mitch thought. We're staying on my track until I get what I came for. "Let's go back to what happened after you and Tamarah left the cafeteria."

"I believe I've covered that more than satisfactorily." Qualls made a show of looking at his wristwatch. "Your few minutes are up."

Mitch made no move to leave. "Did you touch Tamarah after the two of you left the cafeteria?"

Qualls stood abruptly. "This is preposterous! You seem to be fixated on whether or not I touched Tamarah more than twelve hours before she was killed. I don't remember doing so, but if I had, it would have no relevance to your investigation."

He didn't remember. Qualls was covering his butt, in case someone saw him with Tamarah outside the cafeteria. Mitch stood, too. He was three or four inches taller than Qualls and thought it might give him an advantage. It didn't seem to. Qualls braced himself with his palms flat on the desk and thrust out his chin. That look probably scared the crap out of the kids.

Miming Qualls, Mitch flattened his own hands on the desk and met Qualls's glare. "You lost your cool and grabbed Tamarah. You shook her, didn't you? In fact, you gripped her so hard that she cried from the pain. Harder than you intended, I imagine, and that's when you realized you were too angry to deal with her then. Isn't that the little detail you forgot, Mr. Qualls?"

The slight widening of Qualls's eyes told Mitch he'd hit upon the thing the principal had been so intent on denying. "I must ask you to leave my office," he said, his voice as tight as an overfilled balloon stretched to the bursting point. "I have work to do."

"There were old bruises on her upper arms," Mitch said, "bruises that match the shape of an adult's fingers. What if I told you I have a witness who saw you grab Tamarah and shake her."

Qualls hesitated for an instant and Mitch thought the
bluff might work. But then Qualls said, "I'm beginning to
regret my decision to cooperate with you, Chief Bushyhead. Perhaps I should remind you I can rescind that decision at any time. Good day."

Mitch stood his ground. "Have you cleared it with the
school board for me to see the personnel files?"

Qualls stared at him in stony silence for a long, charged
moment. "You may look at the files but you can't take them
from this office. And you can't make copies."

"All right. Where are they?"

"You'll have to wait until later. I have an appointment
now."

This little delaying tactic was Mitch's payment for back-
ing Qualls into a corner. But if Mitch pressed the man now,
he could throw up other roadblocks and delay the investigation further. Mitch wondered how long it had been since
the board gave permission for him to see the files and
whether Qualls would have passed along the information at
all if Mitch hadn't asked.

"I'll be back. Tell your secretary to expect me, in case
you're not here." With that, Mitch left. One of his suspicions had been confirmed, even though Qualls had stopped
short of an admission. He was convinced Qualls had made
the bruises on Tamarah's upper arms. Clear evidence of the
principal's hot temper, but since the bruises were made
hours before Tamarah was killed, they didn't tie Qualls to
the murder. Mitch's urgency returned. At that moment, he
wanted very much to see Qualls implicated.

But the bruises on Tamarah's arms didn't do it. In fact,
the incident outside the cafeteria might have frightened Tamarah so badly that she couldn't bring herself to face the
ogre again the following morning. What if she hadn't been
lured into the woods by the killer, after all? What if she'd
run there to hide rather than keep her appointment in the
principal's office?

It was a possibility that threw the case wide open as far as
suspects were concerned. Tamarah's meeting with her killer
might have been pure chance. If so, the murderer wasn't

necessarily somebody employed at the school. He could have been a complete stranger to Tamarah.

Still, she would probably have had time to cry out, to struggle. She could have been heard by somebody crossing the school grounds. But from what he'd learned, everyone was inside at that time, getting ready to go to town.

Except, of course, for Jerry Bookland. Lyman Shoemaker had run into Bookland the morning of the murder on his way from the cafeteria to his living quarters. Bookland had been making a final round of the campus preparatory to going off duty. According to Bookland, he left shortly after eight but he could have been there as late as eight-thirty. Still, if he'd heard sounds in the woods that morning, he'd have mentioned it.

At this point, there were too many possibilities. Tamarah could have kept the appointment with Qualls and done or said something that caused him to lose his temper again, which seemed to have a hair trigger. In the heat of anger, could he have decided to administer corporal punishment and killed her accidentally?

That theory had more holes than a sieve. Corporal punishment to a principal meant paddling. How could Qualls have accidentally broken her neck while paddling her? It didn't happen that way.

Qualls had shaken her earlier. Could you shake an eight-year-old child violently enough to break her neck? Unlikely. Furthermore, how could Tamarah have entered Qualls's office without being seen by Darlene?

Mitch stopped at the secretary's desk to ask, "Darlene, yesterday morning, did you leave your desk at any time before nine-thirty?"

"Gee, let me think." Darlene popped her gum and pushed her glasses up her nose with her index finger as she thought it over. "I might have gone to the ladies' room. I can't say for sure that it was before nine-thirty."

"If you remember, will you let me know?"

"Sure thing, Chief."

Mitch brooded on his conversation with Qualls as he drove to the high school football field where the morning session of the pow-wow should be winding down.

He found an empty slot in the line of cars behind the bleachers. As he left the squad car, he noticed John Irons, better known in Cherokee circles as Crying Wolf, the old medicine man with whom Mitch had had dealings on previous occasions.

Inexplicably, he was drawn to the old man. For one thing, Crying Wolf gave off an aura of being at peace with himself and his world and you felt calmed in his presence. For another, Mitch enjoyed hearing the old man talk in the guttural tones of one who was more accustomed to speaking Cherokee than English.

Seated at the center of the field were five men, beating drums in rhythm with Charley Horn, who was singing a dance song in Cherokee. A gourd dance was in progress. Men and boys danced sedately on one side of the field, with women and girls performing a shuffling step on the other. Fancy costumes and more elaborate dances were reserved for the crowds who attended the evening sessions.

With Crying Wolf was another elderly Cherokee. The other man had a blanket wrapped around his shoulders, in spite of the mild temperature. Both men wore their hair in long braids. They were seated in folding chairs at the edge of the field on the fifty-yard line. A woman sat facing them on the bench occupied by sidelined players during football games.

As Mitch walked toward the three, they seemed to be engaged in serious conversation. Upon noticing him, they stopped talking and watched his approach.

"Hello, Grandfather," Mitch said to Crying Wolf. The respectful title felt natural, though a year ago Mitch would have felt self-conscious using it. He was still—would always be—an outsider to some of the conservative Cherokees, not because he was half-white but because he hadn't been raised in the Cherokee way and could not speak the language. "How are you, sir?"

"I am well," Crying Wolf said gravely. "This is my friend from North Carolina." He indicated the blanket-wrapped old man seated next to him. Rheumy eyes fastened on Mitch's face as the other man accepted Mitch's proffered hand.

"Mitch Bushyhead, Grandfather," Mitch said.

The old man eyed Mitch's uniform. "You are the law for the white man," he said, grinning to show there were no hard feelings. His four upper front teeth were missing, causing a slight lisp. "I am called Wandering Deer. As a boy I liked to go on journeys."

Most of the older traditional Cherokees had two names, a "white man's name," as they called it, used on legal documents and in dealings with whites, and an Indian name, usually given to them at a young age. The two-name tradition wasn't so common among younger Cherokees.

The old man's introducing himself as Wandering Deer was a sign of acceptance. It was a way of saying, "I recognize you. You are one of us."

"It's a pleasure to meet you," Mitch said.

"He makes medicine on the Qualla reservation," Crying Wolf said.

Mitch glanced at the young Cherokee woman sitting on the bench and found her watching him curiously. "The daughter of my daughter," Crying Wolf said, "Rhea Vann."

She was in her early thirties, Mitch judged. Her black hair was brushed back and caught behind her ears with combs; it fell, thick and straight, to below her shoulders. She wore a pink blouse with lace around the collar and padded shoulders. Her skirt was blue denim. She wore low heels and Mitch noticed that her bare, brown legs were taut and smooth. There was something sad behind the curiosity in her eyes as she met Mitch's gaze. Something caused by the serious conversation he had interrupted? Mitch wondered.

They shook hands. Hers was small and firm, with neatly clipped, unpolished nails.

"She is medicine woman," Wandering Deer said. "All three—we make medicine." The two old men laughed, and

Rhea's dark eyes twinkled at them. They were having a joke on her.

"I'm a family practice physician at the tribal clinic," she explained to Mitch.

"You took Dr. Waters's place?" Mitch asked. About two months ago, Waters had retired as head of the clinic and the only full-time medical doctor on staff.

"Yes." Her brief smile faded. "We've been talking about Tamarah Birch."

"Did you know her?"

"I saw her as a patient at the clinic a couple of times."

"Recently?"

"The first time was a few days after I began working there. She had an ear infection. Then, about a week ago, her dorm mother brought her in again. Tamarah had been complaining of a stomachache and had missed two days of school." She frowned slightly.

"You look skeptical."

"Upon examination, I could find nothing wrong with her. I talked to her for ten or fifteen minutes and became convinced she was faking the stomachache. So I sent the dorm mother, Aggie Horn, outside and asked Tamarah if something was troubling her." Her voice trailed off for an instant. Then, "She said she had done something bad."

"She didn't tell you what?"

She shook her head. "Not really. I prodded her a bit, and she finally said—" Her eyes moved away from Mitch. "Let me think now. I want to get it right. She said, 'I saw a secret and I promised never to tell.'"

"Saw? She said she *saw* a secret?"

"Those were her exact words, and the only other thing I could get out of her was that she had broken her promise. That was evidently the 'bad thing' she had done. Then she asked me if I thought God would punish her by taking her father away from her."

"I understand her mother died about a year ago," Mitch said.

She nodded. "I was aware of that, of course. It's not unusual for a child to feel somehow to blame when a parent dies. In Tamarah's case, after the loss of her mother, she was sent to the boarding school. It may have been the most sensible thing for her father to do in his circumstances, but Tamarah may have seen it as a rejection. I sensed that being separated from her father made her quite anxious."

"How could she be sure he wouldn't die, too?" Mitch mused.

"Exactly. She may have feared any small infraction, such as breaking a promise, could bring on his death and leave her alone in the world."

"Step on a crack and break your mother's back," Mitch murmured. "The things that go on in kids' minds, without the people around them ever suspecting."

"Childhood is not necessarily the carefree time we like to believe it is," she agreed. "Tamarah Birch was a very tense and worried little girl. She needed to talk to someone, and I asked Mrs. Horn to have Tamarah's father come and see me when he arrived at the end of term to take her home. I intended to recommend that he put her in counseling this summer." Sadness clouded her dark, expressive eyes. "Instead he'll take her home to bury her."

The blanketed old man, Wandering Deer, muttered something in Cherokee, switching to English to add, "Her soul is not at rest."

Mitch turned to him. "What do you mean, Grandfather?"

"She is in *Tsusgina'i*."

At Mitch's questioning look, Crying Wolf said, "He does not understand. He was not raised with his father's people."

"He says she is in the ghostland," Rhea translated. "The realm where spirits of murder victims wander until their deaths are avenged."

"She cries to go to *Usunhi'yi*," muttered Wandering Deer.

"She longs to go to the dark land in the west," Crying Wolf explained, "but she cannot go to the Night Land and be at peace until her death is avenged. You must find the

evildoer, Mitch Bushyhead. When he is punished the child's
soul can be at rest."

"He will be punished," Mitch assured him.

"The white man's law works too slow," hissed Wandering Deer, then switched to Cherokee, grimacing as though
there was something particularly nasty about the words. He
was angry suddenly and his black eyes were fierce.

"What did he say?" Mitch asked Rhea.

"He is incensed because an innocent child has been murdered," she told him. Mitch found it curious that she gave
him an interpretation, rather than translating the old man's
words.

Crying Wolf gazed at his granddaughter, then said to
Mitch, "At dawn, I made medicine." He switched to Cherokee and conversed with Wandering Deer for several moments. In English, he said, "The killer is at the tribal school.
The smoke has told me this."

Mitch glanced at Rhea. She looked back at him calmly,
giving no indication of how she felt about her grandfather's medicine. She stood. She wasn't as tall as Mitch had
guessed, perhaps five feet five. "The dancers are taking a
break now. Let me drive you home, Grandfather," she said
to Crying Wolf. "You need to rest, after getting up so early
and walking so far. We'll come back tonight if you want."

"You treat me like a child," Crying Wolf scolded, but he
got to his feet nevertheless. She folded his chair flat and,
carrying it in one hand, she took her grandfather's arm with
the other. With a backward glance at Mitch, Wandering
Deer walked with them toward the cars parked behind the
bleachers. The two old men continued their conversation in
Cherokee.

Mitch sat down on the bench and waited for Charley
Horn to take leave of the drummers. Rhea Vann's remark
about Tamarah Birch's revealing a secret she had promised
to keep had jogged Mitch's memory. When he had questioned Tamarah's roommates, he'd sensed that Ruthann
Blackfox was holding something back. She had been Tamarah's best friend, the logical person to have been privy to
Tamarah's secret. He had meant to talk to Ruthann again,

but it hadn't seemed urgent so he'd let it slide. He didn't see Ruthann in the audience and hoped Horn would know where he could find her.

As soon as Charley Horn left the drummers, Mitch walked across the field and fell into step beside him. "Charley, could I speak to you a minute?"

"I saw you talking to Crying Wolf," Horn said. "Did he tell you about the medicine ceremony?"

"He mentioned it."

"He says the medicine told him the killer is at the school."

"He told me that, as well."

"Does it help you?"

"Not particularly. We're already working under that assumption."

"Oh."

"I want to talk to Ruthann Blackfox again. I thought you might know where I could find her."

Briefly, Horn scanned both sets of bleachers. "I saw her here earlier. She was with some other girls from school."

"Did they leave together?"

"I'm sorry, I didn't notice." He frowned worriedly. "Aggie could probably tell you where Ruthann is."

"Where can I find your wife?"

"Try Sequoyah Street. On the bus ride to town this morning, she told some of the girls that they could browse in the booths before lunch."

Mitch thanked him and returned to his squad car. Before starting the engine, he checked in with Helen, who said Duck and Shelly Pitcher had responded to a few calls that morning. Nothing major, though. There had been no call from Lisa. He hadn't really expected to hear from her yet—she would spend the better part of today and tonight driving to Boston—but he felt let down, nonetheless.

He told Helen he probably wouldn't get back to the station until mid-afternoon.

TWENTY-ONE

MITCH RAN INTO Emily and Temple on Sequoyah Street. "We'll be at our house for lunch," Emily told him. "We've been through all the booths twice, so we're going to listen to music this afternoon."

"I have a new Janet Jackson tape," Temple put in.

Mitch had no idea who Janet Jackson was. "Is she any relation to that kid with one glove?"

"Michael Jackson, Daddy," Emily said despairingly. "She's his sister. Honestly, you don't know what's going on in the world."

"The problem is I know too much of what's going on," Mitch said.

Emily's look suggested his knowledge was sadly lacking in certain vital areas. Mitch smiled and said, "I confess I lost out on the pop music scene ten or fifteen years ago." Today's pop music all sounded the same to Mitch. When he tuned it in on his car radio, he couldn't understand the words.

"Would you like to borrow my Janet Jackson tape?" Temple asked.

"Uh, no thanks."

"We'll probably go over to Temple's later," Emily said. "Can you pick me up there at five?"

"I'll do my best," Mitch promised. "But if I'm delayed, wait there for me."

Emily groaned. "Don't be too late, Daddy. I have a date with Kevin tonight. I'll be *soooo* glad when I get my driver's license."

"Me, too," Temple chimed in.

"Temple's father is buying her a Plymouth," Emily said pointedly. Before she could get going, for about the mil-

lionth time, on how desperately she needed her own car before the next school term, Mitch said, "Gotta run."

A few minutes later, Mitch caught sight of a group of
young girls in front of the drugstore. They were clustered
around a woman, who had her back to Mitch. Recognizing
the woman as Aggie Horn, he made his way in their direction, stepping off the curb into the street to make faster
progress.

Aggie Horn turned with a preoccupied look on her face.
She saw him and waved and all the little girls turned to stare
at him.

Reaching the group, Mitch realized that Ruthann Blackfox was not one of the dozen or so girls with Aggie Horn,
whose gaze continued to sweep up and down the street, as
though she were expecting someone to join them any minute.

"Hello, Chief Bushyhead." It was Mari Ketcher, one of
Tamarah Birch's roommates.

"Greetings, ladies. You waiting for someone?"

"We lost Ruthann," Mari said.

"We haven't lost her exactly," Aggie Horn amended, still
scanning the crowd. Turning to Mitch, she added, "She went
into the drugstore to use the bathroom."

"But we looked in the drugstore and the bathroom and
she's not there."

"You didn't see her come out?" Mitch asked.

Aggie shook her head. "We probably just missed her."

"You were standing here all the time?"

"Yes, but we weren't really watching for her—until I realized she'd been gone fifteen minutes and sent a couple of
the girls to look for her."

"How long ago was that?"

Aggie consulted her watch. "About ten minutes. I didn't
want to move. I'm sure she's merely wandered off somewhere and she'll eventually look for us here." She said it as
though she was working hard to convince herself.

"I'm hungry," complained one of the younger girls.

"We'll eat in a little while, Dorothy," Aggie said distractedly. "As soon as Ruthann comes back."

Dorothy stared accusingly at Mitch. "Have you caught Tamarah's murderer yet?"

"No, but we will," Mitch told her. "I'm going to talk to the people in the drugstore." Inside, he found Tom Wood, the middle-aged pharmacist and two clerks, a matronly woman, and a teenaged girl.

Mitch went back to the pharmacy to talk to Wood, a laid-back, slow-talking man. "Morning, Chief," Wood drawled. "Have you caught the thieving delinquents who stole my tapes?"

"Not yet, Tom."

"So what else is new?" Wood groused. "I already wrote it off, anyway."

"Duck's working on it," Mitch assured him. "Did you see a little girl—Ruthann Blackfox—from the tribal school come through here about a half hour ago?"

"Yeah. She asked if she could use the bathroom and Tina over there—" he indicated the teenaged clerk "—showed her where it is."

"Did you see her come back through?"

"Naw. I had some prescriptions to fill. Wasn't paying any attention."

"One of the teachers from the school was out front with a group of girls, waiting for Ruthann. She never came back."

Wood scratched his head. "Well, hell's bells, maybe she's still back there, sick or something."

"A couple of the students checked and couldn't find her."

"I better have a look, anyway."

Woods was gone only briefly. "She's not there. Tina—" He raised his voice. "You and Madge come back here a minute."

When the two clerks had joined them, Wood said, "Tina, didn't you take that little Indian girl to the bathroom?"

Tina darted a look at Mitch. "I showed her where it was and left her."

"Did you see her come back out?"

Tina shook her head. "No, did you, Madge?"

"No. I saw a couple more Indian kids go back there and come out again, but now that you mention it, I never did see the first one come out."

"Is there a back exit?" Mitch asked.

"Sure," Wood said. "The state fire marshal requires it. Come on, I'll show you."

Pasteboard boxes were stacked in the back room. A narrow trail between them led to the bathroom with a break to provide access to a heavy steel door that opened to the outside. Mitch stepped into the alley, where there was nothing but trash barrels.

He stepped back into the drugstore. "Has this door been unlocked all morning?"

"Sure," Wood said. "In case of fire, we have to be able to get out quickly. I open it when I come to work in the morning and lock it when I go home for the night."

"She must have gone out that way."

Wood shrugged. "That doesn't make sense. She'd have had to walk half a block down the alley and around to Sequoyah Street." He spoke with the disbelief of a man who rarely took more steps than were necessary. "It's much shorter through the drugstore. She probably slipped past us when we were all busy with customers. We've had a lot of traffic this morning."

"Then why didn't they see her out front?"

Wood scratched his head again. "Beats me."

Mitch turned to the two women. "Can you remember who else was in here when Ruthann went back to use the bathroom?"

"The Kirkwood sisters," said Madge. "Millicent wanted something for indigestion and Polly looked at the support hose, but she didn't buy any. Millicent said if she'd lose some weight, she wouldn't need support hose. There were several other people in here about the same time, too. I didn't recognize them, so they must've been from out of town."

"Tina, do you remember anybody else?"

"Donald Rabbit—I know him from high school, but he goes to NEO now." Mitch nodded. Donald was Virgil's oldest son, a freshman at Northeastern Oklahoma Junior College in Miami. "He came in to buy some shaving cream. I think he was leaving about the time that little girl asked to use the bathroom."

"Anybody else?"

"Let me think...oh, yeah, I almost forgot. Kendall Harlan was here. I know her from high school, too. We're both seniors this year, but I heard she flunked some courses and has to take them over next year."

"Kendall was here? Was anyone with her?"

"I didn't see anybody."

"What did she want?"

"She looked at magazines. Just hanging out, I guess. We said hi, but I don't know her all that well. She's kind of— well, different. I had to wait on another customer and the next time I noticed, Kendall was gone."

Mitch went outside to Aggie Horn and the waiting students. "Nobody saw her leave," Mitch told them. "She must have used the back way."

Aggie was clearly agitated now. Apparently she had failed to convince herself that Ruthann had simply wandered off. "Why would she do that?"

"I don't know, but it explains why nobody saw her leave. Have any of you seen Kendall Harlan this morning?"

All but one of them shook their heads. The student called Dorothy said, "I think I saw Kendall driving her brother's car."

"When?" Mitch asked.

"When we first got here, after we left the pow-wow."

"That was about eleven," Aggie put in.

"Did you see her get out of the car?"

"No, she was just driving down the street real slow—at least, I think it was her. I'm not really sure. She was a long way off. It could've been Mrs. Harlan, I guess."

Mari sent Dorothy a disbelieving look. "How could you get those two mixed up? They don't look anything alike. Was her hair wild and purple, or not?"

"I couldn't tell," said Dorothy apologetically. "I only saw her from the back. I'm sorry."

"That's all right," Mitch told her. "You've been a big help."

"Hey!" one of the younger girls yelled, "there she is!" She jumped up and down and waved. "It's about time, Ruthann! Come on!"

Ruthann was walking toward them, finishing off a hot dog. Mitch hadn't realized how worried he was until the sight of the little girl relaxed the tension in his chest.

"Where have you been, young lady?" demanded Aggie Horn. "We've been worried sick about you."

"Back there," Ruthann gestured vaguely in the direction of the hot dog stand. "There was a long line."

"You didn't have permission to go off on your own."

Ruthann hung her head. "I'm sorry," she murmured.

"I didn't know you had any money with you."

Ruthann merely shrugged.

"I told you we'd eat together at noon," Aggie persisted. "You stick with the group after this. Understand?"

Ruthann nodded meekly and glanced at Mitch for the first time, then her eyes skittered away. "Did you go to the hot dog booth alone, Ruthann?"

The child twisted a strand of black hair around one finger. "I wasn't alone. There were lots of people there. A long line. I told you." She made a face. "I don't feel so good, Mrs. Horn."

There was something else here, something beyond Ruthann's leaving the group without permission. He had to find a way to bring it into the open. But this wasn't the place to question the child further. "I'd like to have a talk with you when you get back to school, Ruthann," Mitch said. "Will that be all right?"

"I guess so," she said uncertainly.

"I'm starving," said Dorothy.

"All right, Dorothy," Aggie Horn said sharply. "We'll eat at the Three Squares Cafe and then we'll go back to the football field for the afternoon session of the pow-wow."

"Can I have ice cream?" Ruthann asked in a small voice.

"I thought you didn't feel well," Aggie reminded her.

"Uh—I mean if I feel better by then."

"That depends on how you behave in the meantime. Stay close to me now."

Mitch watched them leave with an uneasy feeling. Where had Ruthann gone besides the hot dog stand? Even if there was a line, it shouldn't have taken thirty minutes to get her hot dog.

Maybe she would tell him when he talked to her alone. Maybe she'd tell him, too, what Tamarah's secret had been. Ruthann had to be the one in whom Tamarah had confided. That didn't mean Ruthann would admit it. The child was as cautious as a doe with a new fawn. Or a little girl caught in something too big and too frightening for her to deal with. Mitch would have to gain her trust.

And if he accomplished that and she told him what she knew, it might have nothing to do with Tamarah's death. He hesitated briefly, then decided to grab a bite of lunch at the sandwich shop and try to get some paperwork done before going back to the tribal school.

TWENTY-TWO

MITCH WAS BRINGING the Tamarah Birch case file up to date when Virgil strolled into the office.

"Hey, bro," Mitch greeted him. "You like this place so much you can't stay away, or what?" Virgil's shift started at four P.M.; it was two o'clock now. He was wearing jeans and cowboy boots, his usual attire when he wasn't in uniform. A full-blood Cherokee, Virgil had once told Mitch that as a kid, when he played cowboys and Indians, he always insisted on being a cowboy. Bad influence from those Saturday afternoon shoot-'em ups at the local movie house, he'd said.

Virgil lounged in a chair and propped his boots on Mitch's desk. "I had to get examined for some eyeglasses."

"What! You can read road signs a mile away."

"Yeah, but I can't read the newspaper. The print won't hold still. So I'm getting those little Ben Franklin reading glasses. Thought they might make me look intelligent."

"Worth a try, I guess," said Mitch. "Your arms are getting too short. Comes with age, I hear. Like arthritis and low back pain."

"What do you mean, you *hear?* You're only two years younger than I am."

"You had to come in here just to tell me that?"

Virgil grinned. "Sure." He grew sober. "I went out to the pow-wow after I left the doctor's office." He frowned and gazed out the window to the bustle on the main street.

"And?"

Virgil looked back at Mitch. "I heard some of the men talking. Old Man Pigeon, Bradley Muskrat, that bunch."

"Nighthawks," Mitch said. Since Virgil was also a member of the Nighthawk Keetowahs, a secret society dedicated to the preservation of the old ways, he added, "The reactionary arm, I mean."

"The fact that they're Nighthawks really has nothing to do with their attitude, Mitch. They sure clammed up when they noticed me, but I heard enough to get the gist of their conversation."

"Which was?"

"Somebody ought to get a group together and go after Tamarah Birch's killer, like in the old days, since it doesn't appear the police are doing anything."

"A lynch mob, you mean. Vigilante justice." Mitch closed the case file and leaned back in his creaking swivel chair. "Just what we need."

"Yeah," Virgil muttered.

"How can they go after the murderer? Do they have some inside information on who it is?"

Virgil shrugged. "I heard from several people at the pow-wow that Crying Wolf says it's somebody at the school."

"He told me that."

"Regardless, I gather Dwayne Burns is still the popular choice of some of that crowd. Before they saw me, I heard Muskrat say they ought to round up every man at the school plus Burns and do whatever they had to do to make the killer confess."

"That'll be about a dozen suspects, give or take. Could get a bit unmanageable."

Virgil rubbed his chin thoughtfully. "It's probably just bravado, but I thought I'd better let you know. I assured them we've talked to Burns and all the school employees and—well. I said we'd narrowed down the list of suspects and, between them and me, we expected to make an arrest within the week." He chuckled humorlessly. "I don't think they were too impressed."

"Hell, I am. Within the week, huh?" Mitch scratched his jaw, remembering his own feeling of being pressed for time. A week might well be all they had. "Hope you're right. In the meantime, all we can do as far as that little band of merry men is concerned is keep our eyes and ears open."

Virgil nodded and Mitch added, "If the situation heats up, we might ask Crying Wolf to talk sense to them."

"Provided his version of sense agrees with ours."

Mitch wasn't at all sure the old man would agree. At the pow-wow when he'd met Wandering Deer, he'd suspected the visiting medicine man's angry spate of Cherokee—which Rhea Vann had declined to translate—had had to do with the Cherokees meting out their own justice.

Mitch linked his hands behind his head and stared at a crack in the ceiling. "Well, if we make an arrest within a week, we should have no problem."

"What do you think the odds are?"

"Not so good right now, but a lot can happen in seven days."

"Hmmm."

Avoiding more conversation on the depressing subject, Mitch asked, "Do you like having a partner for a change?"

"Does a fat girl like hot-fudge sundaes? Roo's a good kid. Green but eager. How's Duck doing with his new side-kick?"

Mitch grinned. "I'm pretty sure he's not gonna win Mr. Congeniality. But Shelly seems to be taking it in stride. She told him he was fat and consequently too slow." Shelly had dropped by the station on her lunch break to bring Mitch up to date. Later, Duck had come in on *his* lunch break to renew his request to be taken off days.

Virgil laughed. "Went right for the jugular, eh?"

"Duck wants to go on the evening shift, but I told him I was leaving Roo with you for at least three months, then we'll see."

"It hasn't been six weeks since he told me Geraldine would raise the roof if he worked the hours I do."

"That was before Shelly entered the picture. I guess Geraldine's displeasure doesn't look so bad by comparison."

"Well." Virgil clasped the arms of his chair. "You heard from Lisa since she left town?"

Mitch shook his head. "It's too soon. She said she'd call me when she gets settled."

Virgil gave him a long look. "Do I sense storm clouds on the horizon?"

Mitch winced. "She's been offered a job teaching at a junior college in California."

"She gonna take it?"

"She wants to."

"Oh." Virgil levered himself to his feet. "Tough, old buddy. Maybe you can change her mind." Mitch said nothing. He didn't want to be the one to change her mind. Even if he could, which he doubted.

"Well," Virgil said, "I better get on home."

"And I have to go see Porter Qualls. He agreed to let me look at the faculty's personnel files. With great reluctance, I might add."

"You know what you're looking for?"

"Haven't a clue. Maybe something will spark a new idea, open up a new line of questioning."

"Good luck. Check with you later," Virgil said as he left.

Mitch sat at his desk for another few minutes, working on the case file. But Virgil's visit had made him restless. The paperwork could wait. He closed the file. On the way out, he told Helen where he could be reached if he was needed.

As Mitch walked from the parking lot to the school administration building, he met Porter Qualls leaving the building. "Darlene will show you those files," Qualls said shortly. "You'll have to return them to her by four-thirty. That's when she leaves, and I won't be back today."

"Fine," said Mitch. That gave him an hour and a half. If there was anything helpful in the files, he should have found it by then.

Darlene removed the files from a locked cabinet in Qualls's office. She relocked the cabinet and left the files with Mitch in the conference room. He settled at one end of the long table and opened the folder on top of the stack. It was labeled SHOEMAKER, LYMAN.

The counselor was fifty-nine years old. He had been at the tribal school for fifteen years, having worked as a guidance counselor in Hobbs, New Mexico, the six years prior to that. Before Hobbs, he'd spent sixteen years in Albuquerque teaching math in a junior high school. His undergraduate degree was from Oklahoma City University, his master's from North Texas State. On his application for employment at the tribal school, he'd checked "Divorced" under "Marital Status." So he'd been divorced for at least fifteen years. The only other thing contained in his file were two letters of recommendation, from the superintendent of schools in Hobbs and the principal of the last school where he'd worked.

Mitch reached for the next folder. Katherine Hildebrand had been at the school for more than thirty years. She had taught in Tahlequah Public Schools for five years before that. She was sixty-three and widowed. Her college transcript from the University of Oklahoma showed straight As. Both letters of recommendation in her file mentioned that she was a conscientious teacher and a good disciplinarian.

The Stands and the Horns had arrived at the same time, seven years ago, the Stands having come from Muskogee and the Horns from Oklahoma City. All four held degrees from Oklahoma State. The Horns were in their forties, the Stands in their thirties. Their references were excellent.

Nancy Adair had received a bachelor's degree from the University of Colorado the previous June. Her transcript showed mostly As with a few Bs, and the letters of recommendation from three of her professors were glowing in their praise.

Compared to the other faculty files, Ellis Harlan's read like a travelogue. His degrees were from a small college in Washington State and the University of Oregon. He had joined the tribal school faculty at the beginning of the previous school term. Before that, he had taught two years in Great Bend, Kansas; five years in St. Louis; three years in Missoula, Montana; two years in Boise, Idaho; and four years in Elko, Nevada. All lateral moves, it appeared; he had coached and taught PE at each of the schools.

Merv Haines had retired from the army twenty-one years previously and had been at the tribal school as janitor-groundskeeper since then. He was sixty-four years old and divorced. Mitch skimmed the remaining files, finding nothing to hang a line of interrogation on.

He scanned the few remaining files quickly. As he closed the last folder, the only bit of data that had stuck in Mitch's mind was Ellis Harlan's penchant for switching jobs and moving from state to state. He glanced at his watch; it was ten after four. He shuffled through the files, found Harlan's, and leafed through it again.

The coach had a decent transcript of grades from a small college in Washington state, which he had attended on a basketball scholarship. The file contained two letters of recommendation from the principal and vice-principal of the St. Louis school where he'd stayed longer than any of the others. They seemed to like him fine in St. Louis. So why had he left?

Mitch closed the file. He moved his shoulders to work out a kink, then propped his chin in his hand and stared out an open window through which drifted the faint scent of freshly turned earth. Somebody must have planted flowers recently. He watched a male and female cardinal pecking at seeds in the grass and fought a feeling of futility.

He pulled his mind back to the personnel files. To Ellis Harlan's file. Okay, so Harlan had moved around a lot. There was no way of knowing, from the file, whether he'd been fired from any or all of those jobs or had left voluntarily. Maybe he was the restless type—after a few years the grass began to look greener in another pasture.

What, Mitch wondered, in all of this was pertinent to the investigation?

Nada. Zip.

There was a tap at the conference room door and Darlene stuck her head in. "Chief Bushyhead, it's quitting time."

"Okay, Darlene. I'm going. Thanks for your help."

From the school, he drove to the Roberts's house to pick up Emily, reviewing again en route the information in Ellis Harlan's file. There was something . . . something he'd read that nagged at him, but he couldn't quite bring it into focus.

Harlan was a job-hopper, but what did it mean? Maybe he became dissatisfied every few years and wanted a change of scene. Maybe he bored easily. Maybe he grew lazy and undependable on each job, after the new wore off, and he was fired. Or maybe he was let go for losing his temper and sounding off to the wrong person. Like Qualls, Harlan had a short fuse, and his family situation was anything but soothing. The daughter alone was enough to make a man lose his cool.

But he had good references from St. Louis. Wait a minute . . . maybe that's what was nagging him. Why had Harlan submitted two references from St. Louis and none from Great Bend, the last place he'd taught before coming to Buckskin?

Mitch parked in front of the Roberts's house, but remained in his car for a few minutes longer, thinking. When *he* interviewed a prospective employee, he wanted at least one reference from his most recent employer. If he himself were filling out an employment application, he'd omit such a reference only if he knew the report would not be favorable. That was undoubtedly why Harlan had provided no reference from Great Bend. Which meant he'd probably been fired there. But what had that to do with Mitch's investigation?

Maybe if he knew why Harlan was fired.

He left the car, walked up the Roberts's front steps, and rang the doorbell. After dinner, he'd get on the phone to Great Bend. Somebody in the police department should be able to give him the superintendent's name and number.

TWENTY-THREE

"You must have heard from Lisa," Virgil said.

After Emily had left with Kevin for a movie, Mitch had picked up Virgil at the station and headed out to the tribal school for the third time that day.

"Why do you say that?"

"It's obvious you're busting to tell me something."

"I haven't heard from Lisa."

"Oh. You wanta talk about it?"

"What's to say? It's her move." He sounded bitter and hastened to divert Virgil's attention. "But I do have something to tell you. I talked to the superintendent of schools in Great Bend, Kansas, this evening."

Virgil looked nonplussed. "Anybody I know?"

"Jacob Counts."

"Never heard of him."

"The coach at the tribal school, Ellis Harlan, taught in Great Bend for almost two years before he came to Buckskin. I looked at those faculty files this afternoon. Harlan has never worked anywhere longer than five years. Everybody else at the school taught one, at the most, two, other places before coming here. So Harlan's employment record stood out. But what really piqued my interest was that the letters of recommendation he submitted with his employment application were from St. Louis, not Great Bend, the last place he worked. I wondered why."

"They fired him?"

"Technically he quit. When I asked Counts if Harlan had been asked to resign, he said he'd prefer not to answer that question. Everybody's worried about getting sued these days. Employers weigh every word to make sure they aren't invading an employee's privacy."

"No answer is almost as good as a yes."

"Right, and Counts did give me the names of a couple of teachers who taught with Harlan in Great Bend. I got the feeling he really wanted me to know the straight scoop and hoped one of them would oblige. I got lucky with the first teacher I called, Marcia Moorman. She taught girls' PE—still does—and Harlan taught the boys as well as one social studies class."

"How long do you intend to drag this out? What'd she tell you?"

"Quite a bit, after she was assured of anonymity. It seems a ninth-grade girl accused Harlan of molesting her. He was scheduled to defend himself before the school board. That was in March, but a few days before the hearing, the Harlans skipped town 'under cover of darkness,' according to Marcia Moorman and left no forwarding address. They moved to Buckskin in August, so they were somewhere else in the interim, maybe with relatives."

Virgil whistled softly. "He could have done it before. Could be why he left so many jobs."

"I doubt we can get hold of any school officials in those towns before Monday. I'll have Shelly or Duck try to run it down then."

"No wonder Harlan's wife was so uptight when you talked to them. She must be afraid some of those old skeletons are going to fall out of the closet."

"Yeah."

"Only problem is, Tamarah Birch wasn't molested."

"She wasn't raped," Mitch said. "Doesn't mean she wasn't molested."

"But pedophiles get off on all that stuff. There was no semen on the body."

Mitch sighed. "Nor in any of the samples the lab examined from the crime scene."

"I guess he could have worn a condom."

"Or he's impotent."

"Or she wasn't molested at all. She was killed for some other reason."

Mitch pulled the patrol car into the campus parking lot. "Harlan's still our prime candidate."

"He's looking better all the time, too."

There were lighted windows in the principal's house and all the faculty duplexes. It was dinner time and the night air was rich with cooking aromas. Frying meat, fresh-baked bread, and the scent of chili.

As Virgil and Mitch approached the Harlans' quarters, they heard raised voices from inside. Mitch placed a cautionary hand on Virgil's shoulder and they stopped on the narrow walk at the bottom of the front steps.

"That's a damned, disgusting lie!" It sounded like Cody Harlan. "It's sick—you're sick!"

"If I were you, *brother dear*, I'd be worried about my own mental health."

"Oh, right." Cody laughed shakily. "I'm not the one running around with purple hair and safety pins in my ears."

"God, you are uptight."

"You're repulsive, you know that? I don't know why Dad hasn't tanned your hide and given you a good scrubbing."

"Good question, Cody. Why hasn't he?"

"Because Mom always takes your side!"

"That's because she's scared shitless I'll spill the beans. Well, I've done it, and they can't do a damn thing about it."

"Get real, Kendall. Nobody is going to believe your lies."

"You sure about that?"

"Here's what I'm sure of," Cody shouted. "If I ever hear you say that again—to anyone—I'll beat you senseless."

"We better make ourselves known before this gets physical," Mitch muttered. He went up the steps and pounded on the door.

Sudden silence reigned on the other side. Moments passed and Mitch knocked again. Finally, the door opened and Cody Harlan stood there, his face pale and pinched. Whatever Kendall had said to him before Mitch and Virgil were within hearing range had shocked the blood out of his face. Mitch wished their timing had been better and they'd arrived a few minutes earlier.

"Are your parents in, Cody?"

"Uh—no sir. They—" Cody glanced over his shoulder where Kendall stood, scowling. "Where did they—oh, yeah, I remember. They went for a drive. Said they might go to Tahlequah."

"When will they be back?"

"They—uh—didn't say."

"Maybe they ran away from home," Kendall snarled.

"Shut up!" Cody snapped.

"A girl can dream, can't she?" Kendall muttered and pushed past Cody, out the door.

"Dad grounded you, Kendall! Get back in here!"

She whirled around and spat at her brother, "Get off my case, Cody, or you'll be very sorry."

Returning color flushed Cody's face, but he didn't respond. He was afraid to. Kendall's words clearly had been no idle threat. She brushed past Mitch and Virgil and ran down the walk into the darkness.

"Your sister's got a mouth on her," Mitch said.

Cody stiffened. "You heard us?"

"Enough to know the two of you were having a disagreement."

"That's all we ever do, disagree. I can't believe she used to say I was her best friend. God, I hate her." Mitch didn't doubt him for an instant, even though the venomous words sounded out of character, coming from the quintessential All-American boy.

"I'd like to talk to your parents as soon as they return. Would you ask them to call me at home if they get back before eleven?"

Cody swallowed, nodded. "Okay. Sure."

He started to close the door. Mitch forestalled him with another question. "I understand you lived in Great Bend, Kansas, before moving to Buckskin."

"Yes."

"Did you play football there, too?"

"Yeah. I was elected captain and everything. Then Dad came home and announced we were leaving. Right in the

middle of the second semester of my junior year. We stayed
with my dad's uncle in California for a few months, and
Kendall and I finished out the school year there. I didn't like
it."

"Tough."

"Yeah, I had friends in Great Bend I could have lived
with and finished high school there. I begged my folks to let
me stay, but they wouldn't."

"You must have resented them for that."

He shrugged. "I got over it. Is there something else, Chief
Bushyhead?"

"Not right now."

The boy stepped back and closed the door.

"What do you suppose the fight was all about?" Virgil
mused as they crossed the campus.

"Sounded like she told him something he didn't want to
hear."

"Accused him of something?"

"Whatever it was," Mitch observed, "it was bad enough
to knock the props out from under that kid."

At the girl's dorm, Mitch was told by Aggie Horn that
Ruthann Blackfox had skipped dinner and gone to bed with
an upset stomach. She didn't want to wake her, and Mitch
agreed to wait until the next morning to question the girl.
But the upset stomach was suspicious. According to Rhea
Vann, Tamarah had used that excuse when she was troubled—or wanted to avoid a confrontation. Ruthann could
have learned the trick from her best friend.

ELLIS HARLAN brought two bowls of ice cream—chocolate
for Serina, peppermint for himself—to the booth and slid
in across from her. She had said little on the drive to Tahlequah and he had not tried to force a conversation. He
could no longer dredge up the energy to pretend things were
fine between them—or no worse than usual.

He felt empty and could not even fill that emptiness with
the otherworldly, as Serina could. She had prayed for an

hour this afternoon, she'd told him, before the argument with Kendall. He sensed that she had been wrestling with some decision, though he felt no urgency to know more than that. She would tell him in due time. She always did.

He watched her spoon a bit of chocolate ice cream and eat it slowly. She was gazing out the window, but not at what lay on the other side, he knew. She was looking into her own soul. The image of her perfect profile, her alabaster skin, the sweep of flaxen hair against her cheek, filled him with longing. And sweet memories. The sight of her could still do that, after everything.

A strong current of desire flowed through him, the yearning to blot out thought with the taste of her mouth beneath his, the weight of her breasts in his hands, the clean scent of her hair.

Then she put the spoon down and, turning to him, said, "We can't stay in Buckskin, Ellis."

As quickly as it had filled him, desire was swept away by despair. "Why not, Serina? *Why?*"

Without warning, her eyes filled. She squeezed them shut and her fingers gripped her spoon. Her hand was shaking. "The questions, Ellis. They ask so many questions, and they will ask more."

"No," he said, surprising himself with the force of it. "I can't run again."

She stared. Her eyes were deep depressions with blue smudges of fatigue beneath. "Not even for Kendall?"

In the past few days, she had withdrawn from him. It had happened before, many times during their life together. He was losing her, had been losing her slowly for years, he supposed. He could not run fast enough to hold her. Perhaps he was merely too weary to try. If there were another man, something physical that he could fight . . . but she had withdrawn into herself. He had spent twenty years jousting with shadows, and he simply could not do it any longer.

"Not even for you, Serina."

She looked at her ice cream, unwilling to meet his eyes. "You're sorry we adopted her, aren't you?"

"I would be lying if I denied that lately—sometimes... yes, I've thought of how it might have been if we'd been content with one child."

"If I'd been content, you mean," she murmured.

He didn't bother to contradict her. He had always known that her motives for wanting to adopt a second child were complicated, not totally clear, even to her. Partly there had been her need to do penance, to bestow love and care upon a baby unwanted by its biological parents.

"Cody," she said, more to herself than to Harlan. "Our miracle. I suppose I should have realized that wanting more was begging for trouble."

"Because we deserve it. I know that's how you feel."

"No, Ellis. Not when you put it so bluntly."

"Oh, not consciously."

"No," she said again.

"Then why didn't you destroy my letters?"

She hugged herself. "Because I needed them, in the bad times. I needed them for reassurance."

And to be the bomb, ticking away beneath the surface of their lives, that would finally, if fate decreed, explode. But if he suggested she'd had such a self-punishing motive, she would deny it. He said nothing.

"Your ice cream is melting," she said.

"So is yours."

"Suddenly, I don't want it."

"I know. Shall we go?"

She walked ahead of him out of the ice cream parlor and got into the car. Little was said by either of them on the drive home. They had reached the point where words would accomplish nothing. They had said all the words before, many times.

Harlan did not fool himself that their silence resulted from unspoken communion, or that his queer absence of feeling meant he'd finally achieved inner peace. He was merely numb.

AFTER LEAVING THE CAMPUS, Mitch dropped Virgil off at
the police station and drove home, where he made a pot of
coffee and sat down at the kitchen table with a yellow legal
pad and a pen.

He listed the potential suspects in the murder
investigation:

> Ellis Harlan
> Porter Qualls
> Lyman Shoemaker
> Charley Horn
> Stafford Stand
> Merv Haines
> Dwayne Burns

He sipped hot coffee and stared at the names for a while. He
remembered the hatred in Cody's words when he spoke of
his sister. Mitch added another name to the list.

> Cody Harlan

He refilled his coffee cup and wrote headings for two additional columns: "Alibi for Time of Murder" and "Cor-
roboration." After a half hour of thinking and scribbling,
he put down his pen and reread what he'd written.

Suspect	Alibi for Time of Murder	Corroboration
Ellis Harlan	At home. Took allergy medication and lay down. (Tamarah at his table at breakfast.)	Wife & son say he came home & rested alone in bedroom.

Porter Qualls	Breakfasted at home. In office from 8:10 till 9:45 when Tamarah reported missing, except for brief trip to men's room. (Exit from principal's office through conference room can't be seen by secretary.)	Wife asleep, found breakfast remains later. Secretary corroborates time of arrival at office & trip to men's room.
Lyman Shoemaker	At home till he left to board buses at 9:45. Seen by Jerry Bookland en route from cafeteria to quarters (8:00-8:15?)	None.
Charley Horn	At home (apartment in girls' dorm). Met group of students at 9:15 to walk to town. Discovered victim's body and Polly Kirkwood unconscious en route.	Wife corroborates.
Stafford Stand	At home (apartment in boys' dorm).	Wife corroborates.

Merv Haines	At home (room in basement of adm. building).	None.
Dwayne Burns	In coffee shop about an hour (7:30-8:30 A.M.) Walked from town west on Highway 10 to industrial park, and back in time for parade at 10.	Coffee shop owner corroborates. Clerk saw him "loitering" outside jewelry store before parade (time?).
Cody Harlan	Breakfasted at home, then went to town job-hunting.	Mother corroborates, but wasn't with him in town.

Mitch pondered the list for some time and, as an after-thought, added another name:

Jerry Bookland	Left campus at end of shift (Between 8:00-8:30 A.M.) Drove directly home.	None.

What scant corroborating evidence there was on the list wouldn't stand up well under cross-examination. In such circumstances, a spouse's story was generally discounted. But on current evidence, Mitch was inclined to accept the wives' word that Horn and Stand were with them during the time in question.

He didn't think Qualls's secretary was lying, either, but no one could swear Qualls hadn't exited the building through the conference room.

Conceivably, Ellis Harlan could have left his bedroom, where he was supposedly resting, for a brief period without his wife and son knowing.

Jerry Bookland was not really a suspect in Mitch's mind. He'd added his name to be thorough. He knew Jerry and couldn't believe him capable of murder, but he'd misjudged people before. And there was that rough emotional period Bookland had gone through a couple of years back after losing his wife and his mother. Good Lord, he was reaching. Going through an emotional upheaval didn't turn a normal man into a child killer.

As for motives, all he had were weak suspicions based on Burns's past history of exhibitionism, a feeling that the Harlans were hiding something, Qualls's hot temper, and the supposition that Tamarah had confided a secret to Ruthann Blackfox, a secret that was potentially damaging to someone. But what was the secret and who might have felt threatened by it? Mitch hadn't an inkling.

TWENTY-FOUR

MITCH WAS STILL going over his notes and drinking the last of the coffee in the pot when Emily and Kevin returned at ten thirty-five.

"Daddy?" Emily called.

"In the kitchen."

Emily came into the room followed by Kevin Hartsbarger, a blond-haired high school junior whose father owned the local Ford-Mercury agency. A good kid. If Emily had to go steady with anybody, Mitch conceded that it might as well be Kevin.

Evidently there was a local fad for steadies to dress alike. Last week Emily had bought a shirt to match one Kevin had. Tonight both wore jeans and gold T-shirts with Buckskin Bears emblazoned in red across the front.

Yet it had taken Emily a good hour to get ready to go out. Another female mystery that Mitch would never understand.

"Hi, Chief Bushyhead."

"Hello, Kevin. How was the movie?"

"Great."

Emily rolled her eyes. "I wouldn't go that far. Arnold Schwarzenegger."

"Lots of blood and guts, huh?"

"Two or three dozen people killed," Kevin said. "Your regular night's work for Arnold."

Emily got out a saucepan, milk, and a can of Nestle's Quick. "Want some hot chocolate, Daddy?"

"Not on top of the coffee I've drunk."

She started heating the milk and rummaged around in the pantry. "I thought we had marshmallows...but I guess not."

"Put 'em on the list."

Emily made a note on the running grocery list they kept next to the telephone. As she was writing, the phone rang and made her jump and drop the pencil.

Kevin laughed. "She thought old Arnold had tracked her down for sure."

Emily snatched the receiver off the hook. "Bushyhead residence. Yes, he's here. Daddy, it's for you."

The caller was Charley Horn. He identified himself and said, "Ruthann Blackfox is missing."

Mitch automatically looked at his watch. It was ten forty-five. "Was she there for bed check?"

"Yes."

"Then she couldn't have gone far. Have you searched the dorm?"

"Yes. She's not there, but we found a bathroom window on the ground floor open. Mr. Qualls asked me to call you. He said, with what's already happened at the school, we could worry about jurisdictional problems later. We need help. Qualls wants to know how soon you can get here."

Mitch glanced at Emily and Kevin seated at the table. They were watching him intently. "Twenty or thirty minutes," Mitch said and hung up.

"Who was that, Daddy?"

"Charley Horn. He teaches at the tribal school."

"Don't tell me they've found another dead kid!"

"No, but one of the students left her room and they can't locate her." He wanted to reassure Emily. "With what's already happened, everybody's panicking, I guess. Honey, I have to go out there." He glanced at Kevin. "Why don't you call Mrs. Morgan and ask her to come over."

"I'd rather go to Temple's."

"Call her then. I'm going upstairs for a few minutes."

"Good night, Chief," Kevin said.

In his bedroom, Mitch changed to his uniform, giving Emily time to make her call. Then he phoned the station and told Virgil to bring Roo and meet him at the school. "Have incoming calls transferred to Duck's number until you get back," Mitch said. "I don't know how long this will take, but the faster we move now, the better chance we have of finding her." He heard Emily come upstairs and go to her bedroom.

Mitch hung up and found Emily putting some things in an overnight case. "Looks like you're going to the Roberts's house," Mitch said.

"Uh-huh." She didn't look at him.

"Everything okay?"

She sighed. "I wish you wouldn't be so obvious, Daddy."

"I don't know what you mean."

She snapped the case lid shut. "You were dawdling up here until Kevin left. Admit it."

"I wasn't thinking about Kevin. I was on the phone with Virgil."

"You didn't have to tell me to call Mrs. Morgan with Kevin sitting right there. You might as well have said, 'Time to go now, sonny boy.' Kevin got the message."

"Look, I'm sorry if I insulted Kevin. That wasn't my intention."

"Kevin could have driven me to Temple's house. But you weren't about to leave me and Kevin here alone, were you?"

"Well . . . I would have felt sort of uncomfortable doing it."

"Don't you trust me, Daddy?"

"Yes, I trust you." What he didn't trust were adolescent male hormones. But maybe he had been a bit obvious. Besides, kids were probably less likely to make out in the girl's house than in a car or an isolated spot in the country. Particularly if the girl's father could pop in on them at any moment. Kevin and Emily had come straight home from the movie, so maybe he just had a dirty mind.

Mitch hugged her and picked up the overnight case. "Okay, I came off as the big, bad, overprotective father. I'm sorry, honey." He kissed the top of her head. "Come on. I'll drive you to Temple's."

"Just think, Daddy, in two months when I get my license, you wouldn't have to chauffeur me around anymore if I had my own car."

"Yeah, well maybe I like chauffeuring you around."

Emily sighed.

AT THE TRIBAL SCHOOL, additional spotlights had been
turned on to augment the night lights. Teachers and some
older students were milling around in front of the girls'
dorm. Mike Farnwell, the security guard on duty, seemed to
be trying to get them organized. Cody Harlan came up to
Mitch immediately.

"My dad was going to call you, Chief Bushyhead, but we
got word that Ruthann was missing and came to help look
for her."

Porter Qualls, wearing a rumpled sport shirt hanging half
out of the waistband of his slacks on one side, joined Mitch
at the same moment that Mitch saw Virgil and Roo approaching across the lighted campus.

Qualls's hair was mussed, a tuft sticking up in back, as
though he'd been called from his bed. "Mike Farnwell was
just assigning groups to search the buildings, Chief Bushyhead."

"Good. My officers will take over now," Mitch said.
"Virgil, you and Roo get these people organized and go
through every building on this campus—living quarters and
all."

"Now, just a minute—" Qualls sputtered.

"You have a problem with our searching the quarters?"
Mitch snapped.

"It's unnecessary."

"You asked for my help," Mitch reminded him. "I'd
rather be thorough than sorry later."

Qualls finally muttered grudging compliance and Mitch
turned back to his officers. "Check every building thoroughly. Don't skip any place where a little girl could be
concealed. Qualls, where are the keys?"

Mitch's urgency seemed to be communicated to the principal. "I have a set at my place. I'll get them." Qualls hurried toward his house. He returned shortly with the keys and
his wife, dressed to join the search in slacks and a man's
cardigan sweater.

"Mitch," Mike Farnwell said, "if you can spare me, I
need to get back to my post."

"Go ahead, Mike," Mitch said. "Detain anyone coming in or going out until I can talk to them."

"No problem. I've already closed the gates." As Mike hurried away, Mitch noticed Serina Harlan moving hesitantly down her front walk. She paused briefly, seemed to brace herself, and hurried purposefully toward her husband.

As soon as she reached the coach, she asked, "Did you tell them about Kendall?"

"What about Kendall, ma'am?" Mitch asked.

"It's nothing," Ellis Harlan said quickly. "She and Cody had a fuss and she went off somewhere to pout, that's all."

"She's been gone almost three hours," Serina Harlan said, her voice catching. "She should have come home by now."

"That girl comes home when she's good and ready," Harlan growled. "You should be used to it by this time."

"But Ruthann has disappeared. What if Kendall is . . . in trouble? I'm worried."

"Under the circumstances, I don't blame you, Mrs. Harlan," Mitch said. "I want to ask you and your husband a few questions. Virgil, get the rest of them started."

Virgil shouted instructions and four groups headed in four different directions.

"Why don't we go inside to talk," Mitch suggested. The night air was nippy and Serina Harlan, in a thin cotton dress, was hugging herself.

Harlan took his wife's arm and they walked to the Harlans' duplex. The Harlans sat on the couch, and Harlan put his arm protectively around his wife. Mitch sank into a chair facing them. The duplex had the same squeaky clean lemony smell as before.

Although the room was warm, Serina Harlan continued to tremble and hug herself.

"I was here earlier this evening," Mitch said. "I guess Cody told you."

"He said you wanted me to call you," Harlan said, "but before I could, Charley Horn came by and said Ruthann was missing and everybody was gathering in front of the girls' dorm to search the campus."

"Kendall got mad at Cody and stormed out of the house," Serina said, bringing the conversation back to the important point.

"They were arguing when I was here earlier this evening," Mitch said. "Kendall was furious about something. Did Cody tell you what they argued about?"

"Kendall took Cody's car without permission this morning and drove to town," Harlan said. "When she came home about noon, I told her she was grounded for a week. She ignored me, as usual, and left the house this evening. Evidently Cody mentioned the car again and that's what set her off. We didn't think anything about it. Kendall is always spoiling for a fight. If Cody hadn't mentioned her taking his car, she'd have found some other reason to pick a quarrel. In fact, she and her mother had words before Serina and I left earlier this evening. That's why we went for a drive. I wanted to get my wife away from here for a while so she could relax."

"Where did you go?" Mitch asked.

"Tahlequah. We stopped for ice cream and drove back home."

"Where is your car now?"

"There's a paved area next to the alley behind the duplex. Cody's car is there, too," Harlan said.

"Does Kendall have keys to either car?"

"Not anymore. I confiscated her keys after she took Cody's car this morning without permission."

Serina Harlan had bowed her head and was plucking at the fabric of her dress. "Mrs. Harlan," Mitch said, "what did you and Kendall argue about before you left for Tahlequah?"

She looked up sharply. "It was . . . she . . ."

"Some trivial remark Serina made," Harlan put in. "Serina said Kendall took it as a put-down and blew up at her." He drew his brows together and hugged his wife closer. "Serina was in tears when we left the house."

"What did you say to her, Mrs. Harlan?"

She dropped her gaze to her lap again. "It—it wasn't exactly the way I told you, Harlan."

Harlan jerked his head around to stare at her. She looked up and said, "Today when I was cleaning Kendall's room, I found some money stuffed down in the toe of a shoe at the back of her closet. She accused me of snooping." She shrugged helplessly. "Well, I suppose I was."

"We give her the allowance," Harlan said. "She doesn't have to hide it. What's wrong with that girl? Surely she doesn't think Cody would steal her few measly dollars."

"It was more than a few dollars, Ellis," Serina said. "I didn't tell you because I knew you'd jump all over her and make the situation worse. You can't force Kendall to tell you anything she doesn't want to tell. I was going to talk to her again about where she got it when she calmed down."

Harlan drew away from her impatiently. "For God's sake, Serina, how much money did she have?"

"Six hundred and seventy-five."

"Six hundred and seventy-five *dollars?*"

She nodded. Harlan jumped to his feet. "I'll confiscate it, damn it. She'll tell us where it came from or she'll not see a dollar of it again!"

"It's gone, Ellis."

He halted in his tracks and glared in helpless frustration.

"I checked as soon as we got back and Cody told us she'd left," Serina murmured. "I searched her room. The money's not there. She—she's run away. Probably hitchhiking, a seventeen-year-old girl, carrying more than six hundred dollars in her pocket." Tears thickened her voice. "She'll be mugged—raped... She could be lying somewhere beside the road this very minute, hurt or—or worse." She sobbed and couldn't go on.

Harlan clapped a palm to his forehead. "Judas Priest! What next?"

"Have either of you missed any money from your wallet or purse?" Mitch asked.

Serina shook her head mutely, and Harlan barked, "School teachers don't have that kind of cash to carry around."

"Have you heard of any money missing from the school, Mr. Harlan?"

"No. I doubt if even Qualls keeps that much cash in the safe in his office. Bills are paid by check."

"What about the cafeteria money?"

Harlan shook his head. "Boarding students' meals are paid for along with tuition and dorm fees at the beginning of each semester. Day students buy their lunches by the day or week, but that money is counted and turned in to Qualls every day. It's deposited in the bank twice a week." Harlan sank back down on the couch beside his wife. "It wouldn't surprise me if Kendall has been picking pockets. Maybe that's why she took Cody's car this morning. With so many people in town—"

Serina choked out, "Stop it, Ellis! Stop saying those things about Kendall!"

"It's the God's truth. Nothing Kendall does would surprise me any more," Harlan muttered.

Serina had dragged a tissue out of her pocket and was wiping her eyes. "She's not a thief, Ellis. She's just very confused."

"Oh, hell," Harlan exploded. "She'd do it just to spite us. When are you going to run out of excuses for that girl?"

"Why is Kendall so angry at the two of you?" Mitch asked. Serina's look was stricken, Harlan's resentful. Serina clutched Harlan's hand.

"Is it because she's adopted?" Mitch asked.

"Somebody told you, then," Harlan said. "Well, it's no secret." Serina's fingernails dug into the back of his hand. He shook her off, then took the hand in both of his. "Cody's birth was very difficult. The doctors advised us that Serina shouldn't become pregnant again. But she—we wanted another child, so we adopted Kendall."

Mitch didn't miss the slip. Evidently it had been Serina who'd insisted on adopting.

"She was only three weeks old when we got her, and she's always known she was adopted."

"We talked to her about it first when she was two," Serina said shakily, "in terms we thought she could understand. We said that Cody grew in Mommy's tummy, and after that we wanted a little girl to go with our little boy. We said we had chosen her from hundreds of other babies. It wasn't quite like that, of course, but we wanted her to feel that she was special and loved."

"Yet you think being adopted is what's behind Kendall's anger and resentment?" Mitch asked.

Serina's head bobbed quickly in assent.

"It has to be," Harlan said. "When she started having trouble in school she said it was our fault, she accused us of being sorry we'd adopted her. She said we'd never loved her as much as Cody."

"We told her over and over that we *do* love her. We tried to help Kendall—even Cody tried—but nobody can get through to her." Serina leaned toward Mitch and added urgently, "Please find her for us, Chief Bushyhead."

"We'll do our best," Mitch said, adding in what he hoped was a confident tone, "chances are she'll come back on her own when she cools off."

"Do you really think so?"

"In ninety-five percent of the cases, runaways are back home within seventy-two hours, ma'am."

"Why don't you go and lie down, sweetheart," Harlan said solicitously.

She shook her head. "I can't."

Mitch considered the woman. Serina Harlan's brittle fragility seemed, if possible, even closer to the shattering point than the last time he'd seen her. "Your husband's right, ma'am. You should try to get some rest."

"How can you expect me to rest when my daughter is God knows where at the mercy of—of criminals and perverts?"

"Serina, we don't know that she's at anybody's mercy," Harlan said.

She bit her bottom lip. "It's just—I keep imagining the worst."

"That's natural." Mitch watched the woman try to get a grip on her rioting thoughts. "Forgive my timing, ma'am, but I have to ask your husband a few more questions."

Harlan frowned, but Serina's expression did not change.
"I've been checking backgrounds, Mr. Harlan. On everybody employed at the school, not just you. But something
has come up. I've been informed that you left your last place
of employment under suspicious circumstances."

"Who told you that?" Harlan demanded, and Serina
darted a terrified look at him.

"A reliable source," Mitch said. "That's all you need to
know. I understand you were accused of molesting a four-
teen-year-old girl."

"That conniving little—"

"*Ellis* . . ." She said his name like a plea.

"I didn't touch that child—or any other," Harlan ground
out. "If you're trying to tie that in with Tamarah Birch—"

Mitch cut him off. "The girl accused you of molesting
her."

"She told me she would, but I didn't believe her."

"Are you saying she warned you?"

"You don't understand, Chief Bushyhead," Serina said.
"In addition to Ellis's physical education classes in Great
Bend, he had to teach one section of ninth-grade social
studies. That girl was in the class, and she was failing."

"She was perfectly capable, but she wouldn't do her
work," Harlan muttered.

"Ellis told her several times that if she didn't shape up,
he'd give her an F." She glanced urgently at her husband.
"Tell him what happened, Ellis."

"A week before third-quarter grades were to be turned
in," Harlan said, "she came to my office after school. All
of a sudden, she was worried about what her parents were
going to say if she brought home an F. She pleaded with me
to give her a passing grade. I told her I couldn't. I'd given
her every opportunity to make up the work, and she'd made
no effort. I said she deserved an F and that's what would
appear on her report card."

"That's when she threatened Ellis," Serina said.

"The little bitch said if I didn't pass her, she'd tell her
parents that I'd put my hand inside her clothes and tried to
kiss her." Agitated, he raked his fingers through his hair. "I

didn't believe her. She was barely fourteen. But she'd been around, obviously. She said she'd see me in court and stalked out. Next thing I knew, her father was on the phone threatening to kill me, the school board had scheduled a hearing, and the whole town was up in arms.''

Mitch studied him. ''If you were innocent, why didn't you go to that hearing and defend yourself? Your reputation was on the line, and leaving as you did makes it seem you *had* no defense. I don't know how you managed to get yourself hired at this school.''

''I got references from another school where I'd taught before,'' Harlan said. ''I hoped they wouldn't notice the omission. I doubted it would work, but it was the only chance I had.''

''Nobody asked you about Great Bend?''

''One of the board members brought it up when I was interviewed. I—I lied. I said I'd sent a letter to the superintendent there for a reference and, when it didn't come, I learned he'd been ill. They let it go and I got the job.''

''If I'd been in your shoes,'' Mitch persisted, ''nothing could have kept me away from that hearing.''

''If I'd shown my face at that meeting, I'd have been lucky to get out with my life. You know how that kind of thing gets blown out of all proportion. The girl was from an influential family. As innocent as a newborn babe, according to her parents. And who was I? A new teacher in town who'd traumatized a sweet, trusting child—that's also according to her parents. Nobody was going to listen to anything I had to say.''

Mitch was watching Serina Harlan, and her face crumpled under his scrutiny. She managed to say, ''That's exactly what happened.'' She was careful not to look at her husband as she spoke. ''We had nothing to hide, but we knew most people in Great Bend were convinced we did.''

We had nothing to hide. Strange way of putting it. ''Do you have a recent photograph of Kendall, Mrs. Harlan?''

She looked at her husband then. She appeared reluctant to leave him. Harlan could not seem to bring himself to meet her gaze. "Yes," she said. "I'll get it." She rose from the couch and went down the hall to a bedroom.

"You've had a lot of jobs during your teaching career, Harlan," Mitch said quietly.

"Is that a crime?"

"No crime. But I can't help wondering why you've hopped from state to state so frequently. All that moving must have been hard on your family."

"My wife and I always discussed it and made joint decisions. The kids adjusted quickly."

"From what Cody told me, he didn't adjust to leaving Great Bend so quickly. He and Kendall had to finish out the school term in California, didn't they?"

Harlan sighed wearily. "Cody was at an age when it's difficult to leave friends behind. But he soon made new friends, he always does." He clasped his hands and stared at them. "Everybody likes Cody." Mitch was surprised to hear his voice thicken. Until that moment, Harlan had appeared tough, belligerently defensive. It was unsettling to see such a man close to tears, as if some inner barrier had crumbled, leaving feelings exposed that had long been held in check.

Serina Harlan came back into the room. "Here's a snapshot from when we lived in Great Bend. It's the most recent one I could find. It was taken shortly before that girl accused Ellis. Kendall was going to a party. It's one of the last times I can remember her being happy."

Mitch studied the smiling girl in the picture. Kendall had been captured sitting on a porch railing. She wore a pink dress. At the instant the picture was snapped, the wind had caught her hair, lifting it around her face. It was the image of a normal, pretty, teenaged girl.

Mitch tucked the snapshot in his pocket. "Thank you, ma'am. I wonder if I could take a look at Kendall's room now."

Serina's shoulders sagged. "Go ahead. But you won't find anything to tell you where she's gone. I've looked and looked."

Kendall's mother was right. The girl had left no clues to her whereabouts. The diary in the drawer of the bedside table contained no entries for the past five months. The last entry was dated December 13.

> English test today. Ugh! I think I passed—barely. Talked to Mom again about looking for my biological mother. She said to wait until I'm 18. Later, I heard her crying in her room. It made me feel awful. I won't mention it to her again. I'll do it without Mom's help.

"Thank you, ma'am," Mitch said. "Let me know immediately if you hear from Kendall."

"Of course."

As Mitch left, Harlan was still seated on the couch, staring at his hands. The searchers were regrouping in front of the girl's dorm. Roo caught sight of Mitch and loped to meet him. "No luck, Chief."

"We'll take the faculty quarters next," Mitch said, "then spread out to comb the woods and other areas bordering the campus." Members of the last search party were straggling out of the administration building, disheartened.

Mitch made his way to the center of the small crowd. "I need some men to search the duplexes and principal's house. Virgil and Roo...Horn...Shoemaker..." He quickly chose six men and dispatched them. "If any of the rest of you have a flashlight or know of any you can borrow, go get them now. And step on it. We're no longer looking for one girl. We're looking for two."

TWENTY-FIVE

THE SEARCH continued all night, parties moving in ever-widening circles beyond the tribal school campus, through woods and fields, along alleys, and across yards in residential neighborhoods.

A misty rain fell during the predawn hours. The searchers returned to the school, weary, wet, and defeated, their clothing streaked and torn, their shoes caked with mud. Mitch had joined the party that searched the woods, the first group to make it back to campus. Exhausted, he waited for the others on the Qualls's front porch, leaning back against the house, his legs stretched out in front of him.

The searchers straggled in by twos and threes, reported to Mitch, and stumbled home. Mrs. Qualls went directly into the house and must have fallen immediately into bed, for no light came on. Virgil and Roo joined Mitch on the porch. Roo sat with his chin resting on drawn-up knees. Virgil groaned as he stretched out on his back on the hard wood floor. Porter Qualls, Charley Horn, and Lyman Shoemaker dropped down on the Qualls's front steps.

They heard Stafford Stand calling the boys who'd taken part in the search, counting noses, then herding them, bedraggled and subdued, to their dormitory.

"Those girls," mumbled Roo, "must have dug a hole and pulled it in after them."

"Or somebody did it for them," Virgil said.

"Every time I turned a corner," Horn said, "I kept expecting to find Ruthann lying there with a broken neck, like Tamarah."

"Do you think Ruthann and Kendall are together, Chief Bushyhead?" asked Shoemaker.

"I don't know," Mitch responded. "You couldn't call them friends. The age difference, the fact that they attended different schools...I'd have guessed they barely knew each other. Were they ever together on campus?"

"Not to my knowledge," said Qualls.

"No," agreed Shoemaker.

"I should go in and call Ruthann's parents," Qualls said. "Can't see how I can put it off any longer."

"Where do they live?" Mitch asked.

"Houston. They'll be here tomorrow—today now. I hope to God we've found Ruthann by then." He rose and crossed the porch. He stopped in front of his door. "We're going to lose students over this. This school is in for some tough times."

Shoemaker yawned and got slowly to his feet. "I'm afraid you're right. I've got to go home or I'll fall asleep right here."

"Me, too," said Horn. The two men left, dragging tired feet.

Mitch stood and nudged Virgil's arm with the toe of his shoe. "Virgil, we're going. Wake up."

"I'm awake."

"Mr. Qualls, I'll be back early tomorrow morning to see Mari and Jamie."

"The Horns questioned them. They know nothing about Ruthann's disappearance."

"Charley told me that, but I want to talk to them anyway. In the meantime, I'll get out an APB on both girls."

For once, Qualls made no objection.

IT WAS JUST seven-forty-five the next morning when Mitch, accompanied by Officer Shelly Pitcher, crossed the grassy oval and approached the girls' dormitory. A clear sky portended warm and sunny weather for this next to the last day of the Cherokee Heritage Celebration. Only a few puddles remained in low places from last night's rain.

Mitch and Shelly's appearance on campus was being duly noted. Students crossing the campus gawked at them.

"They've been to the cafeteria for breakfast," Mitch said. "I don't see either of Ruthann's roommates, though."

Shelly's gaze swept the ring of campus buildings and came to rest on the date "1902" inscribed in concrete above the dormitory entrance.

"This was built five years before statehood," she remarked. "The stone building over there looks even older than that."

"That one houses the cafeteria, library, and gym," Mitch said. "It was probably the original building. Back when they were just beginning to accept the fact that the government wasn't going to leave the Indian nations intact. But they hoped there was a chance of getting a separate Indian state."

"Sequoyah," Shelly murmured. "Isn't that what they wanted to call it?"

"Uh-huh. They even had a constitutional convention in Muskogee, but it was naivete to think they could prevail against the boomers who wanted the land parceled out to the Indians in individual allotments so they could grab what was left over."

Shelly studied the line of duplexes at the western edge of the campus. "It looks so peaceful...and secure. A little world where parents can tuck their children away to keep them safe. But it wasn't safe for Tamarah Birch, was it? Or for Ruthann Blackfox."

"Or Kendall Harlan."

"You really don't think Kendall simply ran away—by coincidence—on the same evening Ruthann disappeared?"

"That's a big coincidence. I'm having trouble swallowing it. The more I think about it, the harder it gets." They had reached the dormitory. Mitch started up the steps between the lilac bushes. He looked back to see Shelly hesitating at the bottom, frowning. "Shelly?"

She stirred. "Sorry. I was thinking about the parents of those girls—Tamarah and Ruthann, even Kendall. They brought their children here. They'll blame themselves."

"Probably," he agreed, thinking of the times when he had to depend on a neighbor or take Emily to a friend's house because he was called out at night. "Parents are good at guilt."

She climbed the steps to where he stood. "Voice of experience, Chief?"

"Yes, but Serina Harlan is a special case. That woman is riddled with guilt."

Her brow knotted suddenly. "There are parents who deserve to be riddled."

"Another voice of experience heard from?"

She gave him a long, sharp look. "Yeah. Maybe I'll tell you about it sometime. As for Serina Harlan, it's probably inevitable that the first reaction of parents with kids like Kendall is, 'My God, where did I go wrong?' And Kendall has a lot of company. Surely it isn't always the parents' fault."

"No," Mitch agreed. "Listen, when I question Ruthann's roommates, you jump in whenever you want to. They might feel more comfortable talking to a woman."

Two little girls dashed past them, giggling, and ran into the building. Mitch caught the door before it closed and held it open for Shelly. Aggie Horn was in the foyer, reminding the incoming children of the time they were to board their buses and cautioning them not to be late.

She greeted Mitch and Shelly and added, "We thought about confining all the children to the dormitories today, but Charley pointed out that they might be safer away from the campus."

"He may be right," Mitch conceded. "I'm sure they'll be well-supervised in town."

"Absolutely," Aggie said. "Even Mrs. Qualls is going to help out today. None of these kids is going to sneeze without an adult knowing it. Oh . . ." She pulled a small photograph from her skirt pocket. "Charley said you need a picture of Ruthann. This is all I could find." Mitch accepted the photograph and Aggie sighed. "I guess you want Jamie and Mari. They went up to their room about fifteen minutes ago."

"They're expecting us?"

"Yes. You know the way."

MITCH AND SHELLY were admitted to the room, after being
asked to identify themselves through the closed door. The
girls' faces were drawn. They looked bewildered and frightened.

Mitch was glad he'd had the forethought to bring a female officer. He introduced Shelly to them. The girls sat,
side by side, on the same bunk they'd occupied when Mitch
had questioned them earlier. Only then, Ruthann Blackfox
had sat between them. They had tried to protect her, and
they must be feeling some guilt themselves about Ruthann's disappearance.

"Have you found Ruthann yet?" Jamie asked fearfully.

"No," Mitch told her, "but we will, Jamie. We're hoping you and Mari can help us."

"How?" asked Mari.

"I don't know," Mitch admitted. "Maybe Ruthann said
something you didn't understand or didn't think was important at the time. And now that she's disappeared...?"
The two girls looked at each other blankly and shook their
heads.

"Do you know who Stone Coat is?" Jamie asked.

Shelly looked at Mitch questioningly. Mitch said,
"There's a Cherokee legend about him. A monster, wasn't
he?"

Jamie nodded. "Stanley Dick says Stone Coat killed Tamarah and now he's kidnapped Ruthann and carried her off
to his cave."

"Well, *I* don't believe it," Mari said. "Tamarah's liver
wasn't gone, was it?"

"No," Mitch said.

Mari nodded. "Didn't I tell you?" she said to Jamie.
"Stanley's trying to scare people."

"I'm *plenty* scared," Jamie said fervently. "I can't wait
for my parents to come next week and take me home."

"Mrs. Horn called a dorm meeting before breakfast,"
Mari told them. "She said we aren't to leave the dorm
without a chaperone except when we absolutely have to, and
then we should only go out with two or three other girls."

"That's good advice," Shelly said.

Mitch touched a pencil sketch lying on the desk beside
him. It reminded him of the ones he'd found in Tamarah
Birch's bureau drawer. "Who did this?"

"Tamarah," Mari said. "Ruthann cleaned out her desk
in Miss Adair's room and found some drawings. Tamarah
was always doodling. Mrs. Horn told us to put everything
in a box for Mr. Birch, when he gets here, but Ruthann
wanted to keep that one. We didn't think anyone would
mind."

Mitch picked up the sketch. It was a crude drawing of a
tree with a double trunk growing from a single trunk near
the ground. Tamarah had drawn a circle on the ground beside the tree. Since the sketch lacked perspective, it was difficult to tell what the circle was meant to suggest. The sketch
had been labeled "Oak" and the initials M.O. in one corner.

Mitch held the sketch out for Mari and Jamie. "What do
the initials mean?"

"Don't know," Mari replied and Jamie shrugged an
agreement. "I didn't even notice them until last night. I was
going to ask Ruthann if she knew, but she was already
asleep."

"We understand, Mari, that you're the one who reported to the Horns that Ruthann was missing," Shelly said.

Mari nodded. "I woke up last night and she wasn't here."

"What time was that?"

"About ten-thirty. I thought Ruthann was in the bathroom, but I went down the hall to check and she wasn't
there, either. So I went straight to Mr. and Mrs. Horn's
apartment, and they said all three of us were in bed asleep
at ten o'clock bed check, so Ruthann hadn't been gone long.
But we searched the whole dorm and couldn't find her."

"Maybe Ruthann was only pretending to be asleep," Jamie suggested, "until Mrs. Horn checked our room."

"Mr. Horn told me that a window was open in a first-
floor bathroom," Mitch said.

"Yes," Mari replied. "She must have left that way because all the doors are locked at ten. You can open the fire

exits from inside, but if you do an alarm goes off loud enough to wake everybody on campus."

Mitch looked at the sketch again. "I'm going to borrow this for a while," he said, folding it and tucking it into his shirt pocket. He glanced at Shelly, who nodded and took up the questioning.

"Mari, you said when you woke up and discovered Ruthann wasn't here, you thought she'd gone to the bathroom. Why didn't you just roll over and go back to sleep? Would you have gone to check if it had been Jamie who was gone?"

Mari was thoughtful for a moment. "Probably not. I hate having to go to the bathroom at night when everyone's asleep."

"Why?" Shelly asked.

When Mari didn't answer, Jamie said, "The dorm's spooky at night. There are lights on in the hall and everything, but it feels strange to be the only one up."

Shelly nodded. "I know what you mean. So, Mari, why did you go to the bathroom in search of Ruthann?"

"She'd been acting funny all day. All afternoon, anyway." Mari darted a look at Mitch. "After she slipped out of the drugstore by the back way and came back with a hot dog, she was real quiet. She acted like she was worried about something. When we got back to the dorm, she lay down on her bed and didn't even want supper."

"When Mari and I came back from the cafeteria," Jamie put in, "Ruthann had fallen asleep in her clothes. We pulled the spread over her and left her like that."

"Did you try to find out what was wrong with her before that?" Mitch asked.

"Sure, I did," Mari said. "I asked her what was bothering her. She said she was sick to her stomach. But that was after I'd badgered her to tell us what was wrong—like saying she was sick was an excuse to make us leave her alone."

"Mari kept telling her that, if she was worried, maybe we could help her," Jamie added.

"What did Ruthann say to that?" Shelly asked.

"She said, no, we couldn't and she wanted us to just shut up."

"Yeah, she was about to cry when she said that," Mari said. "Remember, Jamie?"

Jamie nodded. "I thought maybe she really was sick then. That's one of the worst things about being at boarding school. When you're sick, you wish your mother was here to bring you soup and 7-Up and put a cool cloth on your forehead. Anyway, that's what my mom does. Mrs. Horn takes us to the clinic and gives us our medicine, but it's not the same."

"Why didn't she take Ruthann to the clinic?" Mitch asked.

"I don't think she even knew Ruthann was sick until she missed supper. When Mrs. Horn came to see about her, Ruthann was already asleep."

"Mrs. Horn was going to take her to the clinic this morning, if she was still sick."

"Now that you've had time to think about it," Shelly said, "has either of you thought of any reason why Ruthann would want to slip out of the dorm at night?"

"No," said Mari emphatically. "She was afraid of the dark, more than ever since Tamarah died."

"I see. I suppose you've heard that Kendall Harlan is missing, too?"

"Hasn't everybody?" Mari asked. "I'll bet she ran away."

Jamie nodded. "Kendall was going to have to take her senior year over, you know. She probably didn't want to. I know I wouldn't. It would be embarrassing to have to go back to the same school with the kids who were a grade behind you the year before."

"So you don't think Kendall and Ruthann are together?"

Mari looked nonplussed. "Kendall didn't have much to do with any of the kids here. She's not friendly, like Cody. I don't think Ruthann even knew her."

"Yes, she did," Jamie contradicted. "I saw them talking once."

"Where?" Mitch asked.

Jamie pondered the question. "At the pow-wow."

"When?"

"I think it was Thursday afternoon. I saw Kendall sit down beside Ruthann and say something. Maybe she was asking about the pow-wow—like what dances were scheduled. Or if Ruthann had seen her father. I don't know. They only talked for a few minutes and then Kendall left."

"Did Ruthann mention it later?"

"No," Jamie said, "and I'd forgotten it until you asked about Ruthann and Kendall. Is it important?"

"Maybe," Mitch said. "I don't know."

A look of regret passed across Jamie's face. "I wish we'd made her tell us what was bothering her."

"I doubt that you could have, if she didn't want to," Mitch told her. Something pricked at his memory. "If either of you thinks of anything else that Ruthann said or did that seemed out of character—in any way unusual—ask Mrs. Horn to call us. Okay?"

Both girls nodded. As Mitch and Shelly prepared to leave, Shelly said, "Thank you both for talking to us. We're going to do our best to find Ruthann."

As they left the dormitory, Mitch pulled the pencil sketch from his pocket and unfolded it. "Why do you think Ruthann wanted to keep this particular sketch?"

"Who knows. Didn't you say Mari and Jamie told you earlier that Tamarah and Ruthann were always going off by themselves and whispering secrets? Maybe that tree's on the campus. Maybe it was their meeting place."

Mitch glanced at her approvingly. "That's pretty good, Shelly." He studied the sketch again. "Hmmm. Wish I knew what M.O. meant."

Shelly shrugged helplessly. "Modus operandi, but an eight-year-old wouldn't know that. Let's see ... Could 'M' stand for Mari? But then what would 'O' stand for?"

"My oak," Mitch mused, "or maybe meeting oak. You know, I think I saw this tree."

"Where?"

"When we were searching the woods last night."

"So, maybe it *was* Tamarah and Ruthann's special meeting place. That might explain why Ruthann wanted to keep that particular sketch."

"Could be. They weren't supposed to leave campus without a chaperone, but you know how kids are. Tell them not to do something, and it looks twice as appealing."

"Did you see the oak near where Tamarah's body was found?" Shelly asked.

"I don't think so."

"I was just wondering . . . Maybe Tamarah and Ruthann were supposed to meet there that morning after Tamarah's meeting with the principal. But Ruthann couldn't slip away and missed the meeting."

"Lucky for her," Mitch muttered. "I want to find this tree again and look at it more closely. It probably doesn't mean a thing, but I'll try anything at this point. I'll take you back to town first. Duck will need some help."

Shelly smiled at the mention of her partner. "He was cross as a bear all day yesterday. Even crabbier than usual, according to Helen. He went on a diet."

Mitch grinned. "What kind this time?"

"He's counting fat grams."

"Good. Your comment about his weight must have gotten under his skin."

Shelly chuckled. "My mere existence gets under Duck's skin."

THE DOUBLE-TRUNKED oak was not at the edge of the playing field, where Mitch thought he'd seen it the previous night. He shouldn't have expected to walk straight to the tree, he told himself morosely. His luck had been mostly bad since Thursday.

He was convinced, admittedly without any physical evidence, that the disappearance of the two girls from the boarding school campus was somehow related to Tamarah Birch's murder. But all he had was hunches. So far the murder investigation had been a twisted maze of shaky inferences drawn from scant and unconnected facts that kept doubling back upon themselves.

It wasn't that he didn't have suspects; too many suspects, in fact. Rather, if the pedophile theory was discounted, the problem was the paucity of motives. And Mitch was still inclined to discount the pedophile theory. At first, the missing panties had pointed them in that direction. The panties turning up in Dwayne Burns's yard even pointed to a convenient suspect. But the forensic evidence contradicted this obvious, even blatant, physical evidence.

The killer had taken the panties in order to turn the investigation in the wrong direction, away from himself and toward Dwayne Burns. So it was somebody who knew Burns had been released from Eastern State. That hardly narrowed the list of suspects. Every person on the list Mitch had written the night before could have known that Burns was back in Buckskin. Bookland and Farnwell had brought Burns home and Bookland had talked about it at the school.

With that information fresh in the killer's mind, the decision to take Tamarah's panties might have been made on impulse in the tense, perhaps panicked, aftermath of the murder.

Mitch looked at Tamarah Birch's sketch again, and again had the feeling he'd recently noticed a double-trunked tree. But where? There was nothing to do but retrace his steps of the previous night.

He stuffed the sketch back in his pocket and trudged toward where the search party had entered the woods. The odor of wet leaves, from last night's rain, hung in the air, and his shoes left impressions in places where the still-damp earth lay exposed. His feet felt heavy and his head ached. He didn't function at maximum capacity when he was deprived of sleep, and he'd had barely two hours before returning to the school this morning.

Snippets of information he'd collected during the past few days gnawed at him. Tamarah confides a secret that she wasn't supposed to tell; almost certainly the confidante was Ruthann. Two days after Tamarah's murder, Ruthann disappears. At roughly the same time, Kendall Harlan disappears. From available evidence, it appeared both girls had left of their own accord and that Kendall took nearly seven hundred dollars with her.

Shortly before the disappearances, Kendall and Ruthann were seen talking together at the pow-wow and Kendall, having taken her brother's car without permission, was seen in the drugstore from which Ruthann exited via the back way, turning up again thirty minutes later carrying a hot dog. When Aggie Horn had wondered aloud where Ruthann got money for the hot dog, the child had evaded a direct answer. Had Kendall bought the hot dog, after arranging to meet Ruthann at the booth?

A few hours before the disappearances, Ruthann appeared to her roommates to be worried, though when asked she said she was sick. Kendall's mother found six hundred and seventy-five dollars hidden in Kendall's closet, and Kendall had a heated argument with her brother during which Kendall claimed to have "spilled the beans" and Cody accused her of lying, expressed strong doubts about her mental health, and threatened to give her a licking.

It all fit together somehow—like a code that continued to elude everybody's best efforts to break it.

Having reached the place where last night's search party had entered the woods, Mitch began retracing the route, scanning trees along the way. Twenty minutes later, he passed the spot where Tamarah Birch's body had been found, pausing to scrutinize every tree trunk in sight, but there was no double-trunked oak.

He trudged on as depression settled in the hollow of his chest. Very soon he would have to face the parents of Tamarah Birch and Ruthann Blackfox, and he had very little in the way of answers to offer them.

Mitch sighed, caught sight of a large chunk of sky between the tree branches ahead, and realized he had doubled back toward the campus. He came out of the woods directly west of the faculty duplexes, as they'd done last night. Then, as the search party had, he re-entered the woods, and veered south.

Suddenly the double-trunked oak was right in front of him. He pulled out the sketch to compare it with the tree.

The drawing was far from an accurate representation, about the only similarity being the division of the trunk near the ground. But it was the lone twin-trunked oak he'd seen in the woods, and it was only a few hundred yards off campus, behind the faculty duplexes. Students could duck in and out of here quickly without their absence from the campus being noticed.

Mitch's eyes dropped to a rock, about the size of a small grapefruit, lying near the trunk of the tree. Could that be what the circle in Tamarah's drawing represented? If so, it had had some significance for the child. Perhaps it had been placed there as a marker, which would mean that someone wanted to be able to locate the exact spot later.

Stooping, Mitch rolled the rock to one side. The ground beneath the oak tree was bare, except for a scattering of dead twigs, and the ground where the rock had lain was no different. He fished out his pocket knife and used it to loosen the packed earth where the rock had rested. Within moments, the point of the knife blade snagged on something. Bending over, he scooped and tossed aside the loosened dirt with his hands until he'd uncovered a piece of dark, knitted wool. He tugged on the fabric, pulling it free. It was a ski mask, and when he shook out the loose dirt, a man's gold ring fell out. The ring looked like a high school or college graduation ring. Numerals that must have indicated the year of graduation were so worn down it was impossible to tell what they'd been. But the letter "O" was still decipherable, and from its placement there must have been two additional letters following it.

The mask was solid black or navy. It was hard to tell in this light. Mitch swallowed. His mouth was suddenly dry.

I saw a secret and I promised never to tell.

It was more than a few dollars, Ellis.

He wore gloves and a black ski mask. The mask had red stripes around the eyes and mouth . . . But eyewitnesses at the Muskogee bank didn't recall any red stripes.

He's already taken more than half a million, three hundred thou of it in Muskogee.

Mitch's mind raced. Had Tamarah seen somebody burying this mask and ring? The spot was almost directly behind the Harlan's duplex. Suppose Ruthann had seen Ellis
Harlan digging right here—or Cody—but how did Kendall
come into it? Could Kendall be the one Tamarah confided
in, rather than Ruthann? That wasn't likely; Ruthann was
Tamarah's best friend, but she hardly knew Kendall.

Okay, what about this: Tamarah saw Kendall burying the
mask and ring and told Ruthann. But how could Kendall
have gotten *her* hands on them? Her father or brother gave
them to her? Or she found them among their belongings?

He couldn't figure it out now. But this tree was important to Tamarah. She'd marked the spot where the mask was
buried, so somehow she'd known about the mask and
Ruthann must have known, too. She'd chosen this sketch
from several she'd found in Tamarah's desk. The last time
he'd seen the child, she'd been troubled and afraid. Now
Ruthann and Kendall were gone, and Mitch's instincts told
him they were together. Which must mean that if Kendall
hadn't buried these things, she knew about them and understood their significance, perhaps even knew who had
buried them.

Assume that Kendall had somehow gotten her hands on
the mask and ring and Tamarah had seen her burying it and
had told Ruthann, who had later mentioned it to Kendall.
Far-fetched, maybe, but it explained why Kendall and
Ruthann suddenly had so much to talk about. It was a
workable theory until something better turned up. Suppose
it had happened exactly that way, what did it all mean?

The ring did not belong to Kendall. Furthermore, Mitch
could not believe she was the mastermind behind four bank
robberies, or that she'd somehow come into possession of a
gun and killed a bank guard. Then killed Tamarah when she
learned Tamarah hadn't kept her promise to remain silent
about what she'd seen. Kendall had more than six hundred
dollars she couldn't account for, but if that was money taken
in the robberies, where was the bulk of it? And if Kendall
wanted the mask destroyed because it was evidence against

her, why hadn't she burned it? Why bury it with a man's ring?

Mitch shook the mask again and stuffed it and the ring into his shirt pocket with Tamarah's drawing. His feet no longer felt heavy as he hurried back to the campus. Jerry Bookland should be around and the janitor, Merv Haines. One of them could tell him where to find a shovel.

TWENTY-SIX

AN HOUR LATER, Mitch leaned wearily on the shovel handle. He was dirty and sweating and he'd rubbed a blister at the base of his right thumb. All for nothing; he'd found no money. Well, it had been a long shot. Discouraged, he gazed at his handiwork. He'd dug in a wide circle all the way around the tree and turned up nothing but a few rocks and a jagged piece of an old soda pop bottle.

He shouldered the shovel and walked back to the campus tool shed, a small wood structure beside the administration building. Merv Haines, who was weeding an azalea bed nearby, straightened and walked over to the shed.

"Did you find what you were looking for, Chief?" Curious about why Mitch wanted a shovel an hour earlier, Haines had offered his help, which Mitch had declined. In the past hour, Haines's curiosity must have grown by leaps and bounds. He studied Mitch's face as though trying to decipher what was going on behind it.

"Maybe," Mitch said shortly, hoping to leave the impression that he hadn't come back completely empty-handed. Haines would talk about Mitch's mysterious foray into the woods with a shovel as soon as the faculty returned to campus. If the killer had buried the mask and ring or had instructed Kendall to do so, maybe the news would at least make him nervous about what Mitch knew or suspected.

Mitch thanked Haines for the use of the shovel and left the janitor staring after him, his eyes narrowed in speculation. Driving back to the station, Mitch decided that, when the evening shift came on, he'd send Roo out to keep watch on that tree tonight. In case anybody decided to check on the ski mask and ring.

He found Duck and Shelly having lunch in the patrol car at a local Sonic drive-in. Shelly was eating a burger and fries. Duck, Mitch noted with approval, had ordered a chef's salad.

Mitch got out and walked over to their car. "Anything interesting going on today?"

"Oh, sure," Duck muttered. "I hauled in a real intriguing guy this morning. He puked all over himself and passed out in the alley behind the coffee shop sometime during the night. Guy who works there took out the trash about eight, found him, and called the station. Stink-o was just waking up when I got there, moaning and groaning like he was dying. Said he had a migraine."

"Did he call somebody?"

"His daughter. She's coming up from Stilwell to get him." Duck stabbed a bit of lettuce with a plastic fork. "Oh—" he said, the fork halfway to his mouth, "we might have a lead on those stolen rap tapes. Millicent Kirkwood called to complain that loud voices from a neighbor's house kept her awake all night. The family has a couple of teenagers. Miss Millicent said it sounded like chanting."

"She suspects the worst, of course," Mitch observed.

Duckworth nodded. "A meeting of a witches' coven or something else really evil. Anyway, I called the neighbor and the lady of the house first said her kids didn't have any rap tapes. I asked her to look, anyway, and she came back and said she'd found some in their room. The titles were the same ones that were stolen from the drugstore."

"Did you tell her that?"

"No. I just told her to make sure they keep the volume down so the neighbors don't complain again."

"The kids will be home this afternoon," Shelly said. "We'll go over there and talk to them and the mother together."

"You can handle that alone, Shelly," Mitch said. He handed Duck the ski mask. "I want you to take this to Claude Dunn at the Muskogee P.D. See if it could be the one worn by that bank robber they're looking for."

"Where'd you get it?" Duck asked.

"I dug it up from beneath a tree which I identified from a sketch made by Tamarah Birch. Along with this." He fished out the ring. "Remember that little circle next to the tree, Shelly? It was a rock marking the spot where these were buried."

"Boy, talk about confusing," Shelly said. "What's a ski mask got to do with our investigation?"

"I had a couple of thoughts. Tamarah might have seen somebody burying it. That somebody might have seen her, too. A man wearing a ski mask has been holding up banks in towns around here. I know it sounds farfetched, but if it was the bank robber who buried this stuff or somebody he sent to bury it..."

Duck stared at the mask in his hand. "He killed Tamarah Birch to shut her up?"

"The thought occurred to me. Before we go off half-cocked, though, we need to find out if that could be the mask worn by the robber."

"Do you think Ruthann knew about the mask and ring, too?" Shelly asked.

Mitch shrugged. "Tamarah might have told her. If Ruthann did know and if the robber knew she knew and threatened her—well, it's a possible explanation for her sudden disappearance."

"So where does Kendall Harlan fit in?" Shelly asked.

"I'm still trying to come up with a theory on that one," Mitch told her. "Duck, I'd like you to head for Muskogee as soon as you finish your lunch."

Shelly stuffed her litter into a paper sack. "I'll hitch a ride to town with you, Chief. See you later, partner."

She picked up the ring from the dashboard as they were leaving the drive-in. "It's an old college ring." She held the ring closer. "Looks like an 'O' here, but I can't make out the rest."

"When I let you out in town, take that over to the jewelry store. See if the jeweler can tell us what the other letters were."

"Okay." Shelly pocketed the ring. "If Kendall didn't bury the mask and ring, Chief, she might have found out about it..."

He could see she was trying to make the same connection Mitch had wrestled with earlier. "How?"

"Well . . . maybe Ruthann told her."

"Why would she choose Kendall to confide in? Why not one of her roommates?"

"Mmmm. Good question. But if Kendall and Ruthann are together, they've either been kidnapped or they're running from something...or somebody." Both were silent for several moments. Then Shelly mused, "If you were a troubled seventeen-year-old girl and you were running scared, where would you run to?"

Something stirred at the back of Mitch's mind. "The last place I'd been happy," he said.

Shelly glanced at him. "Do you know where that place is for Kendall?"

"Maybe," Mitch murmured thoughtfully.

When Mitch got back to the station, Ruthann Blackfox's parents were waiting for him in his office. The father was pale but controlled. The mother was a wreck. She couldn't talk without sobbing.

Mitch explained that the investigation was just getting started and told them about the all-night search and the other measures he'd taken. "We're following up on a couple of things that might or might not be connected to Ruthann's disappearance."

"We didn't know until we talked to Mr. Qualls a while ago that another little girl from the school was murdered last Thursday," Blackfox said as his wife sobbed into a handkerchief.

"If we'd known, we'd...have taken...Ruthann...home," Mrs. Blackfox choked out.

"Mr. Qualls said an older girl is missing, too, the daughter of one of the teachers," Blackfox said.

"We have no evidence that the two girls are together," Mitch said.

"We—we'd feel better if we knew they were," Blackfox said. "Ruthann won't be so afraid if—well, if she's not alone—that is if they're not—hurt."

"We've found nothing to indicate that violence was done," Mitch said, glancing at Mrs. Blackfox as she buried her face in her hands. "In fact, it appears Ruthann left the dormitory of her own free will."

"I don't understand that," Blackfox said, his tightly restrained voice suddenly cracking. "Why would she want to leave the dormitory at night? It makes no sense."

"You had no indication, from letters or phone calls, that Ruthann was upset or worried?"

"Nothing. Of course, we haven't talked to her since little Tamarah died. I'm sure she was—upset about that. They were friends, you know." Mitch nodded and Blackfox regained his composure and went on. "The school should have contacted us and that's what I said to Mr. Qualls. I can tell you one thing, if—*when* we get her back, we'll keep her at home. She won't be back here next year."

"Where are you staying?" Mitch asked.

"We've taken a room at the Starlight Motel."

"I'll call you the minute I know anything."

Blackfox took the hint. He rose and helped his wife to her feet. "We'll be in our room, waiting for your call, Chief Bushyhead." As they left the office, he put a comforting arm around his wife's shoulders and said, "You heard him, honey. They didn't find any evidence of violence."

DUCK RETURNED from Muskogee at 3:30 that afternoon with the report that the ski mask had been shown to an eyewitness to the Muskogee bank robbery, who said it looked like the one worn by the robber. Phone calls were made to two witnesses to the Tahlequah and Grove robberies. All continued to insist that the ski mask worn by the robber they saw had red stripes around the eyes.

"The usual contradictions among eyewitnesses," Duckworth said.

"Maybe they aren't contradictions," Mitch said. "Maybe he Muskogee robber isn't the same man who did the other obs."

"A copy cat?"

"Possibly. The other guy getting away with it could have given him the idea. Or it was the same guy with two ski masks. Did Muskogee keep the mask?"

"Yeah, they'll turn it over to us later if we need it in our case. We gotta make an arrest first."

"Sit down, Duck. I need to talk to you, and you can fill in Virgil and Roo when they come in. I'll be out of town for a day or two..."

"Emily," Mitch called as he entered the house fifteen minutes later. "Emily!"

She came out of the kitchen. "I'm making a cobbler, Daddy. What's wrong?"

"Nothing's wrong." He felt a sudden wave of gratitude that she was safe at home. He kissed the top of her head. "How would you like to go out of town for a day or two?"

Her eyes lit up. "A vacation?"

"Not exactly, sweetheart. A couple of girls disappeared from the tribal school last night—"

"Kendall Harlan's gone, too. I heard."

Naturally. "I want to check out a theory. It's several hours' drive—time for us to have a conversation without interruption for a change."

"Can I drive?"

"Sure."

She cocked her head. "Promise not to stomp a hole in the floor board every time you see another car?"

"I don't do that."

"Hah!"

"Okay, okay, I'll control myself."

"When do you want to leave?"

"How long will it take you to pack an overnight bag?"

"Twenty minutes."

"Make it ten. What about the cobbler?"

"I'll stick it in the refrigerator and finish baking it when we get back." Having dealt with the cobbler, she started toward the stairs, stopped suddenly, and turned around. "By the way, where are we going?"

"Great Bend, Kansas."

She frowned. "Kansas?"

"I know it's not L.A. or even Wichita. But you can always find *something* interesting in a new place."

She sighed. "Maybe they'll have a shopping mall. Oh, I almost forgot. Lisa called. She wants you to call her back tonight. I wrote the number by the phone."

TWENTY-SEVEN

THEY REGISTERED at a new hotel near the interstate. Mitch asked for adjoining rooms and handed one key to Emily. She checked out her room, opened the connecting door, came into Mitch's room and flopped down on the bed. She waved a colorful promotional brochure. "This hotel is totally excellent, Daddy. They have a video game room and a swimming pool. They even have a sauna. Oooh, and did you see the gift shop?"

"You think you can entertain yourself here for a few hours while I talk to some people?"

"Sure. Can I have money to buy T-shirts for Temple and Kevin?" Mitch gave her a twenty.

"That may not be enough."

He gave her another twenty. "I want the change back. Don't leave the hotel while I'm gone, okay? We'll go out for dinner when I get back. Ask the people at the desk to recommend a restaurant."

"Something fancy?"

"Why not."

She beamed. "Great. I'm going to put on my swimsuit now. If I'm not in the room when you get back—"

"I'll find you," Mitch assured her.

It took most of the afternoon to make the rounds of Great Bend's motels and hotels, showing the photographs of the two girls to the clerks on duty. At dusk, with only three motels left to visit, Mitch was tempted to leave them until the next morning. He was discouraged and hungry, and Emily would be expecting him back. He had to shower and change clothes before dinner.

And call Lisa.

About halfway through the list of motels and hotels that he'd copied from the phone book, he had become convinced he was on a wild goose chase. Since then, he'd only been going through the motions.

He got in his car and checked the address of the next motel on the list. It was about a mile from where he was, but in the opposite direction from his hotel. Still, it shouldn't take more than twenty minutes to drive there and find somebody who'd talk to him. He'd leave the last two stops until morning.

The Orchid Motel proved to be a U-shaped tan brick structure housing sixteen rooms with the office at the end of one of the U's stems. A fenced pool and play yard occupied the space between the two wings of the building. A small, dark-skinned woman sat behind the desk in the office, reading a newspaper.

Mitch introduced himself and drew the snapshots from his pocket. "I'm looking for these two girls," he said. "This one's seventeen, the other, eight."

She glanced at the pictures without expression, then studied Mitch suspiciously. "What for?"

"They're runaways and their parents are worried sick about them."

She turned back to her newspaper. Mitch stayed put, waiting in silence until she glanced back at him. "They ran away because they're scared," he said. "They're in trouble, and I can help them."

She looked at the pictures again. "How do I know that?"

Mitch showed her his badge. She sniffed, but bent over the counter to examine it at close range. Finally, she said, "A young woman checked into Room Seven earlier today. She looked older than seventeen, but then most of them do these days. Could be this one." She tapped the snapshot of Kendall Harlan. "I'm not sure. Anyway, she was alone."

Kendall was smart enough to keep Ruthann out of sight while she registered. "Thanks," Mitch said.

"I don't want any trouble. No ruckus to disturb the other guests. Understand me?"

"Sure."

"You got no authority here. I hear a row, I call the local cops." She returned to her newspaper.

"There'll be no row. Thanks again. I won't let on how I located their room."

She didn't look up. "Mister, I never saw you before in my life."

Mitch had reached the door. "Right. You're a stranger to me, too."

The glow of a lighted lamp made a circle on the drawn curtains of Room Seven. Mitch knocked and heard movement in the room beyond.

"Who is it?"

"Desk clerk."

The door opened slowly, the night chain still engaged. Blue eyes peered out at him. Kendall's appearance had undergone a transformation. Her hair was a uniform brown and her earrings were small, gold studs. "Hello, Kendall."

She paled. "Oh, shit fire . . ." Unlike her appearance, her language hadn't improved noticeably. "How did you find us?"

"It's a long story. May I come in?"

"Do you have a warrant, or whatever they call it?"

"I'm not here to arrest you, Kendall. I came to talk. Is Ruthann with you?"

She hesitated, seemingly torn between conflicting desires. "Yes," she murmured, "and she's all right." Her tone was touched by defiance. "Thanks to me. She'd probably be dead now if she hadn't come with me."

"I figured it was something like that, but you can't hide indefinitely. You must know that, Kendall. Six hundred and seventy-five won't last long. Why don't we sit down, the three of us, and talk about it."

"How did you know—" She paused to close the door. There was the sound of the night chain being released, and then the door opened again.

Mitch stepped inside and Kendall opened the bathroom door. "You can come out now, Ruthann."

The child sidled into the room. With her hand on Ruthann's shoulder, Kendall guided her to the bed and sat beside her. "It's Chief Bushyhead from Buckskin. You remember him, don't you?"

Ruthann nodded and stared at Mitch. "Your mother and father are in Buckskin, Ruthann. They're very worried about you."

"I wanted to call them," she whispered.

"I couldn't let her," Kendall said. "They'd have made her tell where we were."

Mitch sat in the room's single chair, an oak captain's chair with an orange corduroy seat cushion.

"How'd you get here?"

"Hitched," Kendall said.

"We slept in a farmer's barn the first night," Ruthann said.

"Kendall, when your mother reported you missing, she told us more than six hundred dollars had disappeared from your room."

"It figures," Kendall muttered. "She snooped through my things again. She about had a cow when she found the money in the first place. But she didn't take it, and as soon as she turned her back, I hid it in my bra."

Mitch's attention was on the younger girl. She seemed to be none the worse for wear. He took out the sketch of the double-trunked tree and handed it to her. "You can have this back now. I had to borrow it for a while. I'm curious, though. What does the 'M.O.' stand for, meeting oak?"

"Mystery oak," Ruthann murmured.

"Ah, I see. Yes...Tamarah named it the mystery oak because she saw something mysterious happen there. A secret she promised not to tell. But she told you, didn't she, Ruthann?"

The child darted a stricken look at Kendall. "It's okay," Kendall said. "I guess it's time we trusted somebody." She lifted her chin. "Tamarah saw me bury something there."

"A black ski mask and a man's ring. I dug them up."

Kendall looked frightened again. "How did you know where to dig?"

"Tamarah's sketch. When I found the tree, there was a big rock sitting about where that circle is on the drawing. I had a hunch it was there to mark that spot so that somebody could find it later. So I started digging."

Kendall sighed. "Tamarah was hiding behind a tree, watching me when I buried them. She came out when I'd finished and asked me why I was burying a ski mask. She didn't see the ring because I had rolled it up in the mask. I told her it was a secret and made her promise not to tell."

"She only told me," Ruthann said. "She wouldn't have told anyone else."

"Where did you get those things, Kendall?"

She looked frightened again and shook her head emphatically. "Look," Mitch said, "the ski mask is now in the hands of the Muskogee police. They think it was worn by a man who robbed a Muskogee bank. You could be in big trouble if you don't tell me what you know."

"I—I didn't know he was going to rob a bank when I went with him. You have to believe me!"

"Start at the beginning, Kendall."

Her hands went to her face. Her words trembled against her closed fists. "I had to talk to somebody. I—I had to..."

"The beginning, Kendall."

She didn't speak immediately, perhaps ordering her thoughts. "I—I wanted to find my birth mother, but Mom and Dad wouldn't help me. I knew Mom kept important papers in the cedar chest in their bedroom, and—one night while they were out I went through the chest, looking for my birth certificate. I thought it might tell the town where I was born, maybe even the hospital. It would be a place to start." She closed her eyes and pressed the knuckles of one hand against her mouth.

"Did you find the birth certificate?" Mitch asked.

After a moment, she shook her head. "I found letters written by my—my father to my mother."

"Ellis and Serina, you mean?"

Hot blood surged up her face. She swallowed hard. "They were written when—when she was pregnant with Cody. They were about something—something..." She shuddered. "I couldn't believe it. I told Mom I'd read the letters and she—oh, she tried to twist it around to mean something else. But I knew she was lying. It was true. It was all *true*."

"What did you learn from the letters?"

When she opened her eyes they looked glazed, as though she'd been far away. She shook her head sharply. "I won't tell you that. You can't make me." She reached for Ruthann's small hand as though seeking reassurance from the younger girl.

"I thought you were going to trust me."

"You don't understand. I *can't* tell."

Mitch remembered Serina Harlan's words: *You can't force Kendall to tell you anything she doesn't want to tell.* "All right," Mitch said. "What happened after you read the letters and confronted your mother?"

"I didn't know what to do. I—I had to talk to somebody. I couldn't talk to Mom and Dad. She cried every time I mentioned it, and he just blew up. Besides, I was so angry with them. I felt betrayed and—well, I went to somebody I thought I could trust. We talked about it three—no, four times, and I felt better after. I was so grateful to him for that. So that day, when he asked if I wanted to ride to Muskogee with him, I was glad to get out of town for a while."

Mitch tried one more time. "What's his name, Kendall?"

"I can't tell you that, Chief Bushyhead. Honest."

Ruthann sucked in a breath. "He'll kill us!" She buried her face in Kendall's lap.

"Like he killed Tamarah?" Mitch asked.

Kendall nodded, distractedly stroking Ruthann's hair. Her eyes filled with tears. "It was my fault. I told him Tamarah saw me burying the mask and ring. I guess I was trying to protect myself."

"By telling him Tamarah knew what you'd buried?"

"I wanted him to know that somebody besides me knew where the mask and ring were. He was furious—it was like he went crazy. He—he scared me. It was like he turned into somebody else. Before that, he hadn't been sure. I'd taken the mask, you see, and he thought he lost the ring. He tried to make me tell him where I'd buried them. But I wouldn't—he couldn't make me. I thought as long as I didn't tell, I was safe."

"From him? You thought he'd harm you?"

"I didn't know. I wasn't even sure then why I'd taken that stuff. Something just told me to do it. That day in Muskogee, he said he had to go to the bank and told me to wait in the car and keep the motor running because he would be back in seconds. I thought he was going to make a deposit or something. I know it sounds dumb, but that's what I thought. A little while later, I heard a shot. I thought it was a car backfiring. Then he came flying out of the bank carrying a sack and jumped in the car and pulled that mask and some gloves off. I didn't even see them before that. He yelled at me to gun it. I was terrified."

"That was when you learned he'd robbed the bank?"

She nodded. Ruthann was sitting up again, but she clung to Kendall's hand. "He had bundles of money in the sack," Kendall said, "and he threw the ski mask and gloves on top. He tossed one of the bundles of money to me and told me to keep my mouth shut."

"Where was the ring?"

"In a little plastic holder between the front seats, with another ring and his wristwatch. I guess he took them off because he was going to put on the gloves before he went into the bank. I slipped one ring and the mask in my pocket before we got home. As soon as we were out of town, he took over driving. He said he'd robbed the bank and accidentally shot a guard and that I was in it up to my neck because I drove the getaway car. If they caught him, he said we'd both go to jail."

"You didn't know what you were doing," Mitch said.

"But I was afraid no one would believe me. I was afraid, if he did get caught, he'd try to put half the blame on me. But if it came to that and I gave the mask and ring to the police, they'd see I wanted to cooperate... It doesn't make much sense now... to think I—we were safe because Tamarah had seen me burying them."

"Then you heard Tamarah had been killed."

"At first, I just couldn't believe he had done it. I kept telling myself it was somebody else... an accident, maybe. I didn't do anything when I first heard. It was like I was

petrified. I couldn't sleep. I couldn't turn my mind off. I'd
trusted him, and he'd robbed a bank and shot a guard and
pulled me into it, too. Then it dawned on me that if he'd do
that, he'd kill Tamarah to protect himself. Finally I couldn't
stand it any longer. I asked him flat out if he'd killed Tamarah because she knew where I buried the stuff. He swore
he hadn't. He kept asking, 'What kind of person do you
think I am?' I pretended to believe him, but there was
something in his eyes—something cold. I knew he'd done it
and that he'd kill me, too, if he could. So I made my plans
and split."

"Why did you bring Ruthann?"

"Because word was going around campus that Tamarah
had told Ruthann a really big secret before she died and that
the police were trying to get Ruthann to tell them what it
was. So I found Ruthann at the pow-wow and told her to
meet me at the hot dog stand in an hour. When we met, I
told her we had to run away because the man who'd killed
Tamarah might try to kill her, too. I told her how to slip out
of the dorm that night, after bed check. She did just like I
said. She's been very brave."

"I want my mommy and daddy," Ruthann said shakily.
"I want them to take me home."

"That's exactly what they want to do, Ruthann," Mitch
said. "If you tell me who killed Tamarah, we can arrest him,
and he won't be able to hurt you."

Her eyes widened. "I don't know who killed Tamarah."

"She doesn't," Kendall said. "I never told her. I thought
the less she knew, the safer she'd be."

"Then it's up to you, Kendall."

She shook her head.

"We'll arrest him. You and Ruthann won't have to be
afraid any more."

"I can't," she said miserably. "If I tell you, then he'll tell
what I told him."

"What you learned from the letter in your mother's cedar chest?"

She didn't answer directly. "People would be hurt—really, really bad."

"Okay." It was clear she couldn't be coaxed into divulging the killer's name. But with what she had told him, there were other ways to smoke out the murderer. Mitch was already devising a plan. "Get your things together. You're going with me to my hotel. My daughter is with me. We'll have dinner and the two of you can sleep in Emily's room tonight. We'll call your parents and let them know you're safe, and we'll drive back to Buckskin tomorrow morning."

Mitch made the phone calls to Buckskin as soon as they reached the hotel. In both cases, he asked for and received the parents' word that they would tell no one the girls had been found before handing the phone to their daughter.

Emily pulled him aside and whispered, "Why do you want them to keep it a secret?"

"I want to be there when the news hits the school," Mitch told her. That is, unless the murderer was Ellis or Cody Harlan, who had been forewarned. He shook off the anxiety the thought caused.

Emily was looking at him with exasperation. "Why?"

He patted her shoulder. "Police business, honey. Listen, I'm going to shower now and phone Lisa. I'll knock on your door when I'm ready to go to dinner."

Fifteen minutes later, showered, shaved and dressed, he dialed the Boston number Lisa had given Emily. She answered on the fifth ring.

"I was afraid you weren't going to answer," Mitch said.

"Oh, Mitch, it's so good to hear your voice."

"I miss you."

"Me, too. You called barely in the nick of time. We were on the way out when I heard the phone ringing."

"We?"

"Martha Bass—a teacher from Ohio. We met at the orientation meeting this morning, and she invited me to room with her. The cost of rent here is highway robbery. You wouldn't *believe* what we pay for three little rooms. But it's close to the campus. Martha was lucky enough to get it because she came to town early." She sounded bubbly, excited. Mitch was a little jealous. To be honest, he had hoped she'd be feeling homesick by now. But if that were the case, it didn't come across in her voice.

"Good. I'm glad you aren't alone." He hoped he sounded glad.

"How's the investigation going?"

"I think I'm on to something. We could make an arrest within the next few days."

"Wonderful! So you can come up here while Emily is away at camp?"

"What about Martha?"

"We could get a motel for a couple of days. There's one not far from here. I want to show you Boston, Mitch. It's a fabulous city."

"You're all I want to see."

She laughed, a low, sultry sound. "I wish you were here right now. I'd skip the reception . . . did I mention we were on our way to a reception for the seminar registrants?"

"No, you didn't. I guess I'd better let you go then."

"Only if you'll promise to call again tomorrow night."

"I may be on stake out, but I'll call as soon as I can."

"I really need to see you," she said quietly.

"I need to see you, too. Talk to you soon. Bye, honey."

He set the receiver softly into its cradle. He felt depressed; he suspected she was going to be too busy the next weeks to miss him half as much as he was missing her.

Even so, although he wasn't sure why, he was reluctant to make the trip to Boston. Maybe he was afraid Lisa would see him differently in an environment that she found so stimulating. Maybe he was afraid he'd stick out like a smudge of grease on a white shirt, and their relationship would be subtly altered, permanently. Maybe it would be, anyway, whether he went to Boston or not.

He reached for the receiver again and phoned Virgil at the police station to say that he was bringing the girls back. He cautioned Virgil to keep it under his hat. "I want to deliver the news to Porter Qualls in person. I want to see his face. Did Roo catch anybody near that oak tree?"

"Nope," Virgil said, "but the jeweler says the first and last initials on the ring were 'O' and 'U.' The middle one's 'S' or 'C.' Could be Oklahoma State."

"Maybe. You better stake out the tribal school campus tonight. Somebody might decide it's too risky to hang around any longer and make a run for it."

"Somebody who?"

"Any name I gave you would be a pure guess."

"What did the girls tell you? Why did they run away?"

"I'll explain everything when I get back."

"You said you want to tell Qualls about finding the girls. You think he killed that child?"

"I didn't say that."

"But you've got more than a guess about who did it, don't you?"

"I have a sneaking suspicion."

TWENTY-EIGHT

PORTER QUALLS had a visitor in his office the next morning when Mitch arrived at the tribal school. "It's Mr. Birch," Darlene told him in a stage whisper. "Tamarah's father. He just got to town."

"Tell your boss I'm here," Mitch said.

Darlene looked at him doubtfully, but she picked up the phone and buzzed the inner office. "Chief Bushyhead is here to see you," she said, listening for a moment, and replacing the receiver. "He wants you to come in, Chief."

Seated behind his desk, Qualls looked toward the door as Mitch entered. He was pinching the knot of his tie and his expression was one of vast relief at having his meeting with Tamarah Birch's father interrupted. Even by the chief of police. Two coffee mugs sat on the desk. Qualls's was empty. The one intended for Birch appeared untouched.

"This is our local chief of police, Mr. Birch," Qualls said. "Mitch Bushyhead. He's investigating your daughter's death."

Birch's head swiveled toward the door. He rose from his chair as his suffering gaze raked Mitch's face for a sign. "Have you arrested Tamarah's murderer?" The man looked as though he hadn't slept in a week, or shaved, for that matter. Dark stubble covered his chin and upper lip. His brown slacks and sport shirt were rumpled. His eyes were red-rimmed and aswim with grief. His hands clenched at his sides. "Tell me you have."

"I'm sorry, Mr. Birch. We've made no arrest yet."

Birch breathed an inaudible oath and sank into his chair. He lowered his head as though fighting tears. "He has to pay," he said thickly. "Tamarah's killer has to—" He was unable to go on.

"He will pay," Mitch said.

Birch's head came up. "You know who he is?"

"I'm afraid I can't reveal his identity at this time. I can tell you that we're almost certain he came from this school."

Qualls, who had been toying with the butterfly paperweight on his desk, snapped to attention. "Do you have any evidence yet to back that up?"

Mitch advanced into the room. "We have a great deal of evidence. I've just returned from Kansas. I brought Kendall Harlan and Ruthann Blackfox back with me. They had some extremely interesting things to say. Both girls are with very relieved parents at this moment." Mitch had advised the Blackfoxes and Serina Harlan to keep the girls inside and close to them until an arrest was made.

"What girls?" Birch asked. "What does this have to do with Tamarah?"

"I couldn't see a clear connection at first," Mitch said. "It seems that Tamarah saw something in the woods, something she shouldn't have seen—something incriminating. That's why she was killed, Mr. Birch. But before that she told her friend, Ruthann Blackfox, what she'd seen. We suspected almost at once that this was the reason for Ruthann's disappearance. She was afraid for her life. Kendall Harlan, the seventeen-year-old daughter of Ellis Harlan, a faculty member at this school, was the fly in the ointment. We suspected the two girls were together, but we didn't know why or how Kendall had gotten involved. It turns out that she's known all along who killed Tamarah."

"What are you saying?" Qualls demanded. "Kendall Harlan is not what I would call a reliable source. If she had any such knowledge, why didn't she go immediately to the police? Why run away?"

"She was afraid of being killed, Mr. Qualls. She was, in fact, afraid of more than being killed, but that's another story, and too long to go into now."

Qualls stared at him. Mitch met the look and Qualls was the first to look away. "Well, thank goodness Kendall and Ruthann are all right," Qualls said. Somewhat belatedly, Mitch thought. "So Kendall accused somebody from the school."

"I didn't say that."

"Then why are you so convinced that Tamarah's killer is one of our people? You've hinted at something nebulously mysterious and incriminating, something seen by Tamarah and reported to Ruthann—"

"Kendall was forced to take part in a crime," Mitch told him. "She didn't come to the police for various reasons that I can't reveal at this time. But she wanted to protect herself, so she buried some evidence in the woods."

"And that's what Tamarah saw?" Birch asked.

Mitch nodded. "Sadly, Tamarah was in the wrong place at the wrong time. She didn't even know the significance of what she'd seen, but she must have been frightened by Kendall's reaction. Kendall extracted Tamarah's solemn promise that she wouldn't tell, but Tamarah couldn't keep the secret from her best friend. Not that it would have made any difference to her fate if she had. Once the killer knew what Tamarah had seen, he had to make sure she wouldn't talk."

"But this Kendall is the one who had the evidence," Birch said. "Why didn't he kill her?"

"Because she was smart enough not to tell him where she'd hidden the evidence. That's why he didn't kill her right away. By the time Kendall and Ruthann decided to run, he had probably realized that the evidence would never be found if the two girls were dead."

"This sounds like something conjured up in Kendall Harlan's warped mind," Qualls snapped. "You're saying that somebody from this school killed a child—though you're not willing to name him—and is fully prepared to kill two others?"

"That's what I'm saying."

A small smirk twisted Qualls's mouth. "So you've returned the girls to Buckskin where the killer can get at them."

"Kendall and Ruthann are being carefully guarded."

Birch was shaking his head sadly. "I don't understand any of this. I sent Tamarah here because I thought it would be more like a family setting for her. I thought she'd receive personal attention and close supervision."

"Tamarah did receive those things," Qualls said, "but she chose to break one of our ironclad rules. The students know that leaving the campus without a chaperone is strictly forbidden. Tamarah left the campus when she went into the woods where she saw something 'incriminating,' if Kendall Harlan can be believed. *I'm* not sure she can be, but that aside, surely you can't expect us to keep an eye on every single student at all times. It's an impossibility."

"All I know," said Birch, rising and facing Qualls, "is that my little girl is dead and somebody here killed her."

"Mr. Birch," Mitch interposed, "will you be staying in Buckskin overnight?"

The man gazed at Mitch blankly for an instant, as though trying to make sense of the question. Then his face crumpled under a wave of grief. "I have to get some sleep. And make arrangements with the funeral home. I suppose there's some place I could get a room."

"The Starlight Motel on Highway 10," Mitch said. "I'll be in touch with you later today or tomorrow."

Birch made a helpless gesture with both hands. "I'm not accomplishing anything here, anyway." He shot an anguished glance at Qualls as he left.

In the silence that followed Birch's departure, Qualls turned on Mitch. "Your irresponsible accusations are smearing the reputation of this school. You'd better be able to back them up, or you'll find yourself a defendant in a slander suit."

"Everything in due time, Qualls," Mitch said. "Good day."

Qualls followed Mitch out of the office. As Mitch descended the stairs, Qualls said in a voice loud enough for Mitch to hear, "Darlene, get the school attorney on the phone."

AT 5 P.M., Mitch and Virgil left the station to go to the tribal school where they would relieve Duckworth, who had had the campus entrance staked out since eight o'clock that morning. With the exodus of the Heritage Celebration visitors, the station had been relatively quiet all day. Shelly had been able to handle the calls that came in; Mitch, after returning from Great Bend that afternoon, spent a couple of hours on paperwork.

That morning, Shelly reported, she had finally had her interview with the two teenagers with the rap tapes and their mother. With a little pressure from Shelly, the teenagers confessed to having swiped the tapes. They would be cleaning up at the drugstore until they paid for them.

After the evening shift started, Mitch and Virgil left Roo to cover the station and drove down Sequoyah Street, which resembled a football stadium after a big game. A piece of paper blowing across the street in front of the squad car prompted Virgil to observe, "The street cleaners will have their work cut out for them tomorrow."

"They'll probably hire some high school boys to help the regular crew for a couple of days," Mitch said.

"Speaking of the street department, I heard Dwayne Burns went to work for them."

"Doing what?"

"Driving a maintenance truck."

"Good. Maybe Mrs. Burns can quit worrying."

"About where her next meal's coming from, anyway."

"Yeah, she's still going to worry about Dwayne exposing himself again."

"If Dwayne's got a lick of sense, he won't. He has to know this job is a gift. The first day of the rest of his life. If you ask me, it's damned big of the city council to take a chance on him."

"On the other hand, if Dwayne gets his act together, they'll have a hard-working employee who can fix anything with a motor in it."

"Yeah." Virgil peered out the side window of the squad car as they approached the campus entrance. "I don't see Duck's car."

"It's in the woods to the right there."

"Great camouflage."

Mitch tapped the horn as he stopped the car. They got out and walked into the woods. The driver-side window of the squad car was down. Duck's elbow stuck out of the opening and his head rested on the back of the car seat. He was asleep.

When they reached the car, Mitch barked, "Officer Duckworth!"

Duck started, his head jerking up. "Wha—what? Oh, jeez, Chief, you scared the crap out of me."

"Duck, how the hell will you know if our guy takes a powder if you're asleep? I asked you to stop every car that leaves the school and search it."

Duck rubbed his eyes. "I wasn't asleep," he grumbled. "I was just resting my eyes for a minute."

Mitch sighed. "What's been happening?"

"Not a thing. The only traffic into and out of that school today has been the cafeteria workers and a janitorial supply salesman."

"Well, he's probably not dumb enough to make a run for it in broad daylight."

"I hope he does it tonight," Virgil said. "I sat out here last night by myself. Longest night I ever spent in my life."

"I'm going home," Duck said. "I'll see you men tomorrow."

After Duck left, Mitch parked his car in the space Duck had vacated, next to a big hackberry tree. Virgil reached for the thermos on the car's back seat, poured two cups of coffee, and handed one to Mitch. They'd also brought a sack full of sandwiches, chips, and cookies packed by Virgil's wife, Trudy.

"I called Qualls this afternoon," Mitch said, "and told him we wanted a curfew on the campus for the next few nights. Nobody is supposed to enter or leave after eight P.M."

"He agreed to that?"

"He didn't like it, but he agreed. What else could he do? He wants to appear cooperative."

Virgil sipped his coffee. "So, if we hear a car leaving the campus after eight..."

"Or before—we react as if it's the killer making his getaway. If it turns out to be some terrified faculty wife, well, I guess we'll have blown our cover." Mitch unwrapped a

tuna fish sandwich. "I think it'll be tonight—shortly before eleven, I'd guess. He'll wait until he thinks the campus
is asleep and the guard's in the guard's office, but he'll want
out before the guard comes to close the gates for the night.
Stopping to open the gates would slow him down, besides
which he'd probably be heard. At the first sound of an approaching car, Virgil, you run through the woods to the
gates. Close them as soon as the car is clear. I'll drive the
squad car across the road, and we've got him. He might try
to get away through the woods on foot, so be ready for it."

Darkness came quickly. The sky had been blanketed with
clouds most of the day, and when night came there was no
moon. Only a few stars still visible in the patches of sky between tree branches.

They drank two more cups of coffee and ate the last two
sandwiches in the sack. Then Mitch took a flashlight from
the glove compartment. "I'm going to reconnoiter the
campus. You stay here and keep your ears cocked. If you
hear a car, block the road."

Virgil munched a potato chip. "Roger."

The central section of the campus around which the
dorms and other school buildings were situated was well
lighted. Mitch kept to the shadowy periphery, where there
was less danger of being seen. The occasional twig snap-
ping beneath his shoes sounded to his ears excruciatingly
loud, but no one else seemed to hear. Except for Mitch,
nothing moved. Apart from his footsteps the only sound
was the soft sighing of wind through tree branches.

He made a quick circle of the central campus area. Lights
shone from almost every window in both dormitories and
in two windows of the administration building, one on the
ground floor, the other in a basement room. The basement
room would be Merv Haines's, Mitch thought, and the
ground floor room the guard's office. He wondered when
the security guard was scheduled to make his next round of
the campus and hoped it wouldn't be while Mitch was making his. The fewer people who knew that the police had the
campus staked out, the better. Except for foyer night lights,
the other school buildings were dark.

He circled around behind the principal's residence. Lights
were on at the back of the house. Framed in the kitchen
window, Mitch saw Porter Qualls and his wife seated at the
table. Qualls still wore his dress shirt, but he'd removed his
tie and opened his collar. Though it was early, Mrs. Qualls
wore the blue bathrobe she'd had on the first time Mitch saw
her. It appeared she intended to retire early. He wondered
if she had another migraine headache.

Lights were on in all the duplexes, too. Shades were
drawn, but he saw shadows moving behind a couple of the
windows. Everybody tucked in nice and cozy, he thought,
as he made his stealthy way back to the woods.

It would be a while yet before anything happened. The
killer wouldn't make his move until the campus was sleeping. *If* he made his move. What if he decided to sit tight and
brazen it out? What if he didn't live on campus, after all?
Two possibilities Mitch didn't even want to think about.

After Mitch returned to the squad car, Virgil put his head
back and dozed. Mitch remained alert to every sound. He
thought he knew the identity of the murderer. If he was
wrong...

He thought about Kendall and Ruthann, hiding in that
motel room, scared half to death. If only he'd known what
to say to make Kendall give him the name. He closed his
eyes, remembering the conversation with Kendall in the
motel room.

*I found letters... I had to talk to somebody... somebody
I thought I could trust.*

Who had Kendall felt she could trust? The initials on the
ring could stand for Oklahoma State or Ohio State, or Oregon State, or any number of other schools. But it was very
old. Mitch thought he knew what those initials stood for.

THEY HEARD the car at fifteen minutes of eleven. It approached slowly, the driver making as little noise as possible. He wasn't about to gun the motor.

Mitch nudged Virgil, who was still dozing. "Something's happening, Virg. Get a move on."

Virgil was instantly awake. "Let's get him," he said as he got out of the car. Mitch started the engine, eased forward until the nose of the car was less than ten yards from the road, and waited. The spot was well chosen. Trees grew up to the edge of the narrow road on both sides. When Mitch drove crossways into the middle of the road, there wouldn't be room enough on either side for a car to pass.

The sound of the approaching car's engine grew gradually louder. Mitch leaned forward in his seat, clutching the steering wheel, trying to judge by the sound when to leave his hiding place. Not too soon, or the car wouldn't have cleared the gates yet, and if he waited too long, the driver might floorboard it and whip past while Mitch was getting into position.

The car slowed, then picked up speed as the driver made the turn and passed through the campus entrance. "Be there, Virg," Mitch muttered and slowly lifted his foot from the brake. His foot poised above the accelerator, he listened as the car picked up more speed. Tension gripped his chest and he was afraid to wait any longer. He jammed his foot on the accelerator and shot into the road, sliced through the beams from the approaching car's headlamps.

He skidded to a halt, cut the ignition and jammed the key into his pocket. The other driver hit his brakes and the car fishtailed, screeching to a stop with its nose inches from the rear fender of the squad car.

Pulling his gun from its holster, Mitch rolled out of the car and, in a crouch, ran around his vehicle, putting it between him and the other car. Resting his arms on the trunk, he positioned his gun in both hands.

"Police! Get out of the car with your hands up!"

He saw Virgil running down the road toward them, his gun drawn. The driver remained in the other car.

"We've got you covered on all sides," Mitch yelled, hoping the guy wouldn't call his bluff and find out how exaggerated the claim was. "Get out of the car! Now!"

The car door opened slowly. "Hands up!" Virgil yelled.

Two hands appeared above the door and Lyman Shoe-maker got out. "What the hell's going on here?" he de-manded, sounding outraged.

Virgil ran forward and pushed Shoemaker over the trunk of his car. He patted him down quickly but thoroughly. "He's clean, Chief."

Virgil stepped back and Shoemaker straightened. "What's the meaning of this?"

Keeping his gun aimed at Shoemaker's chest, Mitch moved around the patrol car until he stood facing the man. "You can lower your hands, but hold them out away from your body so I can see them." Shoemaker's headlights were still on, providing enough illumination for Mitch to detect any sudden move. Shoemaker did as he was told. "It's a bit late for a drive," Mitch said.

"I couldn't sleep. Is that against the law?"

Virgil stuck his head into Shoemaker's car, bending to see the floorboard in front of the back seat. When he backed out of the car, Shoemaker's keys dangled from his hand. "I'll check the glove compartment, Chief." He leaned into the car and fitted the key into the compartment lock. "Hey, look here!" Virgil brought out a handgun, emptied it of ammunition and tossed it back on the car seat.

"You shouldn't have kept the gun, Shoemaker," Mitch said. "Where you headed? Mexico?"

Shoemaker's eyes darted from the gun in Mitch's hands to his face. "I have no idea how that gun came to be in my car."

"Come off it, Shoemaker. According to Kendall Har-lan—"

"Kendall is a world-class liar! I don't know what she told you, but it's not true."

"Interesting," Mitch mused. "How would you know, since you don't know what she told us?"

"I have a pretty good idea. I've seen her in action. That girl can make up a story at the drop of a hat!"

"Know her pretty well, I guess."

Shoemaker didn't respond. Mitch said, "Let *me* tell you a story, Shoemaker. There's this school counselor. Nearly sixty years old, divorced for more than fifteen years. Whatever idealism he had when he first entered a classroom, he lost somewhere along the way. Maybe the daily grind just wore him down. He's staring retirement in the face. Problem is, on a teacher's salary, he was never able to save much. There's his pension, of course, but it's not enough to live on. He's understandably bitter. He's devoted his life to educating and counseling young people, and what's he got to show for it? A pittance and the prospect of living in poverty the rest of his life."

"If this is supposed to have a point—"

"I'm not finished," Mitch interrupted. "Where was I? Oh, yes. Our embittered school counselor is in something of a bind. One day, he's at home with the TV on, or maybe he's driving and listening to the car radio. Or he read it in a newspaper. Whatever, he hears or reads the news that a robber has been ripping off banks and savings and loans in towns near where our counselor lives. The robber hasn't been identified because he wears a black ski mask. What the counselor doesn't know is that the police have kept back one bit of information. The ski mask has red stripes around the eyes and mouth."

Shoemaker sighed heavily and made to put his hands in his trousers pockets. "Keep 'em away from your body," Mitch said sharply.

"I need a smoke."

"Get him a cigarette, Virgil," Mitch said.

Virgil took a pack from Shoemaker's shirt pocket, tapped out a cigarette and handed it to the counselor. He reached into Shoemaker's pants' pocket for his lighter and gave it to him. Shoemaker lit up and sucked deeply on the cigarette.

"To continue," Mitch said, "the news of the burglaries sets our counselor to thinking. Why can't he buy a black ski mask and rob a bank? The police will assume it's just another robbery in a string of them pulled off by the original robber. He'll need a gun, too, just for show, but guns are easy to come by. If he can pull this thing off, our counselor will be able to retire, in Mexico, say, in comfort. He's got it coming, hasn't he? He's given his life to educating kids and it's only right that he should be fairly compensated.''

Shoemaker coughed and Mitch waited for him to stop. ''But he needs a driver, somebody to sit in his car outside the bank with the motor running. The problem is he's new at this robbery game and he doesn't know anyone who would be willing to involve himself in a crime. But wait. There's this crazy, mixed-up seventeen-year-old girl he's been counseling. She's already spilled her family's dark secret, confident that it's safe with him. Something called professional confidentiality. Trusting little thing. And dumb. Why, he can probably manipulate her into being his accomplice without her knowing what's going on until it's too late. How am I doing, Shoemaker?''

''You're a raving lunatic.''

''Wait'll you hear the rest of the story. Maybe you'll change your mind. The counselor tells his seventeen-year-old client that he has to go to Muskogee on business. Would she like to come along for the ride? Well, things aren't exactly rosy at her house, so she jumps at the chance. He drives to a bank and tells the girl he's going to conduct business inside. It'll only take a few minutes, so she is to wait for him in the car with the motor running. At first, things go better than he could have hoped. The teller rakes three hundred thousand big ones into a sack and hands it to him. Too bad he didn't get into this line of work sooner. He'd be a millionaire by now. But the three hundred thou will cushion his retirement nicely. He starts to leave and that's when things get hairy. A bank guard decides to stop him. Well, there he is with the gun in his hand. What else can he do? He pulls the trigger and the guard goes down. He runs out, in a full panic, I imagine—this was supposed to be easy. He jumps in the car, yelling at the girl to drive. She does.''

''How long do I have to stand here and listen to this drivel?'' Shoemaker said.

''Not so long if you'll quit interrupting me. I've spent all day writing this tale in my head, so pay attention. Now, the girl finally puts things together. The counselor's got a sack full of money with a ski mask on top. She may be dumb, but she's not a moron. So he gives her a bundle of money. Hush money. Not much compared to the haul, but to her it's big bucks. As added insurance, he threatens to tell the world her dark family secret if she breathes a word about the robbery to anyone. She seems suitably cowed. He doesn't discover until later that she's stolen the ski mask and his old college ring from Oklahoma City University and hidden it. She's taken out her own insurance policy. Guess he underestimated her, eh, Shoemaker?''

Shoemaker took a drag on his cigarette, squinting at Mitch. ''She refuses to tell him where she hid the mask and ring, but he's still not all that worried. She's too terrified to tell what she knows. But then, alas, he learns that somebody saw her bury the evidence, an eight-year-old child. He's dealt with kids long enough to know that no way is that child going to keep quiet about it. Boarding school can get pretty dull, and seeing a girl burying something in the woods is too weirdly interesting not to talk about. So he kills her. What else can he do? In fact, it's easy. The child in question has an appointment in the principal's office and she's terrified. Our counselor sees her leave her dorm, probably in tears, and comforts her. 'Let's go somewhere and talk about this,' he says, or something along that line. They'll take a little walk in the woods until she calms down. Afterward, he remembers that some poor schlock exhibitionist has just been released from the hospital. He takes the child's panties and leaves them in the schlock's yard. A nice, clear clue. Oh, and later he drops the police a hint that a pedophile might also be an exhibitionist, to make sure they understand the clue he planted.''

In the silence that followed Mitch's recital, a cicada began singing in the woods nearby. In the headlights, he could see Shoemaker staring at him stonily. ''I may be off on a few of the details,'' Mitch said after a long moment, ''but that's the gist of what happened.''

''I don't know what you're talking about.''

''You're telling me you have nothing to hide?''

''That's what I'm telling you.''

"Good, then you won't mind letting me take a peek in the trunk of your car."

Shoemaker went very still. Then, abruptly, he shrugged. "Sure, why not."

"Walk around behind your car," Mitch said. "I'll be right on your heels. Virgil."

Virgil joined them at the back of Shoemaker's car and opened the trunk. The trunk light came on, illuminating three large suitcases. "Well, well, well," Mitch murmured.

"Would you like to search the suitcases?" Shoemaker asked. "You'll find nothing but clothes."

"Open them," Mitch said.

Shoemaker took the keys from Virgil, picked out the smallest key, and unlocked the suitcases. Mitch stepped up and began going through the first case. Virgil pressed a little closer, peering over Shoemaker's shoulder.

Suddenly, Shoemaker whirled, and threw keys and cigarette lighter at Virgil. "Watch it!" Virgil yelled, staggering back but regaining his balance quickly. He wasn't quick enough, though. Shoemaker ran past him and into the woods.

There wasn't time to think. Mitch followed, bringing his gun arm up. Virgil was right behind him. "Stop or I'll shoot!" He waited a moment, then two. Shoemaker stumbled through the trees ahead of him, a dark, moving shadow. Mitch fired.

Shoemaker screamed, slowed and then, turning half around, crumpled to the ground. When Mitch and Virgil reached him, he was lying on his side, writhing and groaning and cursing.

"Where are you hit?" Mitch demanded.

"My arm," Shoemaker grated. "You almost shot my arm off, damn you."

"Be glad it wasn't your head," Mitch said. "Grab his other arm, Virgil. Get up, Shoemaker. There's nothing wrong with your legs."

By the time they got him back to the squad car, he was near to fainting. Mitch helped him into the back seat and cuffed him to the door.

Panting, Shoemaker laid his head back on the seat. His face was white and clammy. Mitch tore off part of Shoemaker's shirt sleeve and tied it around his upper arm, above the gunshot wound, to stem the bleeding. The man was in pain, but he wasn't going to die.

Mitch and Virgil went around to the still-open trunk of Shoemaker's car. The second suitcase contained bundles of money, still in the bank wrappers.

Virgil whistled appreciatively. "Never saw so much money before in my life."

"Probably never will again," Mitch told him. He closed the suitcase and transferred it to the trunk of the squad car.

Shoemaker appeared to be asleep, or passed out, but when Mitch started the engine, Shoemaker groaned. "Take it easy, will you. I'm in agony back here."

"We're taking you to the hospital," Mitch said. "They'll give you something for pain."

Mitch drove away from the school. Shoemaker groaned again. Finally, he muttered, "I only wanted to talk to her."

"Tamarah?" Mitch asked.

"Yes. I wanted her to tell me where the mask and ring were. But she became hysterical...struggling, trying to scream...I only meant to silence her...not kill her."

"Sure you did," Virgil said.

Shoemaker gasped in pain and said through clenched teeth. "I never meant to kill her, I tell you! The guard, either. I...I never broke the law in my life until that day in Muskogee. I read about the ski mask robber in the newspaper. He kept robbing banks and getting away with it. So I thought, why not me? Just once, to get money for my retirement, and never again. I was so scared I was shaking. If the guard hadn't gotten in the way... I didn't even know I'd pulled the trigger until I saw the blood. Everything just got out of hand." The man was actually whining.

"Shut the hell up, you SOB," Mitch snapped. "Save your breath for the jury."

TWENTY-NINE

ELLIS HARLAN was packing. Today the tribal school had celebrated the graduation of its eighth-graders and presented scholastic and athletic awards in an assembly for students and parents. Afterward, amidst flurries of good-byes and promises to write and the loading of family cars with nine months' accumulation of clothes, books, and other paraphernalia, car after car had driven away from the campus. It was seven o'clock in the evening now, and the school grounds were virtually deserted.

On his way there, Mitch had dropped Emily off at the Robertses' house with her suitcases. Early tomorrow morning, Temple's mother would drive the two girls to Norman for a week's cheerleading camp.

Harlan had admitted Mitch to the duplex with a grunt of recognition and returned to packing a cardboard box that rested on the living room couch.

"You'll excuse me for not offering you something to drink," Harlan muttered as he placed a stack of books in the box. "The refrigerator is disconnected and the coffee pot's packed."

"I didn't come for refreshment."

"Why did you come? Isn't your business here finished?"

"Yes. Shoemaker was transferred to the county jail today. He'll stay there until the trial."

Harlan looked up then. His face was an etching in grief. "If that's what you came to tell me, you needn't have bothered. I couldn't care less about Shoemaker. I hope he rots in jail. I've more pressing things on my mind at the moment." He grabbed a stack of magazines and placed them in the box. "You thought it was me, didn't you?" he demanded.

"You were high on my suspect list for a while," Mitch admitted. "You were clearly hiding *something*." Harlan remained silent. "I heard you resigned your job here," Mitch said.

"Thanks to you and your investigation." Abruptly, Harlan turned away from the box. He raked a hand through his hair and sagged to a sitting position on the arm of the couch. "That's not fair. I'm sorry. Your investigation was the catalyst that brought things to a head, that's all. It was only a matter of time until it would have happened, anyway."

Mitch glanced toward the silent hallway leading back to the bedrooms. He had heard no sounds from the rest of the house. "I wanted to thank Kendall. She probably saved Ruthann's life by running away. She's got a lot of courage, that girl."

"I'll tell her—the next time I see her." His voice was heavy, as though it was an effort to get his words out.

"Has she gone away?"

Harlan looked back at him with tortured eyes. "They've all gone away. Cody took an apartment in Tahlequah. He found a summer job there. Serina and Kendall will live in Tulsa for the time being. Serina's looking for a job. I'm going to New Mexico. I've always liked that part of the country." He looked around at the bare walls. "Serina and I are getting a divorce."

"I'm sorry," Mitch murmured. "I didn't know."

He made an odd sound in his throat. "It was inevitable. I can see that now. Surely Kendall told you . . . about us."

"No, she didn't. She merely said that she'd found some letters from you to her mother in the cedar chest. She didn't divulge the contents to anyone, except Shoemaker. He was the school counselor, the one person she thought she could trust not to repeat what she told him. God knows I tried to get her to confide the content of those letters to me. She wouldn't. She was determined to protect the family."

Harlan pressed both hands to his face. "It doesn't matter now," he said through his fingers. He dropped his hands and looked at Mitch, or rather through him. "It started such a long time ago."

Mitch eased into a chair. He sensed that Harlan needed to talk.

"Serina was illegitimate," Harlan said after a moment. "Her mother raised her in Indiana, and she would never talk about Serina's father. All Serina knew was that she was born in San Francisco. One summer, after her mother died, Serina went out to California to try to track down somebody who knew her mother when she lived there, with the hope that she could learn who her father was. About a month later, she traced her mother to the neighborhood where I lived and began canvassing houses. That's how we met."

Mitch was worn out. He hadn't slept in thirty-six hours and had meant only to pop in and out of the Harlan house, tie up the last strings in the case, then go home to a shower and bed. But he stifled the desire to interrupt Harlan.

"She was so beautiful," Harlan was saying. "I was knocked completely off my feet at first sight. In order to keep in contact with her, I volunteered to help her find her father." He sighed heavily. "We fell in love and married two months after we met. Serina got pregnant with Cody right away. We were deliriously happy... everything was perfect—almost. Serina couldn't forget about her father and so we continued searching for him. We..." He paused to take a long breath. "Serina was six months along when we began to suspect the truth. Another month passed while we tried to deny it, but finally there were too many pieces to make them mean anything else. I'm only half-Cherokee, through my mother. My father, who died a couple of years before Serina and I met, was white, and he was Serina's father, too. She's my half-sister."

Mitch had thought he was prepared for anything. He wasn't. "My God, man..."

Harlan's hands went to his face again, his knuckles wiping at tears. "As soon as we knew the truth, she left me." It was a shaken whisper.

"Seven months pregnant," Mitch murmured. "She must have been terrified that the baby would be—"

"A monster. She kept saying it, over and over. 'The baby will be deformed. I'm carrying a monster, Ellis.' All I could think about at the time was that she'd left me and I couldn't live without her. She wouldn't admit me to her rented room. She wouldn't take my phone calls. So I wrote letters."

"The letters Kendall found?"

He nodded and knuckled his eyes again. "I thought she had destroyed the letters long ago. Until Kendall found them. Serina said she'd kept them for comfort when she needed it. When I wrote them, I was obsessed with her. Getting her back seemed far more important than the fact that she was my half-sister. To me she was my wife, the only woman I'd ever loved or would love. I used every argument I could think of." He uttered a shaky laugh. "I told her about Egyptian and Polynesian royalty and other cultures where marriage between full siblings was accepted. I copied reams of research material and sent it to her. Finally, she said that she'd been praying for a sign. As you may have guessed, Serina has a strong religious streak. She said if the baby was normal, she'd accept it as a sign that God approved of our love."

He shook his head helplessly. "The night Cody was born was the worst night of my life. Serina was in labor for ten hours. I was with her the whole time, and she was in an absolute panic. I think I talked nonstop for the full ten hours, calming her, reassuring her. But I was falling apart inside. It was the first time I'd really faced the fact that the baby *could* be a monster. Then Cody was born and he was perfect."

"You must have felt like a man reprieved from the gas chamber at the last second."

Harlan nodded. "I took Serina and Cody home and things were all right for a while. Of course, we couldn't risk having another baby, but Serina wanted one. I was completely happy with our family as it was, but I would have done anything to keep Serina content. So we adopted Kendall. Naturally, I came to love her—almost as much as Cody. She wasn't as bright or outgoing as Cody, but she was a pretty child with a sunny disposition." Harlan gazed around the room again, at the empty space where once a family had lived. "Until she found those letters, and then she underwent a complete transformation overnight. She threw it up to us all the time, especially Serina. How disgusting we were, how perverted. I could have lived with that, but...she told Cody. I could have killed her for that bit of vindictiveness."

"That's what the argument was about the night Officer Rabbit and I overheard them?"

His Adam's apple rose and fell convulsively. "Cody thought she'd concocted a fantastic lie to hurt him. She'd been doing everything she could think of to embarrass and humiliate the family for weeks. But he couldn't get it out of his mind, so he came to Serina and me and told us what Kendall had said. He said he didn't believe there was a word of truth in it, but he had to hear it from us. Serina started crying and eventually she told him everything. I guess she couldn't live a lie any longer."

Mitch waited until he seemed more composed. "Will Cody be all right?"

"In time. Cody's a fighter. Right now, though, he's trying to deal with the shock. Do you know what he said to me?" He looked at Mitch helplessly. "He said he'd never risk fathering children, for fear there'd be something wrong with them. He—he doesn't want to see me or his mother. He says he needs time to get his head together again, then he'll contact us." There was a desperate edge to his tone as he added, "We've showered him with love for nineteen years. In the end, that's what will count. He'll be all right and we'll still be his parents."

"And Kendall?"

"I think she'll be all right, too. She was different, after you brought her back from Kansas. Subdued and sad, but not angry anymore. Serina says Kendall's the one who needs her now, and that the girl can't be happy with the two of us, together." He gave a helpless shrug. "The marriage would have ended eventually, anyway. I've spent twenty years holding it together and, frankly, I'm too tired to do it any longer. Through the years, the love got tangled up with guilt and fear that we'd be exposed and too many other emotions."

"I understand now why you didn't stay in Great Bend and fight for your job," Mitch said. "You didn't want anybody digging into your past."

"They probably wouldn't have learned about me and Serina, but Serina never wanted to take the chance. That's why, every time any problem arose, she wanted to move. She's spent the last twenty years running scared." He took a deep breath and moved his shoulders as though to shake off a heavy weight. He reached for a roll of tape to seal the cardboard box. "Now she won't have to do that, anymore."

"I'm sorry, Harlan. It seems inadequate, but I don't know what else to say."

"Nothing else to be said. I'll find another teaching job—in New Mexico. Qualls has agreed to give me a reference. I can make a new life out there. Cody might come and stay with me next summer. And Kendall, if she wants to. Having that to look forward to is enough for now."

"Well," said Mitch after a pause. "I'll get out of your way."

"The funny thing is," Harlan said, "along with everything else, I feel free. For the first time since I can remember."

At the door, Mitch said, "Good luck, Harlan."

Mitch walked across the deserted campus in the soft darkness of the May night. Harlan's anguish still clung to him. He drew a measure of solace from knowing that Emily would have a grand time in Norman, meeting new friends, giggling and gossiping half the night with Temple. His daughter had suffered the trauma of her mother's death but, as bad as that had been, it was a loss that everybody had to deal with eventually. Natural and clean, somehow. Not like what the Harlan children were having to cope with.

He was booked on a flight out of Tulsa tomorrow morning for Boston. Not that he expected the trip to settle anything between him and Lisa. But it was time to face whatever had to be faced.

The faint odor of the bloom-laden lilac bushes wafted to him on the soft evening breeze. Thinking of the broken man he'd just left, Mitch drew the sweet, refreshing smell into his lungs. Things could be worse for him, he told himself. Not that there wasn't plenty to worry about, but there was enough good to balance the scales. For now.

Hard Luck

A Cat Marsala Mystery

Barbara D'Amato

First Time in Paperback

HIGH STAKES

Chicago journalist Cat Marsala has just begun her assignment on the state lottery when murder falls into the picture—literally—as a lottery official takes a leap in the middle of the multistate lottery conference.

Suicide... or murder? It's curious to Cat—and to the police—that the guy took his mighty plunge right before his meeting with her. Especially curious since he'd hinted at some great exposé material, like "misappropriation" of lottery funds.

"Cat Marsala is one of the most appealing new sleuths to come along in years."
— *Nancy Pickard*

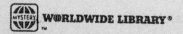

WORLDWIDE LIBRARY®

HARDL

A TONY AND PAT PRATT MYSTERY

Murder Takes Two

BERNIE LEE

First Time in Paperback

FINAL CUT

An unexpected trip to recording studios in London for advertising writer Tony Pratt and his wife, Pat, sounded fun and exciting—in spite of the rather off-the-wall bunch they'd be dealing with.

The tension was thick as London fog, but there were commercials to be made and sights to be seen. Until the eerie quiet of the studio was shattered by an unusual sound effect—that of a falling corpse—as a murderer began a very personal job of editing.

"One of the more engaging husband-and-wife sleuthing teams."
—*Flint Journal*

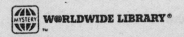

WORLDWIDE LIBRARY®

MTTWO

A PORT SILVA MYSTERY

GRANDMOTHER'S
HOUSE

JANET LAPIERRE

First Time in Paperback

PORT SILVA—LAND TO KILL FOR?

Situated on California's beautiful northern coast, Port Silva had escaped the rash of land developers eating up the state's prime real estate. But when a posh San Diego firm finally offers small fortunes to persuade the people on historic Finn Lane to sell out, everyone jumps at the chance. Except thirteen-year-old Petey Birdsong. The house belonged to his grandmother. He's not selling. Charlotte, his mother, stands adamantly beside him.

But how far will Petey go to defend his home?

"LaPierre is something else . . . real talent."
—*Mystery Readers of America Journal*

Available at your favorite retail outlet in May, or reserve your copy for April shipping by sending your name, address, zip or postal code along with a check or money order for $3.99 (please do not send cash), plus 75¢ postage and handling ($1.00 in Canada) for each book ordered, payable to Worldwide Mystery, to:

In the U.S.

Worldwide Mystery
3010 Walden Avenue
P.O. Box 1325
Buffalo, NY 14269-1325

In Canada

Worldwide Mystery
P.O. Box 609
Fort Erie, Ontario
L2A 5X3

Please specify book title with your order.
Canadian residents add applicable federal and provincial taxes.

GRANDH

WORLDWIDE LIBRARY®

First Time In Paperback

A JOHN COFFIN MYSTERY

Gwendoline Butler

MATTERS OF THE HEAD

Life was good for Detective John Coffin—he'd earned a promotion and had just moved into a new home in the tower of a renovated church-turned-theater. True, he now headed his own force and was no longer a street detective, but his business was still crime and there was plenty in the Docklands.

And then a severed human head was found in an urn on the church steps. A hand turned up in a freezer upstairs. It was one of those cases that stretched out long fingers to touch many lives . . . or, rather, deaths.

"Butler pens a superior procedural." —*Publishers Weekly*

Available at your favorite retail outlet in June, or reserve your copy for May shipping by sending your name, address, zip or postal code, along with a check or money order for $3.99 (please do not send cash), plus 75¢ postage and handling for each book ordered, payable to Worldwide Mystery, to:

In the U.S.

Worldwide Mystery
3010 Walden Avenue
P.O. Box 1325
Buffalo, NY 14269-1325

Please specify book title with your order.
Sorry, this offer not available in Canada. Available in U.S. only.

W@RLDWIDE LIBRARY ®

COFFINM

ZERO

A
KATHERINE DRISCOLL
MYSTERY

at the

BONE

First
Time in
Paperback

Mary Willis Walker

UNSUSPECTING PREY

It had been thirty-one years since Katherine Driscoll had seen her father. Then he sent a cryptic letter. He knew she was in trouble—about to lose her home, her dog kennel and her beloved championship show dog, Ra, to creditors. He was offering his help.

Katherine went to meet him at the Austin Zoo where he was senior keeper of the large cats. But she just missed him—he'd been mauled to death by a tiger.

With nothing to go on but a key and receipt from a storage warehouse, Katherine took a job at the zoo and started probing into her father's bizarre death.

> **"Walker is terrific at goosebumps."**
> —*The Philadelphia Inquirer*

 WØRLDWIDE LIBRARY®
MYSTERY
TM

The Hour of the Knife

SHARON ZUKOWSKI

First Time In Paperback

A BLAINE STEWART MYSTERY

REST, RELAXATION...AND MURDER

Blaine Stewart found work and self-pity moderately effective ways to cope with her husband's death. Tough, tenacious, burned-out, she was getting on everybody's nerves—including her own. A trip to the Carolina coast was going to give her the chance to tie up a case and then the time to catch some R and R.

But when her client—and friend—was found dead in the marsh, Blaine started asking questions.... Vacations had never agreed with Blaine, anyway, and this one wasn't about to change her mind...especially when it was highly likely it would be her last!

"The fast paced action, assortment of characters and the unsolved death will keep you reading far into the night."
—*Polish-American Journal*

 WORLDWIDE LIBRARY®
™